THE LONG GAME

Simon Rowell has worked on outback oil rigs, managed nightclubs, been a tour guide and run marketing campaigns. His first book, *The Echo of Others*, was longlisted for the Ned Kelly Awards for Best First Crime in 2018. He lives with his wife, Karen, in rural Victoria on a farm full of rescued animals.
simonrowell.net

THE LONG GAME

SIMON ROWELL

TEXT PUBLISHING MELBOURNE AUSTRALIA

textpublishing.com.au

The Text Publishing Company
Swann House, 22 William Street, Melbourne Victoria 3000, Australia

The Text Publishing Company (UK) Ltd
130 Wood Street, London EC2V 6DL, United Kingdom

Copyright © Simon Rowell, 2021

The moral right of Simon Rowell to be identified as the author of this work has been asserted.

All rights reserved. Without limiting the rights under copyright above, no part of this publication shall be reproduced, stored in or introduced into a retrieval system, or transmitted in any form or by any means (electronic, mechanical, photocopying, recording or otherwise), without the prior permission of both the copyright owner and the publisher of this book.

First published by The Text Publishing Company, 2021

Cover design by Jessica Horrocks
Cover images by Stephen Mulcahey/Arcangel and Sarah Dawdy/FOAP/Getty
Page design by Rachel Aitken
Typeset by J&M Typesetting

Epigraph © Colum McCann, 2009. Reproduced from *Let the Great World Spin* with permission of Bloomsbury Publishing Plc.

Printed and bound in Australia by Griffin Press, part of Ovato, an Accredited ISO AS/NZS 14001:2004 Environmental Management System printer

ISBN: 9781922330710 (paperback)
ISBN: 9781922459176 (ebook)

A catalogue record for this book is available from the National Library of Australia.

 This book is printed on paper certified against the Forest Stewardship Council® Standards. Griffin Press holds FSC chain-of-custody certification SGSHK-COC-005088. FSC promotes environmentally responsible, socially beneficial and economically viable management of the world's forests.

*For Karen, my first reader,
whose love and support means everything.*

Nobody falls halfway.

Colum McCann, *Let the Great World Spin*

PROLOGUE

He sat in his car, high above the Portsea back beach, near the very tip of the Mornington Peninsula, watching the waves rolling in off Bass Strait, a single bead of sweat on his temple. His was the only car at this end of the car park. Behind him were scrubby dunes, and before him was an endless stretch of ocean. The summer sun, now high in the sky, blanched the scene like a faded polaroid. He held the large knife loosely, bouncing it gently in his right hand, happy with its weight. He turned it to and fro, glinting the sun's rays off its silver edge. Twelve inches long, the knife had a series of black dots on its handle, making it easy to grip.

When he'd been a young boy, his mother would take him to the bayside beaches a few kilometres north, across the peninsula, where the water was calm enough for him to paddle about. He could only remember his father taking him to the beach a couple of times, and it was always here, on the wilder ocean side, amid the saltbush and wallaby grass that clung tightly to the dunes.

'Tasmania is out there. Can you see it?' his father had asked, pointing.

He'd squinted and lied that he could.

He shook his head at the memory. Despite himself, he looked up at the horizon and stared again.

Out beyond the break, teenagers sat on surfboards, laughing and calling to one another. He'd been parked for ten minutes, watching them ignore one perfect wave after another. He knew what they were thinking: that there were plenty of waves, and there always would be. He remembered thinking the same thing. That everything lasts forever.

As a wave broke to his left, he traced his knife through the air, following the slice of white water across the deep blue.

Through the open window, he caught the tart scent of green apple. He turned sharply, staring for a long moment, an impossible expectation filling his mind. Then the perfume was gone, leaving a memory in its place.

It was time.

He returned the knife to his backpack on the passenger seat, and stepped out of the car. He walked around it, checking that the number plates were screwed on tight. Then he took a few steps towards the sea and breathed in as he watched another wave forming. When it started to break, he exhaled until the wave petered out near the turquoise water close to shore. He did this several times. It calmed him. He was in control. He had no other choice.

Shutting his eyes, he sucked in one last deep breath. He got back behind the wheel and eased out of the car park, pulling his baseball cap down low. He kept under the speed limit, as the road curved through dunes, passing a row of drooping sheoaks and clumps of green tussock grass. After a minute, he turned left into Latham Drive. As he'd expected, the street was empty. It was too hot for gardening and everyone would have walked their dogs earlier. People would either be inside staying cool, out back by their pools, or at the beach.

He took his foot off the accelerator and let the car glide the last thirty metres into the empty driveway.

After checking the rear-view mirror, he grabbed the backpack, opened the door silently and stepped out. Using the door as cover, he slipped the knife into the back pocket of his jeans, before letting his shirt fall back over the handle.

He felt good. He could hear the orchestra's drums thumping, racing towards a crescendo. Soon, it would be over.

1.20 PM, SUNDAY 2 FEBRUARY

The familiar metallic smell enveloped Zoe as she reached the end of the hallway. Under her old dark work suit she was wearing a new white shirt, not yet washed enough to feel comfortable against her skin. Her black Doc Martens, polished soft over many years, were encased in powder blue plastic booties. She adjusted her forensic mask and from the doorway looked down at the man slumped against the far wall. Zoe thought he looked about forty, fit with sun-bleached blond hair and a deep tan. His pale blue eyes stared back at her in surprise. His mouth was open and his arms were spread out, as if he were still pleading for life.

Zoe could see the blade of a large knife, an intricate pattern of dots etched into its silver handle, disappearing into a short-sleeved shirt, once white, now stained a rich burgundy.

On the wall above the body a mirror was shattered, shards still held loosely together by its frame. She saw herself reflected from across the room, her tanned face and dark ponytail shattered into a dozen abstract angles. *Looks about right*, she thought with a wry smile, considering the reason for the four months of enforced leave she'd just taken. At that moment, one of the pieces of glass fell, bouncing off the victim's head and landing, point first, in the thickening blood pooled around the body.

Zoe swept her eyes around the room. The furniture looked cheap and new, except the television, which was high-end and huge. Nothing seemed to match, as if it had all been bought in a hurry.

In the distance, she could hear waves crashing and children squealing. Even inside, the late-summer heat baked her throat and she wished she'd left her jacket in the car. She cursed the idea of the dark suit as the standard homicide uniform.

When her phone had rung, just before lunch, she felt a rush seeing the number on the screen. She called Charlie straight afterwards to say they had a job. He moaned when she told him it was in Portsea, an hour and a half's drive south of Melbourne, around the arc of Port Phillip Bay.

'Welcome back,' he had mumbled, before hanging up.

While being part of the weekend on-call team wasn't Charlie's idea of a good time, Zoe was ready to go, happy to be back. Now she was here, though, she needed to keep her game face on. She heard footsteps coming up the hall.

'Detective Sergeant Mayer. Good to see you.' It was Oliver Nunan, the pathologist. He wore a white jumpsuit, with a hood and mask. His powder blue plastic booties matched hers. When Zoe was in training, Oliver had performed the first autopsy she'd witnessed. He was sympathetic when, along with most of her class, she threw up into one of the sick bags he'd handed out beforehand. She became a vegetarian that day.

Zoe had always liked Oliver. He had been kind-hearted and patient when she was learning the ropes. She pivoted to face him, smiling behind her mask. 'Hi, Oliver. Good to see you, too. How've you been?'

Oliver gave a resigned snort. 'Okay, though I'd prefer to be at home watching the cricket.' He turned to take in the scene. 'Well, that's just unpleasant,' he muttered, looking down at the body. Zoe noticed that his greying eyebrows had grown longer since she'd last seen him.

Three major-crime-scene examiners from Forensics pushed past them into the room. All were wearing jumpsuits and masks. One had a case of tools, for collecting evidence; one a video camera and the last a large Nikon. The woman holding the video camera took a slow sweep of the room before zooming in on the victim.

'Hey there, Zoe,' said the officer carrying the tools. 'When did you get back?'

'Hi, Jenny. Today. Charlie and I are on call.'

'Glad you're back on deck. Charlie putting off the inevitable?'

Zoe grinned behind her mask. 'Guess so. He's checking outside the house.'

'Being thorough,' said Jenny. Zoe could see her smile lines around her eyes.

Once the scene had been documented, Oliver approached the body. He felt for a pulse that was long gone.

Zoe remained in the doorway.

'Looks like just the one stab wound,' he said. 'Knife is a decent size. Kitchen knife.'

She watched as he pulled a case from his pocket. Opening it, he picked out a thermometer and measured the temperature in the room, before taking a couple of readings from the victim. He pulled out a notepad and did some calculations.

'When?' asked Zoe.

'Between ten-thirty and eleven-thirty this morning. I'll be able to pinpoint it at the autopsy tonight.'

Zoe made a note. It was now almost one-thirty. The killer might have a three-hour head start.

Picking up one of the victim's hands, Oliver pulled his mask aside and sniffed.

'What?' asked Zoe.

'Bleach,' answered Oliver, without looking up. He turned the hand, looking under the fingernails.

'Fuck,' said Zoe.

'Exactly.' Oliver turned towards Jenny. 'If your team finds a nail brush anywhere, can you bag it?'

Jenny nodded. 'Will do.'

Oliver let out a small groan as he stood up, his knees creaking. 'Okay, I'm done. Tonight at eight work for you?'

'It's a date,' said Zoe.

Oliver nodded. 'Right, I'm off. See you then.'

Zoe walked to the corner of the room, her plastic booties scrunching on the wooden floorboards. She crouched down and watched as the officer with the video camera walked towards the back of the house, recording. Thirty seconds later she came out. 'There are drops of blood leading into a bathroom. No nail brush that I could see. Bathroom's clean though. Heavy smell of bleach and there's a mop and bucket next to the toilet.'

'The killer knew they had time,' said Zoe. 'Flushed away evidence. Can we check for prints on the buttons on the toilet?'

'No problem.'

From above, she heard an intake of breath.

1.30 PM, SUNDAY 2 FEBRUARY

Zoe looked up to see Charlie standing in the doorway, staring at the body, his face pale. At six foot two, Charlie had a good four inches on Zoe and was lean, with close-cropped blond hair. He looked every part the poster-boy homicide detective until he was near a body. After nine months in the squad, he still saw every new murder scene as though it were his first. She thought he might have toughened up while she'd been away. *You haven't even seen a truly horrifying one yet.*

'You okay?' Zoe asked, standing up.

'Yeah, all good,' said Charlie, his voice a pitch higher than usual.

'Any signs of forced entry?'

Charlie turned. 'No, I did a visual on the front and back doors. Neither has been forced. Windows are all shut.'

'Our secondary team here yet?'

'Yeah, Angus and Hannah are outside interviewing the neighbours and gawkers.'

'Good,' said Zoe, glad to be teaming up with Hannah Nguyen and Angus Batch on her first case back. They'd be on board for at least forty-eight hours. For most cases that would be enough time to have someone charged.

'These morning murders are always different,' Zoe said. 'They're more likely to be well planned, clinical.'

'Domestic?' Charlie asked, his eyes again fixed on the body.

'Maybe,' said Zoe. 'This place looks like a bachelor pad, though. New furniture, but none of it matches. I'd reckon our victim is recently single.'

Charlie looked at the large window stretching up towards the cathedral ceiling, and then at the thick marble benchtops. Through a set of french doors, he could see a large deck with an inground spa. 'Doesn't look like any bachelor pad I ever lived in.'

'Domestic or not,' said Zoe, 'I'd bet your next pay cheque that the victim knew his killer. This is no break and enter gone wrong.' The rug lay straight on the floor in front of the victim. The coasters were stacked on the coffee table. 'The victim is near the back of the house and there's no disturbance until here,' she said, pointing to the area around the body.

'Small gash in the back of the head,' said Jenny, beside the victim. 'A piece of glass. Looks like he was caught in a surprise attack and he smacked the back of his head on the mirror. Instinctively backing away, you know?'

'He probably hit his head twice in the struggle,' Zoe said. 'With the first hit he shattered the mirror; with the second, the shard was embedded in his head.' Zoe mimicked the action, before turning to Charlie. 'You got details on the victim?'

Charlie opened his folder. 'Yeah. Wallet was on the sideboard next to the front door. Mobile phone's there too. His name is Ray Carlson. Thirty-nine. Apparently he's a local. Grew up in Sorrento.'

'Not far from here, then.'

'Yeah,' said Charlie, 'and you were right about him being recently single. Separated, no kids.'

'That's a lot of information from a wallet,' said Zoe.

Charlie smirked. 'I asked a couple of the local uniforms outside. One of them knew him from the footy club.'

'How well?'

'Enough to say g'day. Said he was a friend of a friend.'

'We know what Ray did for a living?'

'Yeah, he works…worked…at a winery up at Red Hill.'

'Did he own it?' asked Zoe, looking around the room again.

'No. Apparently he managed the cellar.'

'Any form?'

'No. I ran his name through the system. Zilch.'

'Wallet still full?'

'About two hundred in cash and credit cards are still there.'

'You're from down this way, aren't you?' asked Zoe.

'Kind of. I grew up in Mornington,' said Charlie, pointing vaguely over his shoulder. 'Far more middle class than here.'

'Who found him?'

'An old mate of his, Dwayne Harley. Friends since primary school.'

Zoe pushed a loose strand of hair back with her left hand. 'Right. Where's Dwayne now?'

'Outside. Sitting in the shade, talking to the local sergeant.'

'That his ute in the driveway?' asked Zoe.

Charlie nodded, wiggling his pen between his fingers.

Zoe watched the pen. 'Ask one of the forensics team to open up the garage and see if the victim's car is still there. I can't see car keys anywhere. The killer may have taken it.'

'Will do,' said Charlie.

Zoe stood up and made her way back down the hallway, squinting as she walked out into the glare. She looked back at the house as she pulled off her face mask, and removed the plastic booties from her shoes. The house was modern; its large windows were framed by angled, polished concrete, intersecting with sheets of corten steel, which gave a rust-like finish. The grass in the front yard was lush under foot. She sighed, not seeing any CCTV cameras under the roof line, and put on her sunglasses.

Charlie came out a moment later. 'There's a new Ford Ranger in the garage. All the bells and whistles. Key's on the passenger seat. Called the rego in. It's Carlson's. The only vehicle registered in his name. How much, you reckon?' asked Charlie, gesturing at the house.

Zoe gave the smallest of grins, remembering their old game. When Charlie was first partnered with Zoe, he and his girlfriend were looking for a house to buy and every job gave him a chance to check out the real estate. 'Around here, over three million, maybe four,' she said. 'Less now it's a murder scene, though.'

'You'd need to either be lucky or ruthless to afford to live around here,' said Charlie.

'That counts us out then,' Zoe said. She looked across to where a golden retriever was lying in the shade of a tree. The dog wore a harness that read 'Victoria Police Service Dog', with a blue and white checkerboard strip that matched the police tape sealing off the area. A special exemption had been made for Zoe to get Harry, but only after her boss kicked up a fuss and the Commissioner's office finally relented. The dog sat up when he saw Zoe, alert and ready. She put up her hand, palm out, and he slumped back down on the grass.

A local uniformed sergeant walked across to them, his face a hotchpotch of wrinkles and sunspots. 'Terry Gunny,' he said, his hand outstretched.

'Zoe Mayer and Charlie Shaw,' she replied, shaking his hand.

'Yep, I recognise you from the news,' Terry said.

Zoe blushed as Charlie darted a look at her.

'That Dwayne Harley?' she asked, pointing at a man sitting on a low rock wall near the garage.

'Yeah, that's him,' said Terry. 'He seemed pretty freaked out when the first units arrived. He's calmed down a bit since then.'

'Has he said anything that'd be useful for us?' asked Charlie.

'Nah, nothing. Sorry.'

'Did you know the victim?' Zoe asked.

'No, Ray Carlson wasn't on our radar. Nothing on the system when I ran his name.'

'What about his mate Dwayne?'

'Same. I've seen him about once or twice, but I ran his name as well. He's clean.'

Zoe looked across at the spectators. The younger ones stood on the baking road, hopping from foot to foot. The older ones were on the grass on the far side of the road, whispering to each other. Zoe had an eye out for someone standing alone, looking anxious. All she could see were gawkers.

Hannah and Angus were off to the back, talking to people and making notes. They would ask everyone the same questions: Do you know the victim? Did you see anything suspicious? Hear anything? They would be scanning faces for signs of nervousness. Sometimes a killer would come back to oversee the action.

Zoe turned back to Terry. 'You had any serious crimes around here recently? Anything involving weapons? High levels of violence?'

Terry shook his head. 'Nah, nothing. Had a non-fatal stabbing in Rosebud last year, but the junkie gave himself up two days later. He's in prison now. Most of what we deal with is traffic-related, or people drinking too much at the pub and fighting. Occasionally we get a break and enter of someone's shed. Almost every house at this end of the peninsula has a monitored alarm system, so the crooks go elsewhere.' Zoe remembered the pulsing green light of the alarm system when she had first entered the house.

'Makes sense,' she replied. Over Terry's shoulder, Zoe saw the media arriving and unloading equipment. Beyond their vans, she noticed a dark blue Toyota Camry. She pointed at it. 'You got any local detectives here? That looks like a CI car.'

Terry squinted down the road. 'No, not one of ours.'

'Okay, thanks Terry. I reckon we've got it from here.'

'No worries,' he said, wandering back towards the police tape.

Zoe turned to Charlie. 'Oliver gauged the preliminary time of death to be between ten-thirty and eleven-thirty. Tell Hannah and Angus. They can be more specific in their questioning.'

Charlie set off in their direction.

Zoe walked across to where Dwayne Harley was sitting, staring at his hands. She crouched in front of him. 'Dwayne, I'm Detective Sergeant Zoe Mayer, from Homicide.'

Dwayne lifted his head, but didn't meet her gaze, staring vacantly towards the fence across the yard. Like the victim, he had a tanned complexion. His dark hair was cut short and Zoe could see his lean muscles under his tank top and board shorts. There seemed to be no scratches or bruises on his body.

'Hey,' he said meekly, barely a whisper.

'You want some water or something?'

'No, I'm okay. The other copper gave me some.'

Charlie approached. Zoe pointed over her shoulder with

her pen, keeping her eyes on Dwayne. 'This is Detective Senior Constable Charlie Shaw. So, what happened here today?' she asked, keeping her voice soft and sympathetic. She let her gaze fall to Dwayne's hands, looking for fresh cuts or dried blood around his fingernails or in the creases of his knuckles. They were clean. She saw sand caught in the hairs on his forearm.

Dwayne sucked in a breath. 'Me and Ray were supposed to go surfing this morning. He was a no-show, so after maybe an hour I came into shore and tried to call him a few times, but he didn't answer.' Zoe looked up at Charlie, who was writing notes. He nodded.

'What time was that?' asked Zoe.

'Dunno, probably about a quarter past eleven? It was weird, because he always answers, so I drove up here and... found him. I stood there for a bit, kinda in shock. He looked like a wax model. I thought he was playing a joke. Kept expecting he'd sit up and yell "Boo."'

Zoe leaned forward, breathing in deeply, as if considering her next question. She smelled no trace of bleach. 'What time did you arrive?'

'It was about eleven-thirty by the time I'd got changed, tied down the board and driven up here. The surf beach is just around the corner.'

Zoe pursed her lips. She knew that the same mobile phone tower would service the beach and the house. There'd be no way to verify Dwayne's whereabouts through tower pings.

'That your ute?' Zoe asked, pointing at the new Toyota Hilux in the driveway. It had a surfboard in the back.

'Yeah.'

There was sand on the end of the surfboard. Zoe turned back to Dwayne. 'Did you touch the body? Check if your friend was still alive?'

Dwayne blinked and shook his head. 'No...I didn't. The other copper asked me the same thing. There was too much blood and he wasn't breathing. Fuck, I couldn't do anything...He was already dead,' he said, exasperated. 'If I could have helped him, I would've.' Dwayne started to breathe heavily, raising his fingers to his face.

Zoe put up a reassuring hand. 'I understand, Dwayne. What did you do after that?'

'I came out the front and called triple zero. The first coppers arrived about five minutes later and I've been sitting here ever since.'

'You have your phone on you now?'

'Yeah...why?' Dwayne said, reaching into his pocket.

'Just want to have a look at the phone log so we can add your calls into the timeline.'

Dwayne pulled out his phone, punched in a code, and handed it to Charlie.

'So, were you and Ray friends for a long time?' Zoe continued.

'Ever since I can remember. Went to Sorrento primary together, then to Rosebud secondary.'

'Did you have a key?'

'To what?'

'To the house. A key to get in?'

'No, the door was wide open when I got here.'

Zoe nodded. 'Tell me about Ray's enemies.'

'He didn't have any.'

'Well, someone wanted to hurt him. You probably know him better than anyone, Dwayne. Are you sure there isn't anything that can help us?'

'No. I can't think of a single person who had a problem with him.'

'Any drug issues?'

'Nah. He never touched them.'

'Gambling?'

'Twenty bucks here and there on a Saturday down at the pub. Nothing big.'

'What about relationships?'

'Single. Has been a while now.' Dwayne crossed his arms and looked at the ground.

Zoe watched him. 'He was married though, right?'

'Yeah. He was married to Donna for a long time. Sixteen years or so. They broke up a while back. Getting divorced. She lives in Sorrento, on the bay.'

'Lot of aggro between them?'

'A bit,' said Dwayne, again looking at Zoe. 'Arguing about money, that sort of thing.'

'You think she could've done this, Dwayne?'

'Nah, doubt it. Donna is a piece of work, but I can't see her doing this.'

'Okay. Charlie will take your formal statement now. We'll also need Donna's address and the names of any other friends or family.' Zoe waited, looking Dwayne square in the eye. 'We're sorry for your loss.'

'Yeah, thanks,' said Dwayne.

Charlie sat down beside Dwayne on the rock wall. Zoe walked to her car and opened the back door. She took out a bowl and water bottle and went over to where Harry was sitting, his tail sweeping across the grass. She filled his bowl. As Harry drank, Zoe looked down the street. The blue Camry was gone.

She glanced at the properties beside Carlson's house. The one on the left had an Audi in the driveway and some bicycles strewn across the yard. The other looked vacant, with window shutters closed and grass that was a week overdue for a mow. Probably someone's holiday house, she thought.

The media were milling together in the shade. She could see six TV crews, reporters from a couple of radio stations and the crime beat journos from the major Melbourne papers. There were a couple of people she didn't recognise, who she supposed were from local media. She waved for them to come over.

As everyone was getting set up, Zoe waited impatiently. The sun was burning and she wanted to get her jacket off as soon as possible.

3.30 PM, SUNDAY 2 FEBRUARY

Zoe's gaze travelled up the red lacquered door. It was at least twelve feet high. Around it, the front of the house, all glass and steel, rose like the bow of a ship out over her head. It made Zoe uneasy, as if the house were about to run her down. Harry sat quietly, his eyes on her.

The house was in a quiet cul-de-sac running off Point Nepean Road in Sorrento, and set back deep on the block. Charlie stood behind them on the paved path that cut through the garden of succulents. There was a platinum BMW convertible in the driveway. 'An 8 series. That's serious money.'

Zoe knocked once.

The red door immediately swung open. 'Hello,' said a woman, stretching the word out. She was tall, in her late thirties, with short blonde hair, and wore a clinging blue summer dress that showcased her cleavage. She was wiping her hands with a kitchen towel.

'Ms Carlson?' asked Zoe, holding up her badge.

'Hello, I was wondering when you'd arrive,' she said breezily, without looking at the badge. 'Come on in. I'm just cooking.' Behind her, a white shih tzu barked angrily as he ran back and forth behind her legs, the noise echoing in the atrium-like foyer.

Harry tilted his head, staring impassively at the smaller dog.

'Quieten down, Bobo. Bring your dog—mine will be good. I like his little vest.' The woman pointed at Harry as she bent down to pick up her dog, who stopped barking. 'Service dog, eh? I've never seen a police service dog before,' she said, already walking back through the house.

'He's new,' said Zoe, giving Charlie a sideways glance, not sure how to interpret the upbeat manner. Two detectives arriving unannounced usually provoked anxiety. This woman was acting as if a neighbour had stopped by.

As they entered, Harry darted around Charlie, coming up close alongside Zoe.

'Cup of tea? It's Donna, by the way.' They entered an open living area. The smell of a freshly baked cake filled the air. Floor to ceiling windows gave them a view of an infinity pool, which met the waters of Port Phillip Bay. They could see north around the arc of the peninsula towards the city in the distance.

'Thank you, but no,' said Zoe.

Charlie shook his head, still staring out over the bay.

'You know why we're here, then?' asked Zoe.

'Those hoons. I don't care what judge or surgeon raised

them, they shouldn't be screaming around the streets in their parents' Porsches at two in the morning.'

Zoe put up a hand. 'Ms Carlson, Donna, that's not why we're here.'

'Oh, sorry. I made a complaint to the local station and thought…So, why are you here?'

Donna sat at the dining-room table, indicating chairs for them. 'Ms Carlson, my name's Zoe Mayer and this is Charlie Shaw. We're from Homicide and we have some bad news for you.' Zoe waited a beat. 'Ray Carlson was found dead this morning at his home.'

Donna looked directly at Zoe. A few seconds passed. She shut her eyes until she was almost squinting. 'What… What do you mean?' she asked.

'He was murdered,' said Zoe, her tone neutral.

Donna said nothing, clear-eyed, before shaking her head twice and staring out towards the bay.

Again Zoe waited. 'When did the two of you separate?' asked Zoe.

Donna took a breath. 'About eight or nine months ago. It was winter. June. Yes, it was at the end of June.'

'Who instigated the separation?'

'I suppose it was me, although we'd both been unhappy for a while.'

'Do you know if Ray had a problem with anyone?'

'No. Ray's just a big kid at heart…Murdered? I can't believe it. Are you sure?' Donna shook her head, blinking. Zoe could see her eyes growing moist. She noted that Donna hadn't asked her how Ray had been killed.

'Where were you this morning?' asked Zoe.

'In Rosebud with my sister. At the shopping centre. She lives down there.' She waved a finger towards the window.

'What time was that?'

Donna paused a moment, as if collecting her thoughts. 'I left home around quarter past nine. Arrived just before nine-thirty, I'd say. We shopped for a while and then had coffee. Hold on...' Donna grabbed her handbag and retrieved her purse. She searched through it before pulling out a receipt and handing it to Zoe. It was for a dress bought at 9.58 am for ninety-eight dollars. Zoe turned on her phone, photographed the receipt and gave it back to Donna.

'Bought it for my sister. She doesn't have many nice clothes.'

'What time did you leave Rosebud?'

'About eleven-thirty, I think.'

'Did you come straight home?'

'Yes, why?'

'Have you been to Latham Drive in Portsea today?'

'To Ray's place? No.'

'But you've been there, yes?'

'Only once, and not inside. We had a...a disagreement... outside his place a month back.'

'What about?'

Donna closed her eyes, before shaking her head. 'Money. He was supposed to put some money in my account and hadn't. Wasn't a big deal. He sorted it that night.'

'Does he own the house?'

'No, he rented it when we split.'

'Does Ray have any enemies you know of?'

'No. No one,' Donna said.

'Owe anyone money?'

'Not that I know of.'

'Do you work?'

'What? No, I don't. Why?'

'Well, Ray worked at a winery and the house he was living in would've cost a small fortune to rent. Plus, this place is pretty fancy and there's a new BMW out front…'

'He is…was…the logistics manager. Plus, we were careful with money.' Donna adopted a lofty tone. 'You can save a lot that way.'

'Right,' said Zoe, unconvinced. 'So, why did you and Ray split up?'

'We just grew apart. He wanted to go surfing all the time. I wanted a more grown-up life, a normal life. Ray was like a teenager in a lot of ways. I never wanted kids and I certainly didn't want to be married to one.' Donna paused. 'Sorry, that sounded awful. Bad habit.'

Zoe wanted to catch Donna off guard. 'Did you have anything to do with Ray's death?'

Donna's head jerked back. 'What? No, no, I didn't. How dare you!'

'Who did then?'

'How would I know? I don't have the faintest idea.'

'We would like to have a look at your phone,' Zoe said.

'What? Why?'

'We need to eliminate those closest to him as suspects. It's easier if we look at the phone with your permission rather than wasting time getting a warrant.'

Donna made a show of thinking it through.

'Unless there's something you're not telling us,' added Zoe, one eyebrow raised.

Donna got up and walked to the kitchen bench. She picked up her phone and punched in some numbers as she walked back to the table. 'Go for your life,' she said, sliding it across the table.

Charlie moved in close as Zoe scrolled through the log. 'Who's Brenda?' asked Zoe. The number had been called earlier that day and twice on Saturday.

'My sister, the one I met with this morning.'

'Okay,' said Zoe. All the other numbers had female names attached to them. Charlie wrote down the names and numbers.

Donna pouted. 'This going to take long? I need to call his parents.'

'Not too long,' said Zoe.

Donna rolled her eyes, crossed her arms and looked out over the bay again.

Zoe opened Donna's text messages. She and Charlie read them together. There were exchanges with about ten people, none of whom seemed of interest. Charlie noted them in any case. Zoe passed the phone back across the table.

'Is that it, then?' asked Donna.

8 PM, SUNDAY 2 FEBRUARY

Zoe was going over her notes as Charlie drove them down St Kilda Road past the long shadows of high-rises. Harry slept on his mat in the back seat. It was almost sunset but the heat outside was still blistering.

Her phone buzzed. Zoe glanced at the screen before answering. 'Hi Mum.'

'Hi darling. Good luck for tomorrow. First day back and all.' Though she sounded upbeat, Zoe could hear the background anxiety in her mother's voice.

'Already started. Picked up a job late this morning.'

'Goodness, no easing you back in then?'

'Doesn't work like that. Sooner the better, I say.'

'As long as you think you're ready. How's Tom? Things still going well?'

'Everything's fine. Listen, Charlie and I are running late to an autopsy. I'll give you a ring in a few days, okay?'

There was a pause. Zoe let it run.

'That's fine,' her mother said. 'Whenever you find some time.'

She ignored the bait. 'Will do. Love you.' Zoe ended the call, and looked over her shoulder at Harry, who was asleep.

'How's your mum?' asked Charlie.

'She's all right. Just been fussing over me for the last few months, that's all. After everything that happened, she was hoping I'd pull the pin on police work and make use of my commerce degree. When that didn't work, she started trying to fast forward my personal life into marriage and the maternity ward. In either order.'

'That something you want?' Charlie's eyes were fixed on the traffic.

'Marriage. Maybe? One day. Kids, probably not. Reckon I'm getting a bit old for that.'

'Hardly. What are you, like thirty-five or something?'

'Nice one. Thirty-eight at last count,' said Zoe, grinning.

'You'd be a good mother, I reckon,' he said. 'You've got the right balance of patience and toughness.'

Zoe scoffed. 'Thanks. I'll take that as a compliment.' She wasn't so sure about the patience part. 'I worked the Lamente case when I first came to Homicide.'

Charlie glanced across at her. 'I remember that one. I was in uniform then. Three dead kids. Must have been tough.'

'It was awful, but that's not what affected me the most. What got me was when we finally arrested the guy. He was so normal, mild-mannered, polite. Completely unremarkable. I remember thinking that if evil could lurk in plain sight like that, having kids was too risky. It was like a switch flicked off in my head and I couldn't turn it on again.'

Charlie nodded. 'I can understand that.'

Zoe wished she hadn't mentioned the Lamente case. It was a box of memories best left closed. 'Anyway, Mum would much prefer I was working as an investment banker.'

'She was pissed off when you joined the force?'

'You kidding? She told me I was throwing away a great education and the chance of a good life.'

Charlie chuckled. 'Yep, you'd probably have a holiday home in Portsea by now.'

'And its value would have taken a hit today. Anyway, how's Jane?'

'Not sure. We separated a few months back.'

Zoe shot him a look. 'Shit, sorry to hear that. I had no idea.'

'It happened just after you...went on leave. She said I was obsessed with the job and wasn't putting any effort into the relationship.' He was silent. 'She was probably right.'

'What about Alex?'

'He's okay. He stays with me every second weekend and I try to get to his cricket games every week. We chat on the phone every night before he goes to bed. It's as good as it can be, under the circumstances.'

It was almost dusk as they approached the Institute of Forensic Medicine in Southbank, a modern two-storey glass and concrete affair that also housed the Coroners Court. It was overlooked by a forest of apartment towers that stretched on towards the city.

Charlie swung the car around, parking beneath the canopy of a tree on the far side of the road. 'You want me to stay here with Harry?' he asked.

'Thanks,' said Zoe. 'Do you mind taking him for a walk around the block? He'll need a wee. His lead's in the back.'

'No worries,' Charlie said, opening the passenger door, letting a blast of heat in.

'And keep him on the nature strip. The footpath's too...'

Charlie put up a hand. 'Hot for his paws, yes, I've had a dog before. And I'll give him some water when we get back.'

'Thanks,' grinned Zoe, as she reluctantly headed for the front door. As a waft of spice from a nearby Malaysian restaurant caught her halfway across the road, she realised she hadn't eaten all day. By the time she reached the front door, she knew her appetite would soon be gone. Zoe still hated autopsies. At least she no longer threw up afterwards. She counted that as a win. Charlie hated them even more than she did, so walking Harry was a win for him as well.

She showed her badge at the desk, before heading towards one of the homicide rooms. She took a breath, pushed the door open and walked into the viewing room, a long, narrow space dominated by a large window running almost the length of one side. There was a large television screen at each end. From here she could look down onto the homicide room.

Through the window, Zoe could see Ray Carlson's body lying on a light blue gurney. The top of his head was a metre and a half from her. A large mobile operating-theatre light was above him. The room was painted off-white and fitted out with stainless steel benches and sinks. The floor was covered in dull linoleum in a shade which Zoe guessed was called morgue green. Even without the body, the whole scene would've been depressing.

Oliver Nunan was hunched over the victim, starting to cut the clothing from his body. Next to him was a tall woman Zoe didn't recognise. They both wore matching blue hospital scrubs, masks, wrap-around clear glasses, surgical gloves and pink rubber boots.

'Evening, Zoe,' he said through the intercom, without looking up.

'Hi Oliver. Sorry I'm late.'

'No worries. I was just getting started. This is Anna, Dr Anna Sorgstrom.'

Zoe smiled, nodding hello. Anna was slim and tanned, her shoulder-length blonde hair pulled into a ponytail.

'Nice to meet you, Zoe,' said Anna, smiling. Her accent was Australian with a splash of Swedish. Zoe decided that Charlie might become less reluctant about attending autopsies in the future.

'Anna's my retirement plan. Succession planning, they call it.'

'But you're so young,' teased Zoe.

Oliver gave a short laugh. 'Flattery will get you a long way,' he said.

He continued to cut away Ray's clothes, placing them into large bags. Anna took several photos of the knife, still stuck into Ray's body just below the ribcage, before Oliver pulled it out with a pair of forceps and put it on a tray Anna held out for him. 'DNA and latents,' he said automatically.

Anna put the tray down, leaning in to stare at the knife from different angles.

'What is it?' asked Zoe.

Oliver looked up at Zoe, and then at Anna.

'Looks like gauze to me,' said Anna. 'Tiny piece of it came out with the knife.'

'What, like a bandage?' asked Zoe. She knew that the paramedics hadn't bothered trying to revive Carlson. 'There were no bandages at the scene.'

'I know,' said Oliver, straightening.

Zoe shut her eyes.

'Thoughts?' asked Oliver, noticing.

'The killer wore a bandage on their hand so as not to leave prints on the knife. In the stabbing, the knife caught on the bandage and tore some threads away.'

'Why not just wear gloves?' asked Anna.

'If you answered the front door to someone wearing latex gloves on a hot summer's day, your guard would go up. But a bandage wouldn't cause concern. I think the killer was invited in, and attacked the victim at the back of the house.'

Oliver turned to Anna. 'See, I told you she was good.'

Zoe felt herself blush. She watched as Oliver made a small incision above and below the wound, and then hunched over to peer inside. 'Have a look at this,' he said to Zoe. He picked up a device the shape and size of a pen. He pushed a button on the side and one of the screens in the viewing room came to life.

Zoe hated it when he did this.

Oliver used a pair of forceps to hold the wound open and pointed the camera into it. He was looking up at the screen. 'See how far up and down the wound runs inside the body?'

She nodded, squeamish.

Oliver moved the camera back and forth, illuminating the gash. 'You okay?' he asked.

'Yeah,' she said. 'What do you reckon?'

Oliver stood back from the table. 'Okay, the knife went into the torso in an upward motion,' he said, sweeping his clenched fist in an arc, 'and the attacker then pulled the handle sharply upwards, causing the blade to go down. The attacker would've been standing close to the victim for at least a few seconds. They would've got sprayed with blood. That blade will be razor sharp, mark my words.'

'So the attacker was at least as tall as the victim, yes?'

Oliver paused. 'Based on the point of incision and the leverage required to pull the knife handle upwards—yes. The victim is around five eleven in the old scale.'

'About 180 centimetres,' translated Anna from the end of the examination table.

'It looks calculated to me,' said Zoe. 'It wasn't a frenzied event, with multiple stab wounds. This was meant to kill the victim, but not instantly. Not like shooting someone in the head. Somebody wanted Ray Carlson to know he was going to die.' Zoe looked down at Ray's ashen face.

Oliver broke the silence. 'We checked under his nails. Definitely scrubbed clean with a nail brush or something similar. There's bleach residue up to his wrists, consistent with his hands being dipped in a bucket of the stuff. Did Forensics find a brush at the scene?'

'No, nothing,' said Zoe.

'The only other trauma to the body is the gash in the back of his head.'

'From the mirror,' said Zoe.

Oliver picked up the electric saw. 'Yes, that's the one.'

7.55 AM, MONDAY 3 FEBRUARY

The squad room was already buzzing as Zoe and Harry made their way through the open-plan office towards her desk. Zoe carried Harry's dog bed rolled up under one arm. Some colleagues smiled and waved, while others gave her the thumbs-up. One or two she didn't recognise, testament to the burn-out rate of the squad, looked her up and down, before their gaze fell on the golden retriever at her side.

Harry looked up at each person's face as they passed by. The Homicide office took up a large floor of the Spencer Street police complex, only a few years old. It hadn't taken long for the place to look like an updated version of the old squad's office though, with the usual open-plan desks, low partition walls and constant aroma of coffee and mildly burnt toast.

Along one wall were a couple of offices for senior staff, and conference rooms. Behind another wall near the lift were interview rooms, as well as monitoring rooms with banks of TVs and recording equipment. This office felt like home to

Zoe and she was happy to be back.

'So, this is really happening then, is it?' mumbled Iain Gillies, peering down his nose at the dog walking beside Zoe. In his mid-forties, Iain was a large man, over six foot three with a jowly face and greying hair, whose permanent grimace was appropriate to his personality. Zoe often wondered if he came out of his mother scowling.

'Good to see you too, Iain,' Zoe said. 'You're looking well.'

'Yeah, welcome back, Mayer.' Iain grunted as he slumped back into his chair, his belly bulging against his shirt buttons.

Hannah Nguyen walked over and stroked Harry's head. A detective sergeant like Zoe, Hannah was a tough character, unwilling to take a backward step whenever challenged. Although shorter than the rest of the squad, Hannah was lean and strong, with dark wavy, shoulder-length hair. She wore dark pants and a sleeveless white blouse that showed off her toned arms.

'Hey gorgeous,' she said as Harry pulled his mouth back into a smile, his tongue rolling out to the side. 'Hi Zoe, sorry. Got distracted by your handsome new partner. I didn't get a chance to meet him properly yesterday.'

'His name's Harry,' said Zoe.

'Suits him. He's a sweetie. Good to have a handsome man about the squad for once.'

Charlie rolled his chair back. 'Thanks,' he said, in mock offence.

'Someone's not happy about a little competition,' teased Hannah.

'You and Angus good for an update?' asked Zoe.

'Yeah, for sure. I'll grab him.'

Zoe unrolled the dog bed under her desk. Harry lay down on it like it had always been there. Zoe sat and leaned back to speak to Charlie around the partition. 'Where's the floater who was covering for me?'

'Gone,' said Charlie. 'She headed back to Armed Crime last Friday when it was confirmed you were coming back. She couldn't get out of here fast enough.' He chuckled. 'Said she'd transferred out of Homicide years ago for a reason and the reason was still valid.'

'What about the case load?' asked Zoe.

'Manageable,' said Charlie. 'I've got two other jobs open, plus the Portsea job we picked up yesterday.'

'You'll have to catch me up on the other two.'

'Both under control. I've got a guy in custody for a meth-rage killing and I'm wrapping up witness statements and paperwork. The other one's a suspected DV homicide in Toorak. Wife found dead at the base of the stairs in a mansion. The husband reckons his wife tripped. I'm trying to locate a possible witness who is apparently skiing in Canada somewhere and won't be back for a week or so. I'm working both cases with Hannah. The boss said to let you ease your way back in.'

Zoe raised an eyebrow. *What the fuck?*

Hannah and Angus walked over, wheeling chairs behind them, and sat down. A foot taller than Hannah, Angus Batch had a chiselled jawline and a buzz cut. The first few buttons of his shirt always seemed to be open, allowing the world a glimpse of his hairless chest.

'Learn anything from canvassing the neighbours?' asked Zoe.

'Not much,' said Hannah. 'We interviewed all the gawkers at the scene, plus the other houses in the street that you and Charlie didn't cover, as well as the neighbours over the victim's back fence. No one noticed anything strange yesterday or even knew the victim at all, beyond a wave if they crossed paths. Only two people knew his first name. Consensus was that Ray Carlson kept long hours, usually leaving home around seven every morning and often not getting home until after eleven. They said he lived quietly. No loud music or parties. No domestics or disturbances. Anything to add, Angus?'

Angus shook his head. 'Nothing much. One of the houses had CCTV pointed down their driveway. Picked up three passing cars around the time of the murder. Two of them we confirmed as belonging to elderly neighbours. We spoke to them and they're out of the picture. And the third...'

'Yes, the image you emailed us last night,' said Zoe. 'You got that printout, Charlie?'

He passed it to her. 'The dark blue Toyota Camry.' In the photo, the driver was a blurry figure in a hat. They couldn't see the number plate. 'Charlie, any luck getting this enhanced?'

'That *is* the enhanced version. Not much use, I'm afraid.'

'What time was this?' Zoe said, looking at Angus.

'Ten-forty am.'

'Did you get footage of the Camry leaving?'

'Yeah,' said Angus, consulting his folder. 'It was 11.20 am.' He pulled out another photograph.

Zoe stared at the image. 'Thing is, though, I reckon this car was parked down the street when we were there. Wasn't there when we arrived, but I saw it before we spoke to Dwayne Harley, the guy who found the victim. Not the type of car you usually see parked in a Portsea street.'

'So, what? He killed the guy and came back later to watch?' asked Charlie.

'Yes, it happens sometimes,' said Hannah. 'The cocky ones who think they're smarter than us.'

In her peripheral vision, Zoe noticed the squad's detective inspector, Rob Loretti, walk over and lean against a desk behind where Charlie sat. Rob was Zoe's former partner, who had been promoted to detective inspector in charge of Homicide the year before. In his mid-fifties, Rob was a smart, instinctual detective with a high strike rate for solving cases quickly. He was also the only openly gay head of department that Zoe knew of in the whole of the force. Zoe gave him a nod and turned back to Charlie. 'What time did we arrive there yesterday, Charlie?'

'Quarter after one, or thereabouts.'

Zoe looked across at Angus. 'Can you revisit the CCTV footage and see if our Camry reappears? Check after 1 pm. If the same person came back we might get a better shot of them.'

'Will do.'

'Okay,' said Zoe, 'here's what we know. Victim is Ray Carlson. Thirty-nine. Has lived at the pointy end of the

Peninsula his whole life. Separated. No kids. Found by his lifelong friend, Dwayne Harley. One knife wound only. Knife still in the deceased when we arrived. No sign of a frenzied attack. Clinical.'

'Anything distinctive about the weapon?' asked Hannah.

'Large kitchen knife,' answered Zoe. 'Brand is Shabon. Higher-end, but common enough. I've got one at home. We're not sure if the weapon came from the house or was brought to the scene. I assume the killer brought it, as it looks planned. Autopsy showed that the attacker thrust the knife upwards into the body and then sliced down inside.' Zoe mimicked the action for effect.

'Yikes. Sounds personal,' said Rob in the background.

'We thought the same thing,' said Zoe. 'There were no prints on the knife, but they found a piece of gauze caught in the base of the blade. I suspect that the killer wore a bandage on his hand to stop leaving prints.'

'Any DNA traces?' asked Angus.

Zoe shook her head. 'Still waiting to hear about the knife, but it looks like the victim's hands were dunked in bleach after he died and the fingernails were scrubbed clean. The bathroom reeks of bleach and there was an empty mop and bucket sitting by the toilet.'

'Professional job. Flushed the evidence away,' said Hannah, almost to herself.

'Yeah,' said Zoe. 'Perhaps the killer wanted to change clothes. The bathroom's spotless. Not a fingerprint anywhere. Whoever it was had time to clean up.'

'Any attempt to clean up around the body?' asked Rob.

'No, just in the bathroom,' said Zoe. 'Nothing seems to be missing from the house. Wallet and phone were on the side table next to the front door, and his car is in the garage with the keys inside. Last night's autopsy confirmed he was killed between 10.45 and 11.15 am. We've interviewed Dwayne, and spoken to neighbours, the ex-wife, his parents, his boss and some of his friends. No one apparently knows anything. Carlson had no police record and no big debts or drug issues. He was a moderate gambler. Twenty bucks here or there. According to Dwayne Harley he wasn't in any sort of relationship. Real estate agent said that he direct deposited his rent on time every month.'

'Anything else?' asked Rob.

'We have access to the victim's computer,' said Zoe. 'Found his password on a sticky note in the home office. Same one opened his phone. We'll give it to one of the tactical intelligence officers to dig around in.'

'Give it to Anjali Arya,' said Rob.

Zoe gave a confused look.

'Tactical intel officer who started while you were away,' said Charlie. 'She came from the Fraud Squad. I've got her looking at Carlson's phone records right now.'

'Does the ex-wife feel like a candidate to you?' asked Hannah.

Zoe screwed up her nose. 'Maybe, maybe not. She wasn't turning on the tears, but there's something not quite right about her. She didn't ask how he was killed. We'll have another chat with her this morning.'

'She is also flush, by the looks of it,' added Charlie.

'Views of Port Phillip Bay, infinity pool, flash new BMW out front.'

'No crime in being rich, is there?' asked Hannah.

'Err, no,' said Charlie, searching for the right response. 'But it looks like new money to me. She's flashing it about. Said they were good at saving money, but she's living in a multi-million-dollar house, she doesn't work and her ex has a normal sort of job. It doesn't add up.'

'What about the guy who found him?' asked Rob.

'Dwayne?' said Charlie. 'He wasn't acting evasive or suspicious when I took his formal statement. He said that he and the victim were supposed to be surfing that morning. His story seems to check out. He did seem to be shocked when we spoke with him. He's still a person of interest though.'

'Okay,' said Rob. 'What's next?'

'Normal stuff,' said Zoe, bristling slightly at Rob's old habit of hijacking her briefings. 'Looking first at people he was closest to. Checking life insurance policies, any debts, that sort of thing. Hannah and Angus, can you interview Carlson's colleagues today at the winery?'

'No worries,' they both said simultaneously.

Rob stood up. 'Zoe, have you got a sec? We need to meet with the return-to-work guy from HR. Shouldn't take too long. He's in my office.'

'Okay. Give me one minute.' Zoe turned to Hannah. 'When you're at that winery, can you check for the Camry? See if anyone owns one or knows of someone who does.'

'Got it,' said Hannah.

'And also find out Carlson's salary. Maybe ask around

and see if he had a second job...He stayed out late, so something was occupying his time.'

'Will do,' said Hannah.

Zoe looked down at Harry. 'Stay,' she said, before turning to Charlie. 'Shouldn't be long.'

As Zoe entered Rob's office a man stood, extending his hand. He wore a navy suit and a white shirt, no tie. Around his neck was a blue police lanyard. With hair sculpted by gel, he was in his thirties and wore a broad smile, like an old friend. Zoe felt immediately on guard.

'Richard Wilcox,' he said.

'Zoe Mayer.' His hand felt soft in her grip.

They sat down.

'Zoe, my job is to make sure that you have all the support that you need before you start work again today,' said Richard in a syrupy voice.

It sounded to Zoe like he was talking to a five-year-old. 'I actually started yesterday. Charlie and I were on call.'

'Right, okay, that's not ideal,' said Richard, flustered, looking at Rob, who shrugged. 'Anyway, how are you feeling, coming back?'

'Great. I've been wanting to for months. The first month off was probably warranted, but not so much the next three.'

'You've got your service dog with you. Are you comfortable having him here?'

'Yes, absolutely.'

'Any additional support you need?'

'Like what?' asked Zoe, confused.

'A quieter office space, longer breaks, that sort of thing,' said Richard, giving her a sympathetic smile.

Zoe could feel her heart beating hard. 'Look, I'm not a charity case, okay? I just want to get back to work. That's it. The department swapped my old Commodore for a Ford Escape as a CI car so I can take Harry around with me. That's all I need.'

Richard's brow furrowed as he opened a folder on his lap. Zoe could see three scribbled bullet points at the top of the page. She couldn't make them out. 'You've had a gun safe installed at home?'

'That's right,' said Zoe. 'So I don't have to come back in every night and lock away my firearm.'

'You...don't think that with everything that's happened, that...'

'No, I don't think whatever it is you're about to say. I was planning on getting the safe before I went on leave.'

Richard looked across to Rob, who shrugged again. He gave a hint of a smile. *He's waiting for me to lose it at this guy.* Immediately, she calmed down.

Richard looked again at his notepad, hesitating. Zoe saw his shoulders drop slightly. 'Okay, the psych has cleared you for full duties, so all the best.' Richard pulled a card from his shirt pocket and passed it to her. It felt uncomfortably warm. 'If you need anything, call me.'

'Thanks, I will. All the best,' said Zoe, half standing.

Richard stood, said his goodbyes and left the office.

Zoe stood up and shut the door after him.

'I think you hurt his feelings,' said Rob after he had gone.

'Life's like that sometimes,' she said, crumpling the card. 'Can I have a quiet word?'

'Is this about me easing you back onto cases?'

'Yeah. I don't think—'

Rob held up a hand. 'Zoe, you just came back. The psych thinks you are ready, but I want to be sure you are one hundred per cent before I load you with a full book of jobs again.'

'But I...'

'Just trust me, okay? Soon enough you'll be swamped in work and wishing for this.'

Zoe let out a sigh. She had learnt over the years just how far she could push him.

Zoe was almost back to her desk when she heard the call from across the room. 'Heads up.'

Turning, she saw a tennis ball flying towards her. Instinctively she caught it. Across the room Iain Gillies and his partner Garry Burns were laughing. Although shorter and leaner, Garry was a junior version of Iain, aping his senior partner in every way.

'Looks like you haven't lost your touch,' said Iain with a thin smile. 'Just a welcome back gift from us to throw to your little therapy friend at lunchtime.'

'Thanks,' said Zoe, her chin held high. 'Anyone ever told you two that you look like father and son?' She stared at them, watching them both appear offended, before they turned away in unison. She opened her drawer, dropped the ball in and pushed it shut.

9.45 AM, MONDAY 3 FEBRUARY

Charlie reached over and unclipped the gate to Brenda Johannes's front yard in Rosebud. He tried to push it open without success. His second attempt was more forceful, pushing some of the accumulated weeds flat as the gate gave way.

The house was a 1970s brick veneer. The bricks were a sun-bleached brown and the corrugated iron roof was so slightly pitched that it was almost flat. A mess of weeds looked to be winning the war against the patches of different types of grass. A beaten-up red Toyota Corolla sat under a carport that looked ready to fall in the next storm.

Zoe and Harry followed Charlie up the narrow path to the door. Charlie knocked twice.

The door opened. The sweet, strong odour of cannabis hit Zoe and Charlie immediately.

They knew at once that the woman who answered the door was Brenda, Donna Carlson's sister. They had the same eyes, facial structure and height, but the differences were also apparent. Shoeless, she wore loose blue tracksuit pants and a pink t-shirt. Brenda looked beaten down by life, and although three years younger than Donna, she easily looked a decade older.

'Fuck,' she said on seeing their police badges.

Zoe took the lead. 'Brenda Johannes, Detectives Zoe Mayer and Charlie Shaw. Can we have a word? It's about the death of Ray Carlson.'

'Yeah, sure,' said Brenda, nervously looking over her shoulder.

'Maybe we'd be better speaking outside.' Zoe had no time for the paperwork involved in a minor dope bust.

'Yeah, yeah, that'd be better. Yeah. My son had his mates over last night and the place is, um, a bit of a mess.' Brenda looked down, noticing Harry for the first time. 'What's the deal with the dog? Is it here to sniff out the place for drugs? It was my son's friends...'

'No, he's with me,' said Zoe, leading them over to the corner of the yard, under the shade of a neighbour's tree.

'So Brenda, what do you know about the killing of Ray Carlson yesterday?'

Brenda's eyes shot up to Zoe's face. 'Me? Nothing, nothing at all. Only found out last night. Saw about it all on the news—you know, that there'd been a murder—but I didn't even know it was Ray until Donna texted me afterwards.'

'Can I see the text?' asked Zoe.

'Yeah, sure.' Brenda pulled her phone from her pocket

and brought up the text message. Zoe looked at the message. *Ray dead. Someone killed him this morning. Will let you know about funeral.*

Zoe opened her own phone and photographed the message.

'Pretty cold sort of message, don't you think?'

'Yeah, that's Donna though. She's fairly...' Brenda trailed off, pursing her lips.

'Fairly what?'

'Direct is the best way to say it. Everything she thinks, she says. No filter, ya know?'

'Where were you yesterday morning?'

Brenda paused. 'Shopping with Donna down at the plaza. She bought me a dress. Actually, she forced me into letting her buy it for me. Said I was looking shabby, her words.'

'And when did you get home?'

'After ten. Called me mum straight away cause I was pissed off with Donna and the whole dress thing. Spoke to her for half an hour.'

'Can you check your call log for the exact time?'

Brenda shook her head, handing the phone over. 'Wouldn't know how. Sorry.'

Zoe opened the phone log. There was a call to a contact called 'Mum' at 10.22 am. The call lasted thirty-eight minutes. Zoe handed the phone back to Brenda.

'Who do you think killed Ray, Brenda?'

Brenda was already shaking her head before Zoe finished the question. 'No idea. I mean, I was no fan of Ray. He had been fucking around on Donna for years and he had a drug problem.' She shot a look back over towards her house. 'Serious drugs, I mean. Speed, that sort of thing. He also used to push her around. But I don't know who killed him. Haven't even seen him since they separated.'

'Did you see him abusing Donna?'

'Nah. Just something Donna used to tell me. It wasn't like she had black eyes or anything. He'd just give her a smack on the back of the head or push her, that sort of thing. They'd argue all the time about petty shit.'

'Brenda, do you think that Donna killed Ray?'

Zoe watched as Brenda's eyes narrowed as she thought through an answer. 'Nah,' she answered finally, 'probably not.'

'Sounds like she had motive, though, right?'

Zoe could see Brenda reconsidering. Finally she answered: 'Sure, but I still can't see it. They've had a shit relationship for years, so why now? Especially as they're getting...were getting, divorced.'

'Do you know of anyone close to Ray or Donna that may have been involved?'

'Nah, I don't really know anyone in that crowd. I was never invited into their life. All I know was that Ray always had plenty of cash and that the two of them liked to make me feel like shit. Now it's just Donna to do that though.'

'What about Dwayne Harley?' Zoe asked. She saw Brenda physically shudder when she mentioned his name.

'Yeah, what about him?' Brenda pulled down on the bottom of her t-shirt, stretching it out of shape.

'You think he could've been involved?'

Brenda looked up at the tree above them before responding. 'Doubt it. They were always close. He was best man at Ray and Donna's wedding. I haven't seen him in years though.'

'Anything about him that rubs you the wrong way. You reacted when I said Dwayne's name.'

Brenda exhaled deeply. 'Dwayne tried it on with me years ago. Before Ray and Donna were married. Didn't take it well when I said no.'

'Was he violent?'

'No, not really. At first he was sweet as pie, charming and all, but when I said no he shoved me away, called me a slut and a fucking tease. Normal bloke stuff.'

Charlie interjected. 'That's a long way from normal, Brenda.'

Brenda chuckled sardonically. 'Maybe in your world.'

12.30 PM, MONDAY 3 FEBRUARY

Zoe and Charlie turned into Donna Carlson's street. It was narrow and quiet, bordered by tea trees and gum trees swaying gently in the hot northerly breeze.

After leaving Brenda's house they had spoken to other friends of Ray and Donna Carlson. Everyone they had spoken to also saw Donna as the victim in the marriage, but none could directly shine a light on who could have killed Ray and why.

As they approached Donna's house, a blue Camry pulled away from the kerb and drove past them in the cul-de-sac.

'You see that?'

'What?' said Charlie, looking up from his notes. 'Shit.'

'Lie down, Harry,' said Zoe. In the back, the dog dropped flat. 'Good boy.'

Zoe did a quick three-point turn, gunning the car in pursuit. After a hundred metres, she was right up behind the Camry on Point Nepean Road. Charlie hit a switch and the flashing lights and siren came to life.

The car in front slowed before suddenly accelerating away. Zoe punched the accelerator flat to the floor.

Charlie was on the radio as the Camry drove erratically in front of them, crossing partly into the oncoming lane and then across to the verge. 'Rosebud D-24. All available units in the Sorrento area. We are in pursuit of a blue Toyota Camry. Registration alpha, tango, romeo, three, nine, eight. Headed east on the Point Nepean Road.'

On the radio they heard the duty sergeant arrange for back-up. Ahead of them, the Camry weaved its way through the traffic. Using the car's built-in keyboard, Charlie punched in the Camry's number plate.

'He's a local. Car's registered to Joshua Priest, address in Rosebud.'

A hundred and fifty metres ahead, Zoe saw a group of children on the side of the road, waiting for an opportunity to cross. One of them stepped out before hesitating and pulling their foot back. She glanced at the speedometer. They were doing over a hundred.

'Shit, I'm pulling this,' said Zoe.

Charlie flicked off the lights and siren, and got on the radio to let Rosebud know that they were abandoning the chase. Slowing, Zoe watched as the Camry roared away.

'We'll pick him up later at home,' she said, 'unless the locals get him in the meantime.'

They passed the group of kids on the side of the road, still waiting to cross, and made their way back to Donna's red door.

They rang the buzzer. After a few seconds, she answered, her face creased in annoyance. Donna was wearing a loose white shirt, half buttoned up, and linen shorts. Zoe could see her thin pink lace bra through the gap in her shirt and noticed that her lip gloss was slightly smudged. 'Detectives...how can I help you today?'

'Ms Carlson, we have a few more questions.' Zoe stepped forward through the doorway before Donna could respond, Harry and Charlie following close behind.

'Sure, come in,' she said reluctantly, as they passed by.

They made their way through the light-filled foyer, past some potted ferns, into the expansive living area overlooking the bay. They sat once again at the long dining-room table. Through the window the sun was glistening off the water of the pool in the background. Harry lay down on the cool tiles next to Zoe. Donna's shih tzu eyed him suspiciously from the dog bed in the corner.

'Ms Carlson—'

'Call me Donna, please.'

'Donna, did you have a visitor just now?' asked Zoe.

'What do you mean?'

Zoe, still riled by the abandoned chase, inhaled deeply, glaring at her. 'I don't know how to be clearer. Was there someone here five minutes ago?'

'Yes. A friend of mine dropped by.'

'Joshua Priest?' asked Charlie.

Donna glanced across at Charlie, then back to Zoe. 'Yes. Why?'

'He took off when he saw us. What's the deal with that?'

'No idea. You'll have to ask him.'

'What's your relationship with him?'

'Relationship? He's just a friend. Well, a friend of Ray's, mainly. He popped in to see how I was going. You know, after everything that's happened.'

'How was his relationship with Ray?'

'Good.'

'Any issues? Disagreements?'

'No, why?'

Zoe waited. 'Well, people who tear off when the police are trying to pull them over look kind of suspicious, don't you think? Plus, I suspect Mr Priest's car was in Ray's street yesterday when he was killed. At the exact same time, in fact. What do you think about that?'

Donna shook her head. 'Josh and Ray have been mates for years. There was never a heated word between them.'

'How often would Ray see Joshua?'

'All the time.'

'Any business dealings between them?'

'No.'

'What does Joshua do for a living?'

'This and that. He buys and sells stuff.'

'Seems vague. Like what?'

'Cars, houses, scrap metal, anything. He sees opportunities and makes money.' From the corner of the room they heard a low, slow growl and then a sharp bark directed at Harry, who looked lazily across at the smaller dog.

'Bobo, that's enough,' snapped Donna. The fluffy dog lay down and stared at them with contempt.

'He sells drugs too, right?' asked Zoe.

'Drugs? Nah, doubt it.'

Zoe's phone buzzed. She glanced at the number. It wasn't familiar, but she saw the location was Rosebud.

'Excuse me a moment,' she said to Donna, before answering the call. 'Mayer.'

'Detective, it's Terry Gunny from Rosebud. The guy who was doing a runner on you just before. We've got him in custody. Wrapped the car around a light pole. He's on his way to Frankston Hospital as we speak.'

'What's his condition?'

'Sounds like a fractured leg and collarbone. A slight concussion, but he'll live. We'll charge him with dangerous driving and evading the police, at the very least. Is he in the frame for the murder you are working?'

'Maybe. We'll interview him when he's recovered enough. Can you make sure he's kept under guard until then?'

'No worries.'

'Appreciate it, Terry.' Zoe ended the call and looked up at Donna. 'Your friend Joshua's in the hospital with some broken bones. Smashed his car, I'm afraid. Fortunately no one else was hurt. Anything else you want to tell us before we go visit him?'

Donna looked Zoe defiantly in the eye. 'No.'

A door opened behind them. A slim, tanned woman in her early twenties walked into the dining room, dressed only in a bath towel. She had high cheekbones, with blue eyes and full lips. Zoe immediately thought that she could be a model for a surf wear company. Her long blonde hair was only partially dry and she was carrying a hair brush. Behind her, Zoe could see that she had come out from a bedroom. She stopped, surprised, when she saw the two detectives staring at her.

'Hello,' said Zoe, 'who are you?'

'This is Yvette,' said Donna, before the woman could speak. 'She's a friend of mine who is staying here.'

Zoe noticed Yvette's eyes narrow.

'Yvette, we're homicide detectives. We will need to speak with you in a few minutes. Can you leave us for the moment, though?'

'*Oui*...Okay,' said Yvette, blushing. She went back into the bedroom, and shut the door quietly behind her.

'How long's your friend been staying with you?'

'A few weeks.'

'Right,' said Zoe. 'We spoke to your sister this morning.'

'Okay. And?'

'What time did you say you got home on the morning that Ray was killed?'

'Can't really remember. About eleven-thirty, I think. I wasn't really paying attention.'

'And how long do you reckon it takes to get from Rosebud back to here?'

'About twenty minutes or so. Why?'

'Because Brenda said you dropped her off at home at twenty past ten.'

'Who would know exactly what time it was? We didn't

expect to be quizzed about it by the police, did we?'

'Your sister was sure. You see, after you dropped her off, she rang your mum. She showed us the log on her phone. The call started at 10.22 am and lasted thirty-eight minutes.'

'Earlier than I thought. So what?'

'After dropping Brenda off, where did you go?'

'Back here.'

'Anywhere else on the way?'

'No.'

'So you would've been back here by 10.40, 10.45 am?'

'Suppose so, in that case.'

'Did you go out again after that?'

'No.'

'Did you see Joshua Priest yesterday?'

'No.'

'Was Yvette here when you got back?'

'No.'

Outside the window, Yvette walked into view, now wearing a high-cut pink bikini. She spread a towel out on a lounge and lay down on her front. She reached back and untied her bikini top, letting it fall loose at her sides. From across the table, Zoe heard Donna exhale sharply in displeasure.

'She'll want to put on sunscreen in this weather,' said Charlie, watching her.

'Perhaps you should offer your services,' said Donna, her tone flat. 'You seem to be enjoying the view.'

Zoe and Charlie shared a glance. Zoe flicked her eyes towards the pool.

'Good idea,' said Charlie, standing up. He took his folder and walked over to the sliding door.

Donna watched him as he slid the door across, before closing it and walking over to Yvette.

'I don't want him harassing her,' said Donna.

'Don't worry. He's not that sort of guy. Plus, I think he took French at school. They'll be fine.'

Donna's eyes remained fixed on Charlie and Yvette, who were now chatting.

Zoe decided to change tack. 'Donna, did you suspect your husband of being unfaithful?'

'Ex-husband. I don't think so, but who would really know? He'd go off surfing or fishing a lot. It's not like I had him followed.'

'What about drugs? Did Ray have a drug habit?'

'No. Not while we were together, at least. I would have known.'

'Any abuse in the marriage?'

'What do you mean?' Donna shifted uncomfortably.

'Was Ray ever violent with you? Push you? Hit you?'

'No. We argued, like clockwork, but he was never physical with me.'

'Are you sure? We have spent the morning speaking to people who are close to you and Ray. All day we've been hearing rumours that Ray had affairs when you were married, that he had a drug habit and that he was an abusive husband.'

'People will say things once a person's dead. It's just gossip.'

'Everyone says it was you who told them,' Zoe said.

Donna looked up at her, and out towards Charlie and Yvette.

'What's the truth, Donna?'

Donna glanced down at the table, as if searching for answers. 'Look, people must have misunderstood. I might've been talking about things I believed *could* have been true when we split...the drugs or cheating...As for the abuse, I might have said we'd been fighting. They might have taken it as a physical fight and not just arguing.'

Five cakes sat cooling on the kitchen bench. Behind them were about twenty plastic containers, all lined up, waiting to be filled. 'Are you doing meals-on-wheels?' Zoe asked.

'What?' Donna said absently, before looking over her shoulder. 'Oh, no. It's just a hobby. I like to bake, that's all. I drop them off around the place. To friends. Especially the ones with kids. They love my cakes.'

'Must make you popular.'

'I don't do it to be popular,' snapped Donna, reddening in the face.

'Right,' said Zoe, knowing she'd struck a nerve. 'Who's organising the funeral?'

'I am. There's no one else. His parents are next to useless. I was on the phone with the funeral home this morning. The morgue said that Ray's body will be released tomorrow and they can do the funeral on Thursday.'

Zoe got the feeling that Donna was happy to be burying Ray in such a hurry.

'Are you his next of kin?'

'Yeah, and as you would have found out by now, he hadn't got around to writing me out of his will or anything.'

Zoe saw Donna give the slightest quiver of a grin, a glimpse of something dark. 'Did Ray have any life insurance?'

'Yeah, we both had policies. Two million each.' She tilted her head back, looking Zoe right in the eyes.

'And you are each other's beneficiaries?'

'That's right, but if you're saying that I had anything to do with Ray getting killed, you are way off track.'

'You're divorcing. You get everything now, not just half. Plus, a two-million-dollar insurance pay-out. That sounds like a motive to me.'

'I didn't have anything to do with what happened to Ray. I may not have been the greatest wife, but I'm no killer.'

'Was Ray still supporting you financially?' asked Zoe.

Donna glanced through the glass at Charlie, who was rubbing sunscreen lotion on Yvette's back, before turning back to Zoe. 'Yes.'

'How much per month?'

'I don't know. It varied.'

'Rough guess?'

'Maybe ten or twelve.'

Zoe's eyes opened wide. 'Thousand?'

'Yes, so?'

'Seems like a lot.'

'Does it? Things cost more down this way.'

'Seems so,' said Zoe. 'Donna, where'd he get that sort of money every month?'

'No idea. He had a job. Plus, he had money invested in

shares I think. Or cryptocurrencies. Not sure. He never filled me in on the details.'

'You never asked what happened.'

'Huh?'

'To Ray. You never asked how he was killed.'

Donna let out an exasperated sound. 'I was in shock when you told me yesterday. I found out last night that he'd been stabbed. The papers called wanting a comment. They told me.' She shook her head indignantly.

Zoe knew she was getting nowhere. 'Okay,' she said. 'Thanks for your help. We may need to get back in touch.'

'Glad to help,' Donna said with a thin smile. She pushed herself up from the table.

Zoe walked over to the window and knocked twice on the glass. Charlie turned, smiling, and nodded. Yvette pushed herself up onto one elbow, grinning up at Charlie, and shook his hand. Zoe heard Donna inhale at the sight of Yvette's breasts.

Charlie walked to the door and slid it across. 'It's a hot one out there,' he said.

'Apparently,' said Donna. 'I'll see you out.'

Once they were in the car, with the aircon running, and Harry in his harness, Zoe looked back at the house, where Donna stared at them stony-faced from the red door. Zoe could see through the house to the bay, shimmering in a brilliant sapphire blue.

'You think she's a candidate?' asked Charlie.

'Not sure,' said Zoe. 'She's tall and strong enough. She's got motive, and we now know she had time to go there.

He would probably have let her in. Could she have done it? Absolutely. She's obviously a natural manipulator, but she didn't cry over Ray or care too much about us going through her phone. And she's not trying to make us like her. She didn't fuss over Harry to get on my good side. Nothing.'

'She could be in cahoots with Joshua Priest,' said Charlie. 'He could have done it for her.'

'Yes, I agree. We'll know more after we speak to him. What'd you get from Yvette?'

'Nothing. She said she'd never met Ray Carlson and that Donna never mentioned him before last night. She was sightseeing in Melbourne yesterday when Ray was killed. She pulled out her phone and showed me selfies taken with her friends at the Arts Centre.'

'She shed any light on her and Donna's status?'

'Yes, they met online when she was still in France. They're a couple, although I reckon Yvette is just in it for the travel and the sunshine. Donna paid for her flights and is giving her spending money.'

'A sugar mummy,' Zoe said, giving Donna a last glance as she pulled away from the kerb.

6.30 PM, MONDAY 3 FEBRUARY

Zoe squirmed on the hard couch in the waiting room. She had grown to hate this office. She eyed the indoor plant in the corner. The whole time she had been coming here, the plant had always seemed to be struggling. It seemed to have just enough attention to keep it alive, but not enough to let it thrive.

At first, it was comforting to talk things over, but now the sessions just served as a reminder, stoking up memories. Harry laid his chin on her knee, his brown eyes staring up at her. She gave him a small smile and stroked his head, relaxing a little.

On a table in the corner, along with the usual magazines, was a new framed photograph of a child playing with a labrador on the beach. Alicia Kennedy's assistant, Georgia, sat at her desk, her dark hair pulled back tight, an earpiece in one ear, typing fast. Zoe guessed she was transcribing Alicia's notes from her conversations with her patients. She watched as Georgia's eyes widened every now and again in response to what she was hearing. Zoe would have loved to see the notes Alicia took during her own sessions.

Georgia looked up from her keyboard. 'I thought you'd finished all of your appointments.'

'Final one,' said Zoe.

'That's good. Hey, there's something I've been thinking about and...can I ask you a question?'

'Sure,' said Zoe.

'How'd you deal with the fear that day? I mean, why didn't you just run?'

Zoe had asked herself this question over and over. 'There wasn't time to think about fear. You can't do your job if you're blocked by fear. I saw an opportunity and I reacted. That's all.'

Georgia blinked. 'My brother...was there that day... thank you.' She coughed, trying to recover herself.

The door to Alicia's office opened. 'Hi Zoe, sorry to keep you waiting,' she said. Alicia's smile was disarming and she exuded a kind of effortless confidence that Zoe always found genuine. Alicia was about forty-five and Zoe thought she carried her age well. She wore a blouse with a subtle monochromatic pattern of blue birds on branches and her shoulder-length straight brown hair was pushed back by reading glasses, perched on her forehead. Zoe often had to remind herself that they weren't actually friends, that Alicia was the police psychologist.

'No worries. Is that your dog?' asked Zoe, pointing at the frame.

'Yes, he's a rescue. Was on death row at the shelter. His name's Freddie. Tabitha loves him more than anything. Come on in.'

Zoe stood up and followed Alicia into her office, giving Georgia a reassuring glance as she went. Zoe shut the door behind her.

'So, how's it been?' asked Alicia, picking up her notepad.

'It's just the end of day two, but it's fine.'

'Any anxiety?' Alicia was already writing, her notepad propped against her crossed leg.

'No, not really. We responded to a new job yesterday. They're never a trip to the carnival, but it was okay.'

'When you say "not really", what does that mean?'

'Just the usual stuff. I've always felt a little anxious walking into a murder scene. Most of us do, I'd say. Some things you can't unsee, you know?'

'Nothing debilitating, though?'

'No, felt like a normal job.'

'Apart from that, have you had any panic attacks in the last week? Or blackouts?'

'No, nothing like that.' Zoe could feel the heat rising in her face. Alicia could place her on restricted duties with a stroke of her pen.

'Your work partner, is he acting normally with you?'

'Yes, Charlie's okay. But the boss has got me on a light case load. I'd prefer to get back at full speed. Charlie's working with a different DS on other cases.'

'I understand but why is that a problem? Why the rush?'

'I guess I want to be part of the team again. This feels

weird. The quicker I'm back in the thick of things, the quicker everyone will forget about what happened.'

Alicia's pen was skating above her pad. She was making more notes than seemed necessary. 'What you went through was extreme,' she said. 'I'm guessing your DI wants to play it safe.'

Dropping her shoulders, Zoe looked up at the ceiling. 'It was my job. It could've been any of us.'

Her irritation must've been clear to Alicia, who changed tack. 'Everything okay with Harry? Not hindering you at work in any way?'

'No, he's a natural. Up for anything.' Zoe smiled down at Harry.

'What about the rest of the team? They okay with Harry being in the office?'

'Can't say I've thought too much about it.' Zoe pursed her lips. 'Harry sits under my desk. I'll make sure he gets out a few times a day for a decent walk. The fresh air will do us both good.'

'And the nightmares?'

Zoe regretted letting Alicia know about her troubled dreams, the ones where she didn't make it in time. The ones that still violently jolted her awake in the middle of the night.

'No, they've stopped. Ever since Harry came along a month ago.'

'Good, good,' said Alicia, taking notes and watching her at the same time.

You'd make a decent detective, thought Zoe.

—

Half an hour later Zoe and Harry arrived home in Yarraville, in the inner western suburbs of Melbourne. She had bought the double-fronted Federation-style house cheaply and renovated it over a decade, watching the suburb go through rapid gentrification along the way. It had doubled in value in that time, but she had no plans to cash in. The weatherboard house was painted robin's egg blue, with white trim. It had a small yard in the front, bordered by standard rose bushes, and a good sized backyard for Harry to relax in on their days off. As she pulled into the driveway, she saw Tom sitting on a bench on the front veranda. His suit jacket lay across his knee, and his blue striped tie hung loose around his neck. Tom gave a broad smile as she got out of the car.

'Hey, Mr Hayes, I didn't think we were catching up tonight,' Zoe said, smiling back.

'We weren't. I just wanted to see you, that's all.'

Zoe opened the back of the car and Harry jumped out, his tail whooshing. Tom walked over, leaning in to kiss her softly, before giving her a hug. Harry then pushed his way in between their legs.

'Hey there, Buddy,' said Tom, moving back, brushing the dog hair from his suit.

'Sorry, part of the deal nowadays,' said Zoe, as she unlocked the front door and deactivated the alarm. Harry ran inside, over to his water bowl, as Zoe used the remote to turn on the air conditioner.

'You want a beer?' asked Zoe.

'Sure. Okay being back at work?'

Zoe opened the fridge and pulled out two Peronis.

Opening them, she handed one to Tom, and they sat down on the couch. They'd been dating for about six months, but had actually met twenty years earlier at university when Zoe was studying commerce and Tom was in law school. He moved to Sydney after graduation and had only come back to Melbourne after a messy divorce, when he connected with Zoe again on Facebook. For the past four months, Tom had been a rock for her, riding out the highs and lows as she made her way back, holding her in the night.

'Yeah, it's all good,' she said. 'Picked up a new job. The murder down at Portsea yesterday.'

Tom gave an encouraging smile. 'I saw you on TV last night doing the press conference. You looked great.'

'I was melting. It was like an oven down there.'

'Got any suspects yet?'

'Not really, no clear-cut contenders.'

'Random killing?'

'Nah, doubt it. This is too calculated and they were let inside the house. It's someone the victim knew. We'll get there.'

'You back working with Charlie?'

'Yeah. He's still the same. Stands at the scene gobsmacked, like seeing a body at a homicide is a surprise. How'd your day go?' Zoe unlaced her boots and kicked them off, allowing them to fall onto the polished floorboards of the living room.

'Okay. Picked up a new client. Aggravated burglary charge. His parents are footing the bill. They were asking if I could get him acquitted.'

'And can you?'

'Nope, not with his face all over the CCTV footage. I'll be going for a sentence reduction as the best outcome,' said Tom, picking away at the label of his beer. 'So...how was the psych?'

'Ah, now the reason for your visit becomes clear.'

'And?' He hunched his shoulders and gave her one of his patented smiles, a look of feigned innocence.

It worked better when you were twenty, Zoe thought.

'It was okay,' she said. 'Alicia's nice and all, but I always need to keep my wits about me and remember she's working for Victoria Police, not for my benefit. I don't think I raised any red flags. I should be done with them for good now.'

'She thinks you're okay, then?'

'I'm carrying a gun on my hip, so I'd say so, yeah.' Zoe felt the tips of her ears going red.

Tom noticed. 'That's great. What about Harry? How long have you got him for?'

Zoe's head jerked back. 'What do you mean?'

'I just thought that if everything was going well with you, he might be needed elsewhere.'

Zoe hadn't ever considered that possibility. 'No, Harry's a big part of the reason I'm okay. You saw me. I was a wreck. I'm better now because he's there with me, every day.'

Tom nodded, looking at the golden retriever who was lying on his mat. Harry didn't respond to Tom's stare, but kept his head on his paws, his attention solely on Zoe.

'Anyway, I'm glad things are going well,' said Tom, raising his beer as if to toast. 'So, here's to you and here's to Harry.'

Zoe smiled and Tom let his hand fall affectionately onto her shoulder. From across the room, Harry wagged his tail, thumping it softly against the floor.

'Do you feel like Thai food tonight?' she asked.

Tom gave her a warm smile that was his answer.

3.45 PM, TUESDAY, 4 FEBRUARY

Zoe turned the car into a side street in the town of Rye and pulled over, under the shade of a tree. They were six days into a heatwave and the streets away from the beach were empty.

Charlie stared at his phone. 'Email here from Angus. He found that blue Camry again on the CCTV in the victim's street. Goes past at one twenty-one and leaves again at one-fifty on Sunday arvo. He sent pics.' Charlie opened the images on his phone as Zoe parked. He angled the screen so Zoe could see. He zoomed in on the fuzzy-looking figure sitting low in the driver's seat, baseball cap pulled down.

'Shit,' said Zoe.

'Male?' said Charlie, squinting.

'Yeah, looks like it,' said Zoe. 'The guy returns to the scene after we've arrived, pulls up to watch the show, and leaves before us. There were seven or eight patrol or CI cars on site. He's a bold one.'

'Agreed,' Charlie said, leaning forward, letting the air-conditioning blow against his face, 'and going by the way he cleaned up the scene, not stupid either.'

Zoe nodded, looking up at the house. 'Final stop of the day.'

'Let's hope this guy has more information than Ray's other mates. I'll take anything right now.'

'Hope so too.' Zoe adjusted the rear-view mirror and glanced at Harry, who was lying on his foam mat. He looked back at her in the mirror, his mouth falling open into a broad smile.

'No car I can see,' said Charlie, looking up the driveway as they both got out. He waited, shielding his head from the sun with his folder while Zoe opened up the back and unhooked Harry's harness. The house was an updated beach shack, with freshly painted white palings, and a concrete veranda out front with one chair, a single empty beer bottle on the ground beside it. The garden was dominated by a row of pink agapanthus along the front of the house. A sprinkler sat quiet in the middle of the lawn, its hose trailing off around the side of the house.

An unshaven man with scruffy brown hair came out of the front door. He stopped for a moment, staring at the dog. Then he walked towards them with his shoulders held back, which pushed out his belly. His head was tilted to the left.

'Greg Enders?' asked Zoe.

'Yeah. You the cops?' he asked gruffly, pulling his loose grey Nirvana t-shirt out of his baggy navy blue track pants. He wore no shoes.

'Yes, I'm Detective Sergeant Zoe Mayer and this is Detective Senior Constable Charlie Shaw.'

'That don't look like no normal police dog,' he said.

'He's not,' said Zoe. 'We want to speak to you about the death of Ray Carlson.'

'Yeah, I guessed that much,' he said. 'You want to come in out of this heat? Your dog house trained?'

'Yes, and thanks,' said Zoe, noticing that Greg's head remained tilted.

Greg saw her staring. 'Had a work accident a few years back. Hurt my neck and it's been bent this way ever since. I'm on compo for it. Come on in.'

'Sorry about that,' said Zoe.

'It is what it is,' Greg said, opening the door.

They walked into the modest house, all the way to the back where a large kitchen and living area opened up to a courtyard garden. The room was neat and clean, with a cheap-looking sofa and a large flat-screen television in the corner. There was a news story playing about a snowstorm somewhere in Canada.

Greg grabbed the remote from the kitchen bench and turned off the television, and gestured towards the dining table. 'You want a drink or something?' he asked, as they sat down. Harry lay down on the floor behind Zoe.

'No. Thanks though. As I said, we need to ask you some questions about the death of Ray Carlson,' she said.

'Yeah, awful thing that. He was a good bloke.'

'Where were you on Sunday?' asked Zoe.

'I was here. Slept in. Trouble sleeping at night in this

heat. Got up around ten, I think, and stayed near the air conditioner all day.' He gestured up at the reverse cycle system on the wall.

'Anyone with you?'

'Why? You reckon I had something to do with it?'

'Routine question. We need to establish where everyone was at the time Ray was killed.'

'Well, I was here. And I was alone.'

'How long have you known Ray?'

'About six months. Used to see him down the pub a bit or at the beach.'

'Would you say you were close friends?'

Greg shrugged. 'Nah, not really. We were friendly and all, but I didn't know him that well. Ray barracked for Melbourne in the footy, liked a bet on the fillies, and his preferred beer was Vic Bitter. Beyond that, I don't know too much. He wasn't the sort of guy who had anything deep and meaningful to say. He was best mates with Dwayne. They were both keen surfers. They'd be down there every chance they had.'

'You ever hear of Dwayne and Ray arguing?'

'Nah, they were like brothers. Always have been, by all accounts. Apparently they met when they were five years old.'

'What about Joshua Priest? You know him?'

Greg leaned back and rubbed his neck. 'Um, yeah. I know him a bit.'

'What was his relationship like with Ray?'

'They were good mates, but Josh is a bit...uh...

unpredictable. Between us, the guy's a fricken grenade. Got a temper. You have to be on guard in case he goes off.'

'Did you ever see him argue or disagree with Ray?'

'No, they always seemed to get along fine. They all go way back. Josh went to school with Ray and Dwayne too.'

'Do you know Ray's ex-wife?'

'Donna? No, but I've seen her around. Ray pointed her out once when we were sitting outside at the pub having a beer. They weren't close.'

'How do you mean?' asked Charlie, taking notes.

'Ray thought she was a bitch,' replied Greg. 'Said she was sucking him dry, and not in a good way.' Greg snorted at his joke. 'Anyway, when Ray pointed her out in town that time, she was staring at him from across the road, with hard eyes. She looked pretty mean to me.'

Zoe and Charlie shared a quick look.

'Do you think she had anything to do with Ray's death?' asked Zoe.

Greg considered the question. 'Couldn't say. They weren't fans of each other, but, as I said, I don't know her at all.'

'Did Ray have any enemies?'

'Well, he had at least one, if someone topped him, but I don't know who.'

'Did he owe anyone money?'

'Not that he ever mentioned to me. Always seemed to have a full wallet whenever I saw him.'

'Gambling problem?'

'He'd have a bet on the horses, but nothing over the top.

Ten or twenty bucks on a Saturday arvo.'

'Any drug issues?'

'No, I don't think so.'

'Was he seeing anyone?'

Greg grimaced. 'Not sure. He was a bit coy about that sort of stuff. I remember Dwayne telling Ray a few times he needed to get himself a girlfriend, but Ray always changed the subject. Struck me as a bit strange, but who knows.'

'Anything else you can think of who would be useful for us?' asked Charlie.

Greg stared at the table for a moment. 'I don't think so. Sorry I can't be of more help. Hope you get the person who did this. Ray was a good bloke.'

'Thanks for your time,' said Zoe, pulling out her business card. 'If anything else comes to mind, give us a call.'

Ray took the card. 'Will do.'

They stood and walked to the front door. Harry followed.

'We may need to check in with you again,' said Zoe.

'No worries, I'll be here,' said Greg.

They said goodbye and walked to the car. Zoe opened the back of the four-wheel-drive and Harry jumped up. She pulled a bottle of water from a chiller bag and filled the bowl.

'What do you make of that?' asked Charlie, as Harry drank.

'Well, Joshua Priest just cemented his place as our chief suspect right now.'

Charlie stretched his neck. 'Sounds like he's got the

temperament for it. Ray's ex didn't come off sounding that good either. '

'Yeah, I'm puzzled about Ray's relationship with Donna,' said Zoe. 'He was giving her so much money each month. Why would she be so bitter? But Ray had some secrets. Primarily, where he was getting all the cash from? Only some sort of Warren Buffett could be pulling that sort of money on the stock market every month.'

'Let's see what Anjali has been able to find on Ray's computer,' said Charlie.

Harry had stopped drinking and was staring at her.

'Enough?' she asked him, stroking his head. She waited a second before emptying the bowl on the nature strip. Her phone vibrated. 'Mayer.'

'Zoe, it's Terry Gunny again. We just had a callout to your victim's house.'

4 PM, TUESDAY 4 FEBRUARY

With her siren blaring, Zoe sped around the base of the peninsula towards Portsea, manoeuvring around cars that pulled over to let them pass. When she glanced in the rear-view mirror Harry was lying flat across the back of the car, as she'd taught him.

As they took the back road behind the main part of town, Zoe pushed the buttons on the armrest, lowering all the windows. Charlie turned off the siren as they pulled up outside Ray Carlson's house. Two police cars stood empty, doors open, lights still flashing. Neighbours were standing at their doors, watching.

'Harry, stay,' Zoe said firmly as she jumped out of the car. She and Charlie were running towards the front door when they heard commotion from the backyard.

'Get off me, you pricks.'

They ran around the side of the house to the back, where they saw three officers standing over a young man on his stomach on the grass, being handcuffed by a fourth officer. The man on the ground was wearing a white t-shirt, faded denim jeans that were slung low on his hips with his underwear pulled high, and new sneakers. His build was slim, but the veins in his arms indicated that he worked out.

'What have we got?' asked Zoe.

'We had a call from a neighbour about a guy acting suspiciously and entering the backyard with a shovel. We found him hiding in the shrubs,' he said.

'Right,' said Zoe, looking at five shallow holes in the garden bed. 'Searched him for weapons?'

'Yeah, he's clean,' the officer said.

'Let's get him up.' Zoe crossed her arms.

Two of the officers took an arm each and lifted the man to his feet. He wore a scowl across his face and his eyes had narrowed by the time he was on his feet. He was of medium height, with close-cropped dark hair and brown eyes. As he tilted his head to look at her, Zoe could see the word 'Rebel' tattooed in a florid script on the left side of his neck. *Classy.*

'What's your name?' asked Zoe.

'Piss off.'

One of the officers restraining him shoved him forward before quickly jerking him back. 'Watch your mouth,' he said.

'That's not the best way to start,' Zoe said to the hand-cuffed man, before turning to the officer.

'His name's John Grant,' the officer reported. 'He's nineteen. He's got form. Moved from shoplifting, loitering, cannabis possession, up to robbery, as well as break and enter. Lives in Pearcedale.'

Zoe gave the officer a questioning glance.

'Top of the peninsula. About sixty clicks north of here.'

She nodded, and turned back to the boy. 'You're a long way from home. What are you up to, John?'

'Gardening,' he mumbled.

Zoe looked at the holes he'd dug, all about a foot deep. A shovel lay nearby. 'Yeah, I doubt that. You know there was a murder here on Sunday, don't you?'

John said nothing.

Zoe waved a hand in front of his face. 'You hear okay?'

'Yeah.'

'Did you know Ray Carlson, the guy who was killed here?'

'Nah.'

'You know about the killing though, right?'

'Yeah, my mum told me. She saw it on the news.'

'Where were you last Sunday morning?'

'Can't remember.'

'Try harder,' Zoe snapped. She was losing patience.

The two officers holding John's arms shared a grin, impressed by Zoe's firmness.

She waited, staring at John.

He stared at the fence. 'Frankston,' he said finally. 'I was in Frankston with some mates. At the Bayside Shopping Centre.'

'Time?'

'We got there around nine-thirty and left after we'd had lunch. Probably after one.'

'Someone be able to vouch for you?'

'No one you'd believe, but there's a ton of security cameras there. Check the tapes.'

'Crims seem to know where the cameras are, eh?'

'I'm no crim anymore. I did my time.'

'John, aiding and abetting a murder is serious business. What are your plans for the next ten years?'

'I don't know nothing about that murder.'

'Yet here you are. Digging up the victim's back garden. Looking for evidence that was left behind, I'd say. What do you reckon, Charlie?'

'Looks pretty incriminating to me.'

'It's hot out here,' said Zoe, turning back to John, 'so let's speed things along a bit. What are you doing here? Don't say gardening again. Judges hate smart-arses.'

'I want a lawyer.'

'Bingo. We have a winner,' exclaimed Charlie, under his breath.

'Sounds like a guilty man to me,' said Zoe. She turned to the officer standing beside John. 'Can you read him his rights and take him down to Rosebud station to call himself a lawyer?'

'Will do.'

'Best get that logged as evidence as well,' she said, pointing to the shovel. 'We'll question him at the station. It's lucky he's nineteen; he'll get to go to big boy prison this time around. They'll love him there,' she added, loud enough for John to hear.

—

Two hours later, Zoe, Charlie and Harry walked into the interview room at Rosebud Police Station. Charlie was carrying a large clear plastic evidence bag full of bundles of cash.

John Grant blanched as he watched the bag bang down on the table in front of him. A middle-aged man in a neat grey suit looked wide-eyed at the bag and then at John, before standing up. 'Allan Fredericks,' he said. 'I represent Mr Grant.'

'Zoe Mayer,' she said, shaking his hand. Zoe noticed that he was wearing the same strong aftershave cologne that her dad had once worn.

'Nice dog,' Allan said, looking down at Harry.

'Thanks,' said Zoe. 'This is Charlie Shaw.' Charlie reached across the table and shook the lawyer's hand.

Zoe turned on the recording equipment and read John his rights. She looked him squarely in the eyes. 'This bag is one of seven we have found so far. It'll be counted soon enough, but I'm guessing that there's at least half a million dollars all up. That's serious dough to be buried in the backyard. So, where are we, John? Anything you want to tell us before we get started?'

John looked down at the table.

'My client would like to assist,' Allan said, 'but he's looking for immunity.'

Zoe felt a buzz go through her. 'Immunity for what, exactly?'

'Immunity in regard to trespassing on Mr Carlson's property today.'

Zoe frowned. 'That all?'

'Yes, just the trespassing, and also any attempted theft charges, if that's where you are going next.'

Her buzz subsided. She understood why he wanted immunity on such a minor infraction. 'Are you still on parole, John?'

'Yes, he is,' said Allan, without looking at his client.

'For what?'

'Break and enter, and robbery,' said John. 'Did a year in youth detention.'

Zoe made up her mind. 'All right, immunity on charges from today's events, but only if John fully cooperates. Okay?'

John glanced sideways at his lawyer, who nodded.

'For the tape, please.'

'Yes, I...will...co...op...er...ate,' said John, emboldened.

Zoe had a strong desire to grab John by the hair and drive him face-first into the table. 'Great. So what were you doing in Ray Carlson's backyard today?'

'Looking for that.' He pointed at the bag of cash.

'For the record, John Grant is indicating the bag of money that was recovered from Ray Carlson's backyard. Where'd the money come from?'

'Dunno.'

'How'd you know it was there?'

'I just heard it might be there, that's all.'

'From whom?'

John was silent.

'I said *fully cooperates*, remember?'

'I was told by a girl called Yvette.'

Zoe and Charlie shared a glance.

'Does Yvette have a last name?' asked Zoe.

'Yeah. It's Yvette Laurent.'

'Where does Yvette live?' asked Charlie.

'She's staying in Sorrento at some posh chick's mansion. Yvette's from France. She's a surfer from Biarritz.'

'Is this mansion in Kildrummie Court?'

'Yeah, that's the one. How'd you know that?'

'How do you know her?'

'Met her down at the surf beach a week ago. She's got, like, a surfer's body and she's real pretty, ya know? Anyway, last night she told me there were bags of cash buried somewhere in this dude's backyard. She said that if I went and dug it up she'd be, um, grateful. You know what I mean?'

John looked at Charlie for support. Charlie stared back.

'Anyway,' he continued, 'she said that we could take a chunk of the money and go to Ibiza together and party. I was supposed to dig it up today and take it to the house tonight.'

'The woman she's staying with—did she know about this plan?'

'Yeah. She was in the kitchen at her house when Yvette was telling me about it outside by the pool. The sliding doors were open—she would've heard. I think it's her money. She's a weird one, that lady. She was all strange about me chatting to Yvette. She asked me where I was from. When I said Pearcedale, she started to snigger. I know what that laugh meant. Stuck-up bitch.'

'When did all this happen?'

'Last night. Sun was still up, so it was probably about eight-thirty.'

'Then what?'

'Then I left. Yvette gave me the address and told me to come back tonight with the cash.'

'Anything else?'

'She kissed me out the front of the house. I was getting into it with her when she pulled back and told me we could continue things when we had the money.'

Zoe leaned forward. 'You know you were being played, don't you, John?'

He looked down, pink creeping across his face.

Zoe looked across at Charlie. *Yvette was playing you, too.*

Charlie walked into the brightly lit interview room, where Zoe sat making notes across the table from Donna. The air was stale in the stark white room. Zoe had left Donna waiting for half an hour with the air conditioning off. Harry was lying beside Zoe, his head in the shadow of the table, now fast asleep.

'About time,' mumbled Donna, arms crossed in contempt.

Zoe looked up. 'Let the record show that Detective Senior Constable Charles Shaw has entered the room. What's the final number, Charlie?'

'Seven hundred and fifty-eight thousand dollars.'

'How's Yvette going?' asked Zoe.

'Great,' answered Charlie, looking towards Donna with a sly smile. 'She's really good.'

Donna glared at him.

'Are we waiting for Donna's lawyer?' asked Charlie, ignoring her.

'No,' said Zoe. 'Donna has informed me that she does not need a lawyer.'

Charlie made a show of being impressed. 'Fair enough.'

Zoe turned to Donna. 'So, how are you going to play this one? Saying nothing won't work forever, so have you got another angle?'

'I don't have any angles.'

'Why was the money buried in Ray's backyard, Donna?'

'No idea. I don't know about any money.'

'Come on, Donna,' said Charlie, 'you do. Your girlfriend, Yvette, she's told us everything. About getting her to find someone to dig up the cash, and how you were going to split the money.'

Donna said nothing, shaking her head.

'She's very...compelling, that Yvette,' added Charlie. 'A jury is going to love her.'

Donna stared at him again, exhaling through her nose.

'I don't think Donna likes you, Charlie,' Zoe said.

'Don't see why not,' said Charlie. 'I have been nothing but hospitable to her. And to Yvette, of course.'

'Yeah, right,' spat Donna. 'I saw the way you were looking at her at my house. Couldn't keep your eyes off her tits, you dirty perv.'

Zoe clicked her fingers. 'Earth to Donna—hello. Charlie interviewing your girlfriend is neither here nor there. We are talking about the bags of cash we recovered from your dead husband's backyard.'

'Ex-husband,' retorted Donna.

'Wrong point again,' said Zoe. 'How'd you know about the money?'

Donna was staring at the wall behind them. Zoe knew that she was considering what she would say next.

'Look, I just knew there'd be money there,' she said. 'Ray's been doing it for years. Used to bury money at the house in Sorrento as well, before we split up.'

'So, what was the plan? Get Yvette to use this boy, John, to dig up the cash and then kill him as well?'

'As well? As well as what?'

'Not what, who. Kill him like you had Ray killed.'

'No way. I had nothing to do with Ray getting killed. Nothing. This was about getting the cash before you guys found it and pocketed the lot for yourselves. We were going to give the kid a few grand and send him on his way.'

'So, where'd the money come from? There's plenty of it. What were you and Ray into? Was he skimming contracts? Getting kickbacks from suppliers? Or something else?'

'Don't know. Ray never said where the money came from and I never asked. He used to do extra work on the weekends and some nights. That's all I know.'

'And now that you were getting divorced, your share of the money was going to dry up. That's why you killed him, isn't it?'

'I had nothing to do with that. Listen, I knew that Ray was into something, but I swear I don't know what. Yeah, we weren't getting along, but he was still looking after me financially. I guess he wanted to keep me sweet, so I wouldn't start shooting my mouth off. Him getting killed is a very bad thing for me. I need that money. The insurance company won't pay out his policy until your investigation is finished.'

Zoe sat back. She and Charlie looked at her across the table.

'What?' asked Donna. She gave them a thin smile. 'I'm his sole beneficiary. The money he buried is mine. It's quite simple. Don't you understand?'

Zoe also smiled. 'Donna, the money was almost certainly the proceeds of crime. Once that's proved, it will be forfeited to the government.'

'That's my cash. You're just finding a way to pinch it. That's why I was trying to grab it myself. And what about Yvette?' asked Donna.

'She's going before a magistrate charged with conspiracy with relation to the theft. She's admitted everything. She'll be bailed, but she won't be able to have any contact with you. Don't worry. She probably won't do time. Suspended sentence, I'd say, but then she'll be deported.'

9.30 PM, TUESDAY 4 FEBRUARY

Zoe yawned as they pulled into the car park at Frankston Hospital. It was still warm, but the sun had set, and the air was more comfortable. Charlie got out and stretched. Zoe opened the back door and grabbed Harry's lead. 'Sorry, you'll need to wear this in there,' she said to the dog, attaching it to his collar.

The three of them entered the emergency department. The cool air inside was a relief.

'We're looking for Joshua Priest,' said Zoe, showing her badge to the nurse at reception. 'He was admitted yesterday afternoon.'

The nurse stood. She tilted her head to read *Service Dog* on Harry's vest. She looked back at Zoe, recognition in her eyes. 'He is up in recovery,' she said. 'Third floor, room three-one-two.' She pointed towards the bank of elevators.

'Thank you,' said Zoe.

A young constable was standing outside Joshua Priest's

room. His black uniform looked half a size too large, and he appeared to be around twenty.

'Zoe and Charlie from Homicide,' said Zoe, showing her badge.

'Yes, I know,' he said, reddening, as he looked at her. 'Kevin. Kevin Johanski. From Rosebud station.'

'How's the patient?'

'Not sure. He's awake.'

'Thanks. We'll be here for a few minutes if you want to stretch your legs or grab a coffee.'

'That'd be great. Thanks.'

Zoe pushed the door open and Harry walked in. She and Charlie followed. Joshua watched the procession from his bed. He looked to be about forty. He had bloodshot eyes and smelled of stale sweat. His left leg was in plaster and his right collarbone area was wrapped in a bandage.

'Who are you?'

'Detectives Mayer and Shaw,' said Zoe. 'You bolted from us yesterday.'

'Can't remember. I was in a car accident. I hit my head.'

'Yeah, you drove into a pole.' Zoe grinned. 'Doesn't matter. We aren't here about that. The first part of the chase is all on dash cam. We won't need your memory to solve the case of the moron doing a hundred and thirty clicks with little kids on the side of the road. Rosebud CIU will deal with that. We're here about Ray Carlson.'

Joshua looked at her. 'What...why?'

'Because he's dead, that's why,' said Zoe. 'Because we saw you leaving his ex-wife's house yesterday before you bolted. Because your car was spotted in Ray's street around the time he was killed on Sunday. And because people are saying that you're unstable and aggressive.'

'Who the fuck's saying that?' growled Joshua, agitated.

Charlie looked Joshua in the eye. 'So you don't deny being in his street that day. Why'd you kill Ray, Joshua?'

'I didn't and I wasn't in his fucking street on Sunday.'

'Was it to do with money?' asked Charlie.

'I didn't do it.'

'Donna put you up to it, didn't she?' said Zoe.

'Donna? What are you talking about? I wasn't anywhere near Ray's on the day he was killed. I was up in Melbourne.'

'Doing what?' Zoe said, her heart beating hard. Harry stood up and took a step towards her.

'I was in Albert Park on Sunday morning. I had something to eat at a cafe. It's on Montague Street, just around the corner from Bridport Street. Trendy place. It was pumping. Full of people. Arrived at around ten. Left an hour later and went shopping in the city.'

'Did you drive your blue Camry there?'

'Yep.'

'Who was with you?' asked Zoe.

'No one.'

'How'd you pay? Credit card or cash.'

Joshua waited for a moment. 'Cash.'

'What did you eat?'

'It was called a dragon something. Comes in a bowl. Everything there was rabbit food, but I couldn't be bothered finding somewhere else.'

Zoe knew the cafe well. It specialised in vegetarian dishes. She'd eaten there often herself, even the Dragon Bowl. It was hard to imagine Joshua Priest preferring it to the hamburger joint around the corner. But she did remember that the cafe had CCTV cameras. If Joshua was still there around eleven, he wasn't their killer. 'We'll check it out. So, if you didn't kill Ray, why'd you speed off today?'

'Don't know. Can't remember anything. I told you already.'

'You know who runs from the police?' asked Zoe.

Joshua waited for her to answer her own question. Zoe continued to stare him down.

'Who?' he asked, relenting.

'Crims, that's who. So, who do you think murdered Ray?'

'If I had an idea, I'd tell you. We were good mates.'

'What do you do for a living, Joshua?'

'I'm a trader.'

'Trader in what?'

'Anything, really. If I can sell something for more than I paid for it, it's fair game.'

'Ever do any trading with Ray?'

'Nah, Ray wasn't a risk-taker. He just wanted a quiet life and to go surfing.'

'I don't buy that for one second. We've dug up a ton of cash from Ray's backyard. Ray was into something dodgy. What was it?'

'No idea.'

'I thought you were good mates with him?'

'Yeah I was, but I don't know nothing about that. He never mentioned anything about buried cash to me.'

Zoe turned to Charlie. 'I don't reckon he was good friends with Ray at all. He doesn't seem to know the first thing about him.'

'Yeah,' said Charlie, 'and he doesn't seem to care too much about the fact that Ray was murdered two days ago either.'

Joshua lay in his hospital bed, staring at the wall.

'And you're friends with Donna?' asked Zoe.

'Kind of. They were married a long time. I was never that close to her, but after what happened to Ray I wanted to check in with her, see how she was going.'

'So, how was she going?' asked Zoe.

'She seemed okay, all things considered.'

Zoe gave Joshua a half smile. 'So, you remember *that*?'

Joshua said nothing, glaring at her.

'Do you think that Donna arranged for Ray to be killed?'

Joshua began to laugh. 'Hardly likely. He was her meal ticket.'

'What about Yvette?' asked Charlie.

'Who's that?'

'Donna's...friend. The French girl staying at her place,' said Charlie.

'Haven't met her.'

Zoe could imagine that Donna might have hidden her attractive girlfriend from the prying eyes of Joshua. 'What about Dwayne? You think he could've been involved?'

'You kidding? Never heard them have an argument ever.'

'So, to summarise, you're good mates with Ray. He gets killed and you don't have the first clue as to why. Is that it?'

'We're going to check this alibi of yours,' said Zoe. 'I expect we'll be seeing you again soon.'

6.30 AM, WEDNESDAY 5 FEBRUARY

Zoe woke, stretching her arms towards her bedroom ceiling. Harry was asleep next to her, his head on the pillow. 'Ahem,' she coughed.

Harry opened his eyes and looked at her dreamily. He realised where he was, jumped down from the bed, and circled around to Zoe's side. Resting his chin on the bed, he peered up at her innocently.

'If you are trying to play me with your puppy-dog eyes, it may well work.'

Zoe got up and put on a t-shirt and shorts. It was becoming light and she could still feel the warmth in the air from the day before. It was going to be another stinker. She found her sneakers and phone, and grabbed Harry's lead and a tennis ball.

They walked out of the house, and turned left towards the park three doors down.

Unleashed, Harry ran onto the grass and Zoe threw the

ball. She lifted her phone to check her email. Forensics had come through. Zoe opened the attachment.

Fingerprints at the Portsea house were mainly from the victim. Some secondary prints belonged to the cleaner that Ray used once a fortnight. They'd already checked out her alibi, and confirmed she'd cleaned the house on Saturday, the day before the murder. She'd obviously done a good job, as there was no other significant DNA anywhere. Zoe kicked away the ball that Harry had dropped at her feet. He tore off after it.

She opened a second email, this one from Oliver Nunan, the pathologist. *As previously thought, there was no foreign DNA found under the victim's fingernails due to the use of bleach and scrubbing. The knife was clean of foreign DNA and fingerprints. The small piece of medical gauze on the blade of the knife was devoid of DNA. Bloods negative for alcohol and drugs.* She slipped her phone into her pocket, disappointed.

Two hours later she was at the office and Harry was asleep under her desk, despite the noise of phones ringing and people talking. It was a skill Zoe wished she had.

The Albert Park cafe's CCTV tapes had captured Joshua parking his blue Camry out the front, walking in, ordering and eating his Dragon Bowl.

The flashing light on her phone caught her eye. She punched in her code to retrieve the message. The caller identified herself as Sarah Westbrook, and said she had something confidential to discuss. Zoe recognised the polished voice and the name, but couldn't quite place her.

She called back.

'Hello.'

'Hi Sarah. It's Detective Sergeant Zoe Mayer.'

'Oh, thanks for calling back.'

The way she said it made Zoe instantly remember. Sarah was a former TV journalist, who had become famous for breaking a succession of political and business scandals a decade earlier. She had successfully sued the TV station for age discrimination after she was let go without obvious reason.

'Not sure if you know,' Sarah continued, 'but I produce a podcast called *Westbrook*. I'm a friend of a friend of yours, Tom Hayes. He gave me your number. I need an off-the-record opinion from a police perspective and...it's complicated. Would you have twenty minutes spare? I would prefer to speak about this face to face. It's—um—sensitive.'

Zoe grimaced. She didn't want to get involved, but figured that Tom wouldn't have passed on her number without good reason. 'Okay, when?'

'Can you do today?' Sarah said. 'Sorry, I know it's a lot to ask, but it's important.'

'Okay,' said Zoe. 'Let's say seven tonight down by the river, out the front of the Convention Centre. I'll recognise you.'

'Got it. See you there...and thanks.'

Zoe said goodbye. She looked down at Harry. He opened his eyes and met her stare, his tail wagging.

—

Charlie walked across the office. The top button of his shirt was already undone and he had loosened his tie. Sitting down at his desk with a smile, he started beating out a light drum roll with his fingers as he stared at her.

'You look like a man who's had a win,' Zoe said.

'Good news, bad news.'

'Before you tell me why you look pleased about bad news, I've seen the CCTV. Joshua Priest's alibi stacks up.'

'Shit. So, why'd he run from us then?'

Zoe shrugged. 'He's into something criminal, but he didn't kill Ray Carlson himself. He's still a person of interest. Now, give me the bad news first.'

'Right, bad news comes in two parts. We're losing Hannah and Angus as the secondary team. They're needed elsewhere.'

Zoe gave a resigned nod. 'Thought that'd be the case soon enough. At least we had them for three days. What's the second part?'

'They quizzed the owner of the winery. Doesn't look likely that Ray was skimming anything from there or getting kickbacks. The owner manages the suppliers, contracts and invoices himself. Ray was more like a warehouse assistant than a manager of logistics. The fancy title was to keep him happy. His job was to coordinate deliveries and shipments, and he wasn't selling wine illegally on the side. The owner said he accounts for every bottle. Plus, Ray was on sixty-five grand a year. So, the money's been coming from somewhere else.'

'Okay. Donna said he had a job working nights and

weekends,' said Zoe. 'Let's find out what it was. And the good news?'

'A tip came in last night to Crime Stoppers. Someone reckons that Ray was sleeping with Dwayne's missus.'

Zoe's mouth fell open. 'Crikey, now that's something,' she said. 'It would explain why Ray was so coy with Dwayne and their mate Greg Enders about getting himself a new girlfriend. He already had one. What's Dwayne's wife's name?'

'Katie. Katie Harley. I've got the recording here if you want to have a listen. It's short and to the point.'

Zoe put on Charlie's earphones and listened to the call. The caller was male and well spoken, but didn't identify himself. He said that Ray had been having an affair with Katie Harley for the past few months. He said he didn't know if it was relevant, but thought he should pass the information on. He had a slight Scottish or maybe Irish accent, and sounded older, perhaps over sixty.

'Well, let's go and see Katie. And then chat to Dwayne again.'

A tall woman, about thirty, was approaching them, her straight long brown hair tied back. She wore a turquoise scooped-neck blouse, with fitted black pants and a black silk scarf around her neck.

Charlie smiled. 'Hi Anj, this is Zoe.' He turned to Zoe. 'Anjali is the new tactical intel officer I told you about.'

'Hi Anjali, nice to meet you,' said Zoe, shaking her hand.

'It is a real honour to meet you, Zoe,' said Anjali. 'My

family was thrilled when they heard that I would be working with—'

From two desks down, Iain Gillies turned in his chair. 'Jeez, Anj, turn it down a notch. She was just doing her job.'

Anjali continued to smile at Zoe. 'Anyway, your case. I have gone through Ray Carlson's computer. I was able to log in to his bank account as the username and password auto-filled when I opened the link to his account. He owed a bit on the mortgage for the Sorrento house, though nothing extravagant, only about two hundred grand. Most of his wage was put against the house payment every month. No red flags showing big deposits or withdrawals, but I can't say what he was living off day to day. He didn't seem to be under any financial stress. Other than that, there are some angry email exchanges between him and his ex-wife, mainly about her spending habits.'

'Any deposits into Donna's account?' asked Zoe.

'No, nothing. He must have been giving her cash.'

Zoe pursed her lips. She was hoping for more information.

'Don't worry,' Anjali continued, 'there's more. It looks like Ray had a secret girlfriend. There are a heap of emails from someone called "Muffin" on a Gmail account. Most of the emails are about places and times to meet. I checked his phone and he has a contact named Muffin. I ran the number and it is registered to Katie Harley, the wife of Dwayne Harley.'

'We just got a Crime Stopper tip saying the same thing,' said Zoe.

Anjali's shoulders dropped.

Zoe smiled at her. 'You did good work. Can you print out a list of the messages?'

'Done,' said Anjali, brightening. She pulled a piece of paper from her folder and handed it to Zoe.

'Fantastic,' said Zoe. She looked at Charlie. 'Let's go and visit Katie.'

An hour and a half later, they pulled up outside Dwayne and Katie Harley's house in Rye. It was Georgian-style, with rendered white walls and a manicured garden. A fountain stood in the front yard, with water spouting two feet into the air and goldfish darting beneath.

Zoe sat still, staring into the near distance.

'What is it?' asked Charlie.

'How far are we from Ray's place in Portsea?'

Charlie pulled out his phone and started typing. 'About twenty minutes around the peninsula. At the speed limit that is.'

'Okay, thanks.' Zoe opened her door, prompting Charlie to do the same. Zoe got Harry from the back and they approached the house.

Charlie slapped the flat of his hand against the oak door three times.

'You're not with Organised Crime anymore,' Zoe said.

'Sorry, old habits.'

The door began to open, revealing a tall, slim woman of about forty, her blonde hair styled in an elegant, shoulder-length cut. Wearing pink lycra leggings and a light blue tank top, she pulled her head back in surprise at the sight of the detectives holding their badges, exposing large diamond studs on each of her ears. Despite all of that though, she looked tired and sad.

'Katie Harley?'

'Yes.'

'I'm Detective Sergeant Zoe Mayer and this is my partner, Detective Senior Constable Charlie Shaw. Can we come in for a chat?'

'Of course,' she said hesitantly, looking down at Harry.

'He's friendly,' said Zoe.

'It's not that...it's just that I'm allergic to dogs.'

'Not a problem,' said Zoe. She indicated to Harry to lie down beneath a shady tree near the door and she and Charlie walked inside.

The open-plan living area came straight from the pages of a designer magazine. Cushions were lined perfectly up on the sofas, with a plush throw rug draped over the end of one. A contemporary chandelier illuminated the scene, and a huge abstract painting dominated the room. Everything looked brand new.

'Are you here alone?' asked Zoe, as she and Charlie sat down on the couch opposite Katie.

'Yes. Dwayne's taken the day off and gone surfing. The kids are in school.'

'What does Dwayne do for work?'

'Owns a plumbing business.'

'Do you work?'

'Yes, I am a mum of two. That's plenty of work,' she said, with a hint of defiance.

'Do you know why we're here?' asked Zoe.

'I presume it's about what happened to Ray.'

'Where were you on Sunday morning?'

'I was shopping with my daughter up at Westfield Southland. We came home once Dwayne called us at lunchtime.'

'Why do you think he was killed, Katie?' asked Zoe.

Katie seemed taken aback by the bluntness of the question. 'I have no idea. Dwayne was a wreck when he got home. Walked in as if he'd seen a ghost.'

'What was your relationship like with Ray?'

'We were friends. He was more Dwayne's friend, his best friend in fact.'

'So, if I were to ask whether you and Ray were in some sort of relationship, how would you respond?' Zoe watched Katie's body jerk as she caught her breath.

'Sorry, what exactly are you saying?' said Katie, her face reddening.

'I'm asking if you and Ray were having an affair.'

Katie looked away, desperately searching for an answer. 'That's ridiculous, I'm…I'm…' Her voice petered out. Zoe could see her hands start to quiver.

'Look, Katie, we don't really have time for charades. We have your emails with Ray and your texts to each other,' said Zoe.

Katie sat, mouth open, staring at the space between the two detectives. Zoe could see that her world was falling apart.

'What am I going to do?' she whispered.

'Let's start over. Tell us everything,' said Zoe. She could see that Katie's eyes were moist.

'It started around five or six months ago. Ray was having a hard time with Donna, and he needed someone to talk to. Dwayne and his other mates weren't much help. They just told him to go and get laid. Anyway, we just started chatting. Catching up for coffee and stuff like that. Then one day we were walking on the beach and things…progressed.'

'Does Dwayne know about it?'

'No. He hasn't got a clue.'

'You sure?' asked Zoe.

'If Dwayne knew, the whole world would know, too. He would have lost it at me, at Ray and anyone else within earshot. He doesn't know anything. Ray and I were careful…'

'Katie, do you know of any other reason someone would want to kill Ray?'

'No.'

'Was he in a relationship with anyone else?'

'God, no,' said Katie, looking affronted, before realising the irony of her own situation.

'How about you, Katie? Are you seeing anyone else as well? Another person who may have become jealous?'

'No. No one.'

'Ray have any enemies?'

'No, I can't think of anyone. He was a great guy.'

A car sped past, its V8 motor rattling the windows of the house. Harry barked once by the front door, causing Zoe to turn. A helicopter passed low above the house, its blades thumping the air. Zoe suddenly felt her vision start to flicker and her chest became constricted. A chill rushed through her and everything grew dark.

Zoe opened her eyes and felt herself shiver in the late September chill. She was standing outside the northern section of the Melbourne Cricket Ground, looking out over the surrounding green expanse of parkland. It was Grand Final Day and she had volunteered the night before, without being told anything about the job. Iain and Garry had volunteered too.

Now the crowd was building, and from behind her dark sunglasses, Zoe studied the fans as they approached. She wore black jeans with a light black jacket, just long enough to cover her pistol at her waist, and a red baseball cap, like all the other undercover officers scattered among the crowd. The air was filled with a mixture of cigarette smoke and the smell of fried food.

Through her earpiece, she could hear the section leaders calling in the all clear, one after another. Zoe glanced at the roof of the grandstand towering up behind her. She could see a black-clad figure scanning the area with binoculars. Next to the spotter, Zoe could see part of the long black barrel of a rifle; a police sniper was sitting there, out of sight.

At the front door, Harry barked. The room began to brighten. Zoe blinked, and found herself staring at the folder in her hands, willing the feeling to pass. She tried to breathe deeply. The sound of the chopper faded. She could feel the heat in her face.

'Lots of action around here,' said Charlie. 'Hoons in cars and helicopters. All we need now is a train to go by.'

'It's usually quiet,' said Katie, staring at Zoe. 'That's a local kid. Just got his driver's licence. He's showing off.'

Zoe could feel Katie's eyes on her, but was unable to respond. She was still trying to moderate her breathing.

'Are you...' started Katie.

'Were there any threats from Donna?' asked Charlie quickly, drawing Katie's attention to him.

'No, there was bad blood between them, sure, but nothing that would reach this level. Their fights were all about money. How much she wanted. How much she was spending. That sort of thing.'

Zoe was now recovered. 'Where was Ray getting his money from? His job wasn't paying enough for the house he was living in, much less the mansion his wife's in still.'

'Not sure. We never spoke about money. People around here don't like to talk about that sort of thing. Seems a bit uncouth.' Katie caught herself. 'Sorry, that sounds snobby.'

'We are going to need you to come in and give a statement,' said Charlie.

'What, now?'

'Yes, right now,' said Zoe, standing up. Charlie also stood.

Katie remained seated, staring at the table.

3 PM, WEDNESDAY 5 FEBRUARY

Dwayne Harley stopped short as he entered the interview room at the Rosebud Police Station. He was wearing navy blue board shorts and white t-shirt with a faded Rip Curl logo on the front. He appeared distracted and looked tired.

'What is it?' asked Charlie.

'Is my wife here?'

'Why do you ask that?' asked Zoe.

Dwayne was sniffing the air. 'Smells like Katie's perfume.'

'She's not here,' said Zoe. Harry lay down beside her.

Zoe turned on the digital recorder. 'Interview between Detective Sergeant Zoe Mayer and Dwayne Harley. Also present, Detective Senior Constable Charles Shaw. It is Wednesday, the fifth of February at 3 pm.' She read out the formal caution, and got going. 'Dwayne, since we spoke the other day, have you had any other ideas about what might have happened to Ray?'

'No. It's a mystery to me. I thought you wanted to give me some sort of update.'

'What can you tell us about Ray's romantic life?'

'Romantic life?' Dwayne said, half grinning. 'That's a strange way to ask if he was getting any. He would have told me if he was involved with anyone.'

Zoe stared into Dwayne's eyes, looking for signs that he was lying. He peered back calmly at her, before he began to look confused. 'What?'

'Dwayne, we have spoken at length today with your wife,' Zoe said. 'Katie has admitted to us that she and Ray were seeing each other.'

Dwayne squinted, as if he was waiting for the punchline to drop. 'Seeing each other? No way.'

'I'm afraid it's true. We have emails between the two of them, plus calls and messages from Ray's phone to Katie's phone.'

Dwayne grew pale, shaking his head and staring down. Zoe glanced across at Charlie.

'So, when did you first find out about the affair?' asked Charlie.

'I didn't...didn't know until now,' he stammered. He stood up in a rush and his chair toppled over. He walked to the back of the room, his body shaking. 'Shit,' he screamed into the wall. Harry sat up, watching Dwayne intently. Zoe and Charlie remained in their seats.

After thirty seconds, Zoe said, 'Dwayne, we need to speak with you some more. Can you take a seat, please?'

Dwayne took three deep breaths. He reached down and

picked up the chair. He placed it back in position and sat down.

'Come on,' continued Charlie. 'Be honest with us and we'll help you sort it all out. If you went to confront Ray and it all got out of hand, tell us now and you can get in front of this.'

Dwayne looked up at Charlie. 'Mate, I knew fucking nothing about any of this. I can't believe my best mate did that to me.'

Zoe stared at Dwayne. *Your wife did it to you as well.* He looked concussed by the news, but she'd met hundreds of good liars over her career. Some of them were even great ones.

Harry watched the boat pass underneath as they walked across the Queen Street bridge to Southbank. Zoe looked across at the sprawling casino complex, before she and Harry turned right and walked up in front of the Convention Centre. She felt the cooling breeze coming up the Yarra from Port Phillip Bay.

Zoe spotted Sarah immediately among the tourists taking photographs of the city across the river. She wore designer jeans with a white shirt, had dark sunglasses on, and her brown hair was tied back in a ponytail under a navy baseball cap. She spotted Zoe, gave a small wave and started walking towards her.

'Thanks for coming,' said Sarah.

'No problem. How'd you recognise me?'

Sarah smiled, pointing down at Harry.

'Let's grab a seat.' They sat on a nearby bench. Harry lay down in front of them and then started rolling on his back on the grass.

'Don't mind him,' Zoe said, smiling. Harry's tongue lolled from the side of his mouth.

'Have you had him long?' asked Sarah, taking off her sunglasses.

'Just a month or so,' said Zoe. She still felt self-conscious about having a service dog. 'Now, what did you want to discuss?'

'It's more about getting some advice. My podcast looks at human interest stories. Small stories with universal messages. Redemption stories, that sort of thing.'

Zoe had looked up *Westbrook* after Sarah's call. It was doing well, and was now the fourth-most popular podcast in Australia.

'I am doing a multi-part story on people from my old high school in Hastings,' Sarah continued, 'on the far side of the Mornington Peninsula. It's one of those middle-of-the-road sort of communities—not rich, not poor—where people can go any which way with their lives. I've been looking at successes, disasters, chances taken and missed, you know. Anyway, when I was digging around, I found out that one of my old classmates, Trevor Hill, is on remand awaiting trial.'

Zoe met Sarah's eyes. 'For what?'

'Another guy we were at school with, Eric Drum, was stabbed to death in his backyard in Hastings and Trevor has been charged with his murder. His trial starts soon.'

Zoe vaguely remembered the case and felt her guard go

up. 'You aren't recording this are you? This is off the record, right?'

Sarah raised her hands. 'Completely. No recording at all. Just background research.'

'Okay, but why do you need to see me? I didn't have anything to do with that case.'

'I need advice. Preferably of the level-headed variety. I don't want to get sucked in to doing a sympathetic piece on a killer just because I knew him years ago and he says he's innocent. The thing is, though, I met him the other day and he tells me he was talking to another prisoner and that their cases are identical. Both say they were lifelong friends with the victim, that there were tip-offs about possible motives and evidence that appeared out of nowhere. The victim was stabbed in both cases. He's telling me that they're both innocent and have been framed.'

'You know that the prisons are full of people who claim to be innocent.'

Sarah shut her eyes momentarily. 'Yes, I know that... It's just that I am sitting there listening to this guy, trying to convince myself that he's lying, but every fibre in me says that he's telling the truth. I've been an investigative journalist for years and I know how to pick a liar. I knew Trevor and Eric really well when we were in high school. Something seems off about the whole thing.'

'Okay, let's break this down a bit,' said Zoe. 'Almost all murder victims know their killer, so that part isn't uncommon. We get plenty of tips, so that's not strange either. And knives aren't an unusual weapon of choice. About half of all the homicides I've investigated involve a knife. So, you are probably dealing with coincidence—and not even an improbable one, at that. If your friend is innocent he will get a chance to prove it in court.'

Sarah looked at her feet and sighed. Zoe could recognise something of herself in Sarah.

'Anyway, you should be taking your concerns to the Director of Public Prosecutions,' said Zoe.

'I already tried that. The DPP told me to speak with a senior prosecutor, one of the bigwigs there. She didn't want anything to do with it. Didn't even hear me out when I called her. Sally Johnstone, you know her?'

Zoe bit her lip. 'Yes, I've known her for a long time.'

'She told me I was wasting her time,' said Sarah.

'Did you ask Tom about her?'

'No, why?'

'Sally and Tom dated when we were all at uni together.'

'They did? Sorry, I didn't know or that you're friends with Sally. Small world.'

Zoe laughed. 'We are definitely not friends. Not for a long, long time.'

At university, Zoe, Tom and Sally were part of a tight group of friends. Sally and Tom had dated for a year or so and, even after Tom broke up with Sally, the group stuck together. The next year, a rumour started that Sally was working on weekends at a strip club in Canberra, flying up Friday afternoons and coming back on Sunday. Zoe thought it so ridiculous that she made a joke about it to Sally one day at lunch. Sally tried to laugh it off, but the rage in her eyes was obvious. Instantly, Zoe realised that it was true. Within days, Sally had cut off their friendship, blaming Zoe for starting the rumour out of jealousy.

Since she had been working in Homicide, Zoe now saw Sally regularly around the courts. Sally's disdain alternated between hateful glances and blank stares, as if she didn't know who Zoe was.

'So, what do you want from me?' Zoe asked.

'I don't know where to go next. I mean, if there has been some sort of injustice, I want to help, but I'm not sure how.'

'You tried speaking to your friend's lawyer?'

'Yes, but he sounds only halfway engaged in the whole case. His bills have been paid in advance and that's all he's worried about. He said the evidence is overwhelming and not to get my hopes up. Trevor sold his house to cover his legal fees. He's skint, and his lawyer's interest level has fallen in line with his bank balance.'

'Look,' said Zoe. 'Officially, I can't look into this, okay? If I did, every crook and their lawyer would be on the phone. Do you understand?'

Sarah understood.

Zoe gritted her teeth, reminding herself to thank Tom for giving her number to a journalist. 'What's your friend's name again?'

'Trevor Hill. Charged with the murder of Eric Drum at Hastings on the fifth of February exactly a year ago.'

'And the other guy?'

'Aaron Smyth. He was convicted of murdering a guy called Ben Jennings a year before that, in Frankston. He was found guilty the following November of that year and given life.'

'So how did Trevor and Aaron Smyth meet?'

'They were in the same housing unit at the Melbourne Remand Centre. Got talking about their cases and realised how similar they were.'

'Hold on,' said Zoe. 'Aaron Smyth was convicted three months before your friend's alleged crime was even committed. Why was he still at the remand centre after his sentence?'

'Overcrowding in maximum security at Barwon Prison.'

Zoe stared into space, thinking.

'Should I write it all down for you?' asked Sarah.

'No, definitely not,' Zoe said. 'All right, if I hear anything of interest, I'll call you. If you hear nothing, it means nothing's there, okay?'

Sarah gave a hint of a smile. 'I really appreciate it.'

'There's nothing to appreciate,' Zoe said. 'Understand?'

Sarah nodded, her expression serious again. 'Hundred per cent. Got it.'

'Come on, Harry. Time to go.' Harry bounced to his feet, wagging his tail.

10 AM, THURSDAY 6 FEBRUARY

Ray Carlson's pine coffin was carried from the stone chapel by six pallbearers, including Dwayne Harley. The breeze was once again coming from the north and the air was heating up again. Dwayne's tie was pulled across to the side, as if he'd tried to wrench it off at some point. He was gazing grim-faced at the ground as he walked.

The eulogies had praised Ray's love of surfing, beer and football. *Not a lot for almost forty years on earth*, Zoe thought. Neither Donna Carlson nor Dwayne Harley had spoken.

Zoe and Charlie, dressed in dark suits and wearing sunglasses, had slipped outside towards the end of the service and waited under the shade of a Norfolk pine. Charlie flapped the lapels of his jacket to cool down. 'This would have to be a record for a funeral after a homicide. Four days. Donna couldn't wait to get him buried, eh?'

Zoe was focused on Dwayne. 'Why would he be a

pallbearer?' she asked under her breath. 'He's carrying the guy who was screwing his wife.'

'He's trying to save face,' said Charlie. 'It'd be stranger if he wasn't a pallbearer. He wants to stop people finding out about Ray and Katie. Around here he may as well try to stop a wave crashing to shore.'

They watched people milling around near the hearse. There were a few dozen mourners. Donna Carlson, wearing a black dress, stared across at them, her expression blank.

'Our runner obviously got bail,' said Zoe, nodding towards Joshua Priest. He was in a wheelchair, one leg elevated in a cast, one arm in a sling. He was being pushed by an older woman, wearing a black dress and a pearl necklace, who Zoe guessed was his mother.

'His days of police pursuits are over for a while,' said Charlie.

Zoe had parked her SUV under a nearby tree with the windows down. She knew Harry would be asleep in the back. Near the car, a video camera operator from the Major Crime Scene Unit was recording everything. Videotaping the funerals of homicide victims had become routine after a couple of instances of mourners breaking down and making admissions or even confessions at the graveside. At the very least, the presence of a video camera tended to upset people with something to hide, so the detectives thought of it as a handy tool.

The hearse moved off at walking pace, followed by the mourners, a mixed bunch. Some wore suits and smart dresses, but there were a couple of tattooed guys and a number of younger people in t-shirts. They all passed by Zoe and Charlie, mostly lost in their own thoughts. Joshua Priest sneered at them as he rolled past in his wheelchair.

The sad convoy travelled for five minutes, before reaching the freshly dug grave.

The video camera operator walked at the rear with Zoe and Charlie. As the coffin was carried from the hearse, people gathered.

The detectives instinctively watched Dwayne. He was standing apart from his wife, gazing up at the sky, as if willing the whole event to be over. They could see his body heaving as he tried to hold back tears.

Katie's eyes were on the coffin, her expression distant. To her left, Donna Carlson stood in silence. Everyone seemed to be in their own world.

Zoe's phone vibrated. She walked away. 'Mayer,' she whispered.

'Zoe, its Anjali. The boss asked me to call you. Somebody called in a tip to Crime Stoppers about a guy looking suspicious this morning, dumping a garbage bag into a bin at the Surf Beach car park, at the end of Back Beach Road down at Portsea. The caller said that it was Dwayne Harley.'

Zoe turned back towards the mourners fifty metres away. Dwayne was staring at her. 'Did the caller leave a name?' asked Zoe, maintaining eye contact with Dwayne.

'Anonymous,' said Anjali. 'The only info I have is that the caller was a male. Sounded older.'

'Did he have a slight Scottish or Irish accent?' asked Zoe, remembering the tip they'd got about Katie and Ray's affair.

'Nothing here about an accent. I've rung the Rosebud station to get someone down to the car park to seal off the area.'

'Good thinking, thanks—can you call Forensics and organise for them to get down there as well? We'll go as soon as the funeral's over.'

Zoe ended the call. Dwayne Harley was still staring hard at her.

An hour later, Zoe's phone vibrated again. She looked at the screen: *Forensics are here.*

Her eyes moved from the beach up to Charlie at the top of the stairs that led to the dunes. He gave her a wave. She called Harry back out of the shallows, where he was playing. Harry shook himself dry and they walked from the beach to the car park. Charlie was chatting to Jenny as they approached.

'Hey Jen,' said Zoe.

'Hi Zoe. Down here twice in one week. Should have brought my swimsuit.'

'Or a surfboard,' said Zoe. 'You on your own today?'

'Yeah, we're backed up a bit. What've we got here?'

'Crime Stoppers tip. Someone who's a person of interest in our murder allegedly jammed a garbage bag in that bin over there this morning.'

'Right. I'll get my gear.'

Jenny photographed the area before taking fingerprints from the rim of the bin. Harry watched, sitting on the grass.

'Couple of prints there,' said Jenny, 'but they're from

children's hands. No right-thinking adult touches a rubbish bin if they can avoid it.'

Jenny handed the camera to Charlie. 'Can you video this part?'

'No worries,' said Charlie, taking the video camera and pointing it towards Jenny.

Using a battery-powered screwdriver, she expertly dismantled the lid of the bin. Lifting the large plastic container out from inside, she used metal forceps to remove three soft drink bottles and a takeaway food container, placing them on a plastic sheet she had laid out beside the bin.

She then used the forceps to pick up the bag and placed it on a plastic sheet. She worked it open and looked inside.

'Pullover hoodie. The label says "Large". Looks like there's blood on it. A fair bit actually.' Charlie moved in, videotaping inside the bag. 'There should be DNA inside it from whoever was wearing it. Your person of interest may be about to get an upgrade.'

'Good. We could do with a break,' said Zoe.

'Best get their DNA sample quick-smart. We'll try to see if there are prints on the garbage bag back at the lab.'

'Any chance you can get it prioritised for us?'

'Let me see what strings I can pull,' said Jenny, giving Zoe a wink and taking the camera back from Charlie.

'You two again. What do you want this time? Come to tell me my kids don't love me anymore either?' Dwayne was standing at the door, shirt hanging loose, a beer in his hand. Zoe could smell the stale odour of beer coming from him.

'We need to have another chat, Dwayne,' said Zoe.

'I've told you everything I know. Why don't you both rack off and catch whoever did this.'

Zoe saw a girl of around thirteen come into the room in the background, and watch them warily.

Leaning in close, Zoe whispered, 'Dwayne, you don't want us dragging you away in handcuffs in front of your kids, do you? That kind of image stays with them forever.' She stepped back.

Dwayne went to respond angrily, before stopping himself. 'Tell your mum that I'm headed out for a while,' he said, over his shoulder. He finished his beer, setting the empty bottle down hard on the sideboard next to the door.

At Rosebud station they took Dwayne into the interview room.

'I intend to interview you in relation to the death of Ray Carlson,' Zoe said to Dwayne. 'Before continuing, I must inform you that you do not have to say anything, but anything you say or do may be given in evidence. Do you understand that?'

'Yeah, sure.'

'I must also inform you of your rights. You have the right to communicate with or attempt to communicate with a friend or relative to inform that person of your whereabouts. You have the right to communicate with or attempt to communicate with a legal practitioner. Do you understand these rights?'

'Yep.'

'Do you want to exercise any of these rights before the interview proceeds?'

'No. Don't need a lawyer and my family...' Dwayne faltered, '...my family know where I am. What is all this? Why would I need a lawyer? I just found him there. I had nothing to do with it.'

'Who did?' Charlie asked.

'How the fuck would I know? That's your job to find out.'

Zoe tapped her pen on the table, drawing Dwayne's attention. 'Have you been drinking alcohol today?' she asked.

'Yeah, you know I have. I had a beer in my hand when you arrived to pick me up. Crack detective you're turning out to be.'

'How many drinks have you had today?'

'Two. Two beers, that's it.'

'Any drugs?'

'What? No, I don't do drugs. Why are you asking that?'

'We want to be assured that you are okay to be interviewed, that's all. Not impeded at all, you know?'

'I'm fine.'

'Dwayne, what's twelve multiplied by twelve, minus ten?'

'Um, a hundred and thirty-four,' he shot back. 'Why does that matter?'

'Just confirming your sobriety for the tape,' said Zoe. 'Where were you this morning?'

'Getting ready for the funeral. You were there today, you saw me.'

'Take us through your day, Dwayne. From the beginning.'

'Okay. I got up around six. I am sleeping in the spare bedroom and the mattress in there is crap. Why it's me in there, I don't know. I mean, I'm not the one who's been rooting around. Anyway, I got up and had some toast and a coffee. Then Katie got up. I had to get out of the house. Can't even look at her…So, I grabbed my board and headed out for a surf. Would've been just before seven when I left.'

'Where'd you go? Which beach?' asked Zoe.

'Surf Beach.'

'End of Back Beach Road?'

'Yeah.'

'Isn't that where you and Ray used to surf together?'

'Yeah.'

'Isn't it weird going back there, after what's happened? Don't you want to surf somewhere else?'

'I haven't really thought about it. It's just where I surf. It's like I get in the car and that's where I end up.'

'So, what time do you reckon you got there?'

'Just after seven.'

'Then what?'

Dwayne snorted. 'I pulled on my wetsuit, waxed the board and hit the waves. It's called surfing. Not rocket science,' he said.

'Anything else when you got out of your car?'

'Like what?'

'Anything at all. Talk to anyone, do anything.'

'Nah. Just went into the water. The waves were only average. I wouldn't have bothered except I didn't want to be at the house. There were a few other people already out there. Teenagers. City kids, by the way they were surfing. Didn't know them.'

'Anyone in the car park when you got there?'

'Two or three cars, but I didn't see any people about.'

'How long were you out in the surf?'

'Probably an hour.'

'Then what?'

'I came to shore, drove home, had a shower and got dressed for the funeral.'

'So, between leaving the water and getting in your car, did you do anything else?'

'What is all this?'

'Just answer the question, please.'

'Nothing. Went to the car, took off the wetsuit, tied down the board and came home. That's it.'

'Did you put anything in the bin?' asked Zoe.

'The bin? No.'

'You sure?'

'Positive. Why?'

'Dwayne, we got a call this morning from someone who saw you dumping a garbage bag in a rubbish bin in the car park.'

'That's bullshit.'

'We retrieved a garbage bag this afternoon. Forensics have taken it and its contents away for testing.'

'What contents?'

'A hoodie that looks like it's covered in blood.'

'I don't know anything about that. I didn't put anything in any bin there today. If someone said that, then that person's trying to set me up.'

'Okay,' said Zoe, 'in that case, would you consent to a

DNA test and let us take your fingerprints?' She looked into Dwayne's eyes.

He met her gaze. 'Absolutely, let's finish this bullshit right now,' he said, defiant.

'I'll get a swab kit,' Charlie said.

6.30 PM, THURSDAY 6 FEBRUARY

The office was so quiet that Zoe could hear the murmuring of the air conditioning. Only a few other detectives were around, catching up on paperwork. Zoe knew that the heatwave would be taking its toll—a week of restless sleep and a high workload for the squad. They all knew that violent crime spiked during heatwaves. There had been three new homicides in Melbourne in the four days since the Carlson murder. Harry sat under Zoe's desk, oblivious to all that, happily chewing a stuffed-toy gorilla.

Zoe thought about her conversation with Sarah Westbrook. She knew it would be an itch she needed to scratch. She unplugged her laptop and carried it down the hall to the conference room. Harry followed her through the door, his toy gorilla in his mouth. Zoe glanced down the empty hallway before shutting the door behind her.

She sat on the far side of the long table, facing the door, and logged in to the server. She opened the archive folder, and quickly found the case of Sarah Westbrook's school friend, Trevor Hill.

The victim was Eric Drum. A landscaper, Eric was thirty-eight years old when he was stabbed to death at his home in Hastings, on the far side of the Mornington Peninsula. His body was found at eleven the next morning by his boss, after Eric didn't show up for work.

The alleged motive was that Eric was threatening to out Trevor as gay, something that Eric had found out about a few months beforehand. There was evidence of emailed taunts from Eric in the month leading up to the killing, as well as bloodied clothing buried in the bushland behind Eric's house. Zoe noted that the evidence was recovered after a tip-off, as Sarah had mentioned. The photos from the pathologist showed Eric had been stabbed three times in the upper chest. One of the blows punctured his heart. No weapon was found, but the autopsy showed that Eric had been killed with a large knife, most likely a hunting knife.

She scanned through the pictures taken by the police photographer at the funeral. They showed the usual sombre cast of black-clad mourners.

With a clear motive established and physical evidence found linking him to the crime, Trevor Hill was charged with murder and remanded in custody. The last note in the file stated that the trial was due to start on Monday 17 February. *Eleven days from now.* The homicide detectives listed on the case were Iain Gillies and Garry Burns. The prosecutor was Sally Johnstone. Zoe sighed. No wonder Sally didn't want to listen to Sarah.

Zoe closed the folder and opened the second case Sarah had mentioned, the one she had said was identical to her friend's prosecution.

The victim was Ben Jennings, aged thirty-seven. He had been killed two years ago in the bayside suburb of Frankston. Zoe scanned the case summary. Ben's body had been found by his wife, Charlotte, in the morning. The pathologist determined he had been killed between 1 and 2 am. In her statement, Charlotte had said that Ben and his friend Aaron Smyth had been drinking in their backyard the night before. She had gone to bed at 10 pm and had heard nothing after that.

Zoe opened the evidence folder on the screen. She clicked through the crime scene photos showing Ben Jennings slumped down some wooden stairs at the rear of his house. A bloodied steak knife lay close to his body. The photos from the pathologist's examination at the morgue showed two stab wounds to the upper chest. She glanced at the photos from the funeral, before moving on. The homicide detectives listed on the case were Hannah Nguyen and Angus Batch. The prosecutor was Sally Johnstone. *Fantastic*, thought Zoe. The summary document noted there were no fingerprints on the steak knife.

In evidence to the court it was revealed that Aaron owed Ben ten thousand dollars, but Aaron denied that this had caused any conflict between them. He insisted that Ben was in good spirits when he had left around midnight, walking the two streets back to his house. Aaron lived alone and so there was no one to verify his story.

Later that morning, a bloodied t-shirt was found in one of Aaron's neighbour's garbage bins, three doors down from his house. A keen-eyed constable in a passing patrol car had spotted blood near the lid of the bin, and then found the t-shirt inside. Two hours later, a tip came into Crime Stoppers alerting them that a man acting suspiciously had put a t-shirt into a rubbish bin outside a house that wasn't his. The caller said that the man lived at 7 Mica Street, Frankston: Aaron's address.

The DNA results showed that Aaron's DNA as well as Ben Jennings' blood were on the t-shirt. Aaron was charged with murder. He pleaded not guilty, but was convicted that November.

Zoe thought about what Sarah had said. She was right that each case involved knives, that the victim and suspect knew each other, and that the police had been tipped off. But both cases had strong motives—Eric had been threatening to expose Trevor Hill's sexuality, while Aaron owed his victim money—and undeniable physical evidence. A coincidence, as she had told Sarah.

She was closing down the image files on her screen when something caught her eye. She enlarged the photograph, staring at one of the figures at Ben Jennings' funeral. The man had a beard and was using a cane. He looked to be in his forties, medium height, slim build, and Caucasian. Something about him seemed familiar to Zoe. *Where have I seen you before?*

She scanned the list of witnesses, searching for a name she recognised from another case. None of the names was familiar. She was about to click off the photographs from Eric Drum's funeral, and then stopped. One of the mourners looked similar to the man with the cane at Ben Jennings' funeral. Zoe brought up the two photographs so they sat next to each other on the screen. The fellow at Eric Drum's funeral looked younger, about thirty-five, and was solidly built. His hair was dark auburn and he was clean-shaven. The two men might have been brothers. Again, she scanned the list of witnesses, but recognised none of the names.

Ten minutes later, still thinking about the two men, she went to get a coffee. Harry followed close behind. On her way back to her desk she heard Charlie speaking in Rob Loretti's office.

'I'm not sure,' he was saying. 'Something happened when we were doing an interview down the peninsula. There was some noise, a hoon driving by and then a chopper over the house. It was only for a few seconds, but she froze up. The person we were interviewing noticed. Then her dog barked out the front and she snapped out of it.'

'Okay, keep an eye on her and let me know if anything else happens,' Rob said.

'Will do, boss.'

Zoe was almost back at her desk when Charlie came out of Rob's office.

'Hey, where have you been?' he said, his face reddening.

Zoe felt the anger building in her chest. Her phone vibrated, saving Charlie momentarily. 'Mayer,' she snapped.

'Zoe, it's Melina Fredericks from the lab.'

'Melina,' said Zoe, her tone softening. 'What do you have for me?'

'Blood on the outside of the hoodie found in the bin at Portsea is a match to your victim, Ray Carlson. DNA samples from the inside match Dwayne Harley. Skin cells, hairs on the insides of the sleeves and around the collar. His DNA's also on the zipper. From the blood pattern on the front, it looks like your suspect took the hoodie off soon after the murder and scrunched it up, probably to bag it. No prints on the garbage bag. Whoever dumped it must've been gloved up. I'll email you the report in a minute.'

'Thanks, Melina. Appreciate you fast-tracking it for me,' said Zoe.

'Do me a favour and keep that quiet. I don't need a reputation as a soft touch,' said Melina.

'You've got it,' said Zoe, and ended the call.

'Bad news?' asked Charlie.

'Dwayne's DNA is all over the hoodie. The blood is from Ray Carlson.'

'What? That's fantastic,' said Charlie, triumphant. 'Motive, opportunity and evidence. He's cooked now.'

Zoe was silent.

'But...' said Charlie.

'It doesn't feel right. It's all too easy.'

'If easy is how it comes, I'll take it,' he said. 'It's your first case back after four months off. You sure you're not looking for something that's not there?'

Zoe bristled. 'He didn't ask for a lawyer, didn't even blink about giving a DNA swab, wasn't evasive. I don't think he knew about his wife's infidelity before we told him either. It doesn't feel right.'

'Sorry boss, but we've got what we need to charge this guy, and we need to do it.'

Zoe exhaled. She knew he was right. 'Yeah, okay. Let's go and pick him up.'

Dwayne angrily paced around the interview room. It was just before 11 pm. Zoe, Charlie and Rob Loretti were watching him from the monitoring room.

'He doesn't want a lawyer,' said Zoe.

'He bitched the whole way about false imprisonment and fake charges,' added Charlie.

'Maybe he thinks he is smarter than the rest of us and can talk his way out of it,' said Rob, stifling a yawn.

'We'll see,' said Zoe. She patted Harry on the head, and then gestured for him to lie down. She and Charlie headed down the hall to the interview room.

'Have a seat, Dwayne,' Zoe said.

Dwayne sat down. 'Took your fricken time.'

Zoe turned on the equipment and read Dwayne his rights again. Again, he refused a lawyer.

'Dwayne, is there something you want to tell me? You know, good people make mistakes sometimes.'

'No, there's nothing. Except that I am innocent and this is bullshit.'

'Do you recognise this hoodie?' said Zoe, pulling a photograph from her folder and placing it in front of him.

Dwayne leaned over the photograph and squinted at

it. 'I've got one that looks like it. That's not mine, though. Mine's at home, not covered in blood. I wore it a week ago. Probably still in the laundry basket. I could've shown you back at the house if you'd asked me. Fucking hell, you two are complete drongos.'

'Dwayne, the blood on this is from Ray Carlson,' said Zoe, 'and your DNA is on the inside of the hoodie. Skin cells and hairs. What do you have to say to that?'

Dwayne's mouth fell open. He stared again at the photograph. 'No way. That can't be true.'

'Now's your chance to get in front of this,' said Zoe. 'If there are mitigating circumstances, now is the time to tell us. We can help you.'

'That's bullshit,' Dwayne roared. 'You're trying to stitch me up. You hear about this sort of thing, but you think it's all crap. You know, urban legend. I can't believe you are doing it to me.'

'Why'd we want to do that, Dwayne?' asked Zoe.

'How the fuck would I know?' he bellowed. 'I don't have any issues with the cops, or anyone else for that matter. Maybe you need to solve the case fast. Maybe this is how you guys work all the time. Put my DNA sample in there. All I know is that I didn't kill Ray.'

'You've got a solid motive,' said Charlie. 'Katie and Ray. You found out, and that's why you did it. Look, you panicked, right? You went to confront him and you just lost it. That's why you still had the clothes to dump. Cause it was spontaneous. Unplanned. Isn't that right?'

'No. No. No. I had nothing to do with this. Nothing.'

Dwayne slammed the table with his fist, causing Charlie to flinch. Zoe didn't move. She could see that his hand was starting to shake.

Zoe and Charlie said nothing, staring at Dwayne. If he was going to confess, they did not want to distract him. Zoe knew that silence applied its own type of pressure to a suspect.

Eventually, Dwayne lifted his eyes. 'What do ya want me to say?' he said, exhausted.

Zoe could hear the excitement in Charlie's breathing.

'We just want the truth, we owe it to Ray,' said Zoe, making her voice soft and sympathetic, as she had outside Ray's house on the day of the murder.

At that, Dwayne snorted a laugh. 'Owe it to fucking Ray. What a joke. Okay, the truth is this—I don't have the first fucking clue how that hoodie ended up with Ray's blood all over it. Or with my DNA inside it. What I do know is that I didn't do this. I'm getting set up.'

'Why would someone do that? Who are your enemies that would do this to you?' asked Charlie.

'I have no idea. I don't have no enemies. Until Ray got killed, I thought my life was sweet. Now my best mate's dead and I find out he was shagging my missus. But I didn't know any of that before you two told me. Shit.'

Zoe tapped on the table. 'Dwayne, we've recovered a large stash of money that Ray had buried in his backyard. Do you know how he came to have that money?'

'What do you mean by a large stash?'

'Seven hundred and fifty-eight thousand in seven plastic bags.'

'Shit, where'd he get that from?' Dwayne sat back, staring Zoe in the eye.

'We're asking you. What was he into?'

'No idea.'

'The house he lived in with Donna, the car she's driving, and the place he rented in Portsea. Don't tell me that working in the winery paid for all that. The guy was living like a funds manager or a crook's lawyer. Do you think we came down with the last shower, Dwayne?'

'Look, he was still paying off the house—why would he have all that cash? It doesn't make sense to me.'

'Well, it makes sense to us,' said Zoe. 'He was getting divorced and didn't want to share it with Donna. It's also highly likely the proceeds of criminal activity.'

'I don't know anything about that.'

'The situation is this,' said Zoe, as she tapped the photograph. 'We have evidence, and you had the opportunity, means and the motive to kill Ray Carlson. You will now be charged with murder. I strongly recommend you appoint a lawyer to represent you.'

Dwayne slumped forward and put his face in his hands.

9.15 AM, FRIDAY 7 FEBRUARY

'What time's the game?' Charlie said into the phone. 'Any of the other kids need a lift?...Okay, no worries...see you then.'

He turned to Zoe. 'That was Jane. Alex has cricket tomorrow. Even in this heat. What I wouldn't give for a few hours of rain to cool this city down.'

Zoe was only half listening.

'What's up?' asked Charlie. 'Five days from crime to charge. That's a pretty good result for your first case back.' He tossed a ball of scrunched-up paper into the air, caught it and threw it hard into the bin. 'The guy's guilty. It's a slam dunk.'

'Something's not right.' She was going to say something but stopped herself. She knew that once what she was thinking was out in the open, anything might happen.

'Look,' said Charlie, 'maybe your instincts are a bit off. Maybe you're not back in your groove yet.'

In her peripheral vision Zoe noticed several detectives stop working and look their way. She turned to her partner. 'Which squad are you working in?' she asked, her voice so low he had to lean in to hear.

'Come on, Zoe. I didn't mean—' Charlie said.

'Which squad?'

From under the desk, Harry got up and walked around next to Zoe. He sat down, watching her.

'Homicide.' Charlie looked left and right, his face turning dark red.

'And where do you want to be working next week?'

'I wasn't trying to offend you. I'm sorry.'

'Charlie, I don't appreciate your attitude,' she said, her volume back to normal. 'We don't just need to prove a case, we need to prove it entirely without doubt. That's the only way to stop cases falling to pieces at trial when your evidence is put under the torch by some highly paid barrister who was born angry. If there's an acquittal, the heat is on us. I test my cases from every angle to make sure they can't be pulled apart. That's why *my* cases don't turn to shit in front of a jury, you got that?'

'I understand. Zoe, look, I was out of line.'

'You're dead right there. And while we're at it, I don't appreciate you reporting back to the boss on how you think I'm travelling. If you're worried about that sort of thing, get a fucking transfer. I've got no time, and even less respect, for that bullshit. Do we understand each other?'

The veins on Charlie's neck were bulging. 'Yes, absolutely. It won't happen again. Okay?'

Two desks down, Iain Gillies was chuckling.

'And you can shut the fuck up, too,' growled Zoe, standing up. 'Right, come on,' she said, grabbing a folder from her desk. She headed for Rob's office, Harry at her side.

'Wait—what?'

Zoe knocked and walked in without waiting. Rob looked up as Charlie caught up, almost falling through the doorway.

'What do you need, Zoe?'

'The Carlson case. I think we've got an issue.'

Zoe brought Rob and Charlie up to speed on her meeting with Sarah Westbrook, her review of the murders at Hastings and Frankston, and the parallels with the Portsea case. Rob and Charlie listened in silence.

'Okay,' said Rob, when she had finished. 'But they are just similarities. The motive and evidence both stand up and that's what's important. Plus, we have stabbing homicides every week.'

'I hear you, but look at this.' Zoe opened her folder and put a print-out of a photograph on his desk. 'This is from the Frankston murder two years ago, for which Aaron Smyth was convicted. It was taken at Ben Jennings' funeral. See this guy?' Zoe pointed out the slim, fortyish man with the dark beard and the cane.

Rob nodded.

'Okay,' said Zoe, placing the other photograph on the desk. 'The case from Hastings. A year later. Eric Drum's funeral. That guy is Trevor Hill, who's charged and in custody.' She pointed at a tall man who was openly weeping.

'That's Iain and Garry's case,' said Rob. 'The trial starts in just over a week's time, yeah?'

'That's the one. See this guy?' Zoe pointed to the solidly built man standing next to Trevor. He was clean-shaven, with neatly cut, dark auburn hair, and looked to be in his mid-thirties.

'Can't see it. What are you saying?' asked Rob.

'I think it could be the same person.'

Rob shot her a look, shaking his head.

'It's easier if you see it on the videos. Can you pull it up on your screen?'

'Sure,' said Rob. 'Come around.'

Zoe and Charlie walked around to the DI's side of the desk.

'You drive—you know what you're looking for,' said Rob, standing up.

Zoe sat down and grabbed the mouse. She found the two video files and opened them up next to each other. Then she hit play. They watched people milling around the grave. Zoe forwarded the first video to a specific spot and paused it. Then she did the same with the second video.

'Watch this part,' she said, before clicking play on each of the videos. In the videos, both men looked directly at the camera for a second or two, narrowing their eyes. 'See it?'

'I do,' said Rob. 'It's a similar expression, but it's not the same guy. They look about ten years apart in age, for a start.'

Zoe glanced up in time to see Rob give Charlie a baffled look.

She opened her folder and pulled out a third photograph. 'This is from Ray Carlson's funeral yesterday.' She pointed at a scruffy-haired man in the photo, his head tilted to one side. 'That guy's name is Greg Enders. He was friends with Ray and Dwayne Harley.'

'What? You think that he is the same person as the other two?' asked Rob incredulously.

'Maybe,' said Zoe. 'Have a look at this.' She opened the video from Ray Carlson's funeral, found the right place and let it play. Greg's neck was tilted and his shoulders were pulled back. He was wearing a loose shirt, barely tucked in over a small pot belly. His hair was messy, covering his ears, and he had a new beard, probably about two weeks old. He was standing next to Dwayne, who was also looking towards the camera.

'See the time stamp,' she said, as she held up her phone. 'At this exact moment Anjali was calling me to tell me about the Crime Stoppers tip.' In the video, Greg Enders was looking towards the camera, but off to one side, to where Zoe was standing. 'He's looking right at me.'

In the video Greg narrowed his eyes, and then returned his gaze to the funeral. 'He could've phoned in the tip just before the funeral. If so, he knew I'd be getting the call right then.'

'Whoa, hold on,' said Rob. 'This is all very coincidental. You sure you're not trying to retrofit a scenario from the information you're finding? To my eyes, there's three different people at three separate funerals, with one of them looking in your direction when you received a call. That's it.

Dwayne Harley is staring across at you as well. Perhaps they heard your phone ring and were pissed off since they were at a funeral.'

Zoe made an effort to remain calm. 'We noticed Dwayne staring at us. We weren't paying any attention to Greg Enders. And my phone was on silent. Plus, I walked way back and was whispering. Look, I feel like there's something there. It's something in that look,' said Zoe.

'What do you think, Charlie?' asked Rob.

Charlie sucked in a breath before responding. 'Honestly? I see three different people. So the expression at that moment looks similar, but they still look like different people to me. Maybe Enders was pissed off because we were taking phone calls during his mate's funeral. Who knows? Sorry, Zoe,' said Charlie.

There was a knock at the door. Zoe gathered the photographs together and turned them over.

'Come in,' said Rob.

Two men entered. They looked like brothers, tall and fit, with the same blank expression on their faces. The older of the two was just under six foot tall and had short dark hair, while the younger man was slightly taller with a full head of auburn hair. They both wore blue business shirts and dark pants, their Victoria Police lanyards hanging from their necks.

'Sorry to bother you,' said the older one. 'You Zoe Mayer?'

'Yes.'

'I'm Doug Strong and this is Frankie Chambers from the

Drug Squad,' he said, tilting his head towards his partner. 'We need to chat about Dwayne Harley.'

'What about him?' asked Zoe, standing up from Rob's chair.

'We're charging him with methamphetamine production,' said Doug. 'Dwayne and his mate Ray Carlson have been renting a house outside of Somers, on the eastern side of the Mornington Peninsula. We've had the house under surveillance, inside and out, for the last couple of months. Dwayne and Ray are, or were, cooking meth. Big time. We were due to pick them up this week, once we had all the proof we needed about their supply chain. We've got a mountain of evidence on Dwayne, so our visit is just a professional courtesy.'

Zoe remembered the tattooed men at Ray's funeral.

'We dug up a stack of cash in Ray Carlson's backyard,' said Charlie. 'Over seven hundred and fifty thousand. I think we've just found our motive for Ray's murder.'

'Could be,' said Frankie. 'Seen it happen before. One guy gets greedy. These two have been at it a while, much longer than we've had them on our radar. They've been selling through a middle man, a mate of theirs from high school, who's connected to a bikie gang. It's a fairly low-risk operation, as far as this sort of thing goes. Sell to one trusted buyer only. We've just arrested the middle man.'

'Joshua Priest?' asked Zoe.

Doug nodded. 'Yeah, that's the one. We've had him under surveillance for a while. We were watching when you chased him the other day.'

Zoe had a thought. 'Did you have Dwayne under surveillance on the day that Ray was murdered?'

'No,' said Doug. 'We had plenty of evidence on Dwayne and Ray. We were focused on Joshua and the rest of the supply chain downstream. Sorry.'

Zoe nodded. 'You have audio with the surveillance in the house where Dwayne and Ray were cooking?'

'Yeah,' said Frankie.

'Did you pick up any disputes between them?'

'Nothing. They were a professional unit, as far as drug cooks go. Careful, organised. They weren't users as far as we could tell. That cash you dug up would be a small amount of the money they've been making. They've been smart operators until now. Keeping most of their money hidden away, continuing to pay off mortgages, not buying Ferraris, that sort of thing. We only found out about them because we were following Priest around, trying to work out where he was getting his supplies. We'll be doing a lot of digging over the next few days. Dwayne's backyard is probably full of bags of cash as well. Anyway, he's going to be charged this arvo. Even if he cooperates, he'll do a minimum of ten years on that charge. Hopefully longer.'

'Okay, thanks for letting us know,' said Zoe.

'No worries. But we're gonna need the cash. It's evidence in our case.'

'Sure. We'll get the paperwork sorted and it's all yours.'

'Thanks, and we'll give you a call if Dwayne gives us any information that involves your murder charge,' said Doug, as he and Frankie turned towards the door.

'Now we've got two motives,' said Charlie. 'Dwayne decides he wants all the cooking duties for himself. Knocks Ray off. Maybe greed combined with finding out about his wife doing Ray was enough for him.'

'Charlie's right,' said Rob.

'I understand that,' said Zoe, 'but I still want to investigate these mystery men.'

'Let it go,' Rob said. 'The three men are three different guys. You've been out of the game. Sorry, but you're off base on this one.'

Zoe silently fumed as she collected the photographs from Rob's desk.

1.30 PM, FRIDAY 7 FEBRUARY

Zoe paced in the waiting area, looking at the text message that had summoned her here. Harry sat beside the couch, watching her. 'I thought we'd finished all our sessions,' Zoe said as soon as Alicia Kennedy opened the door.

'Hi Zoe, come on in,' Alicia said, as calmly as ever.

Zoe moved towards the door, Harry joining her.

Alicia walked around her desk and sat down. Zoe remained on her feet. 'I thought I was cleared for full duties,' she said.

'You are. I wanted to see how things have gone in your first week back.'

'The boss called you.'

'I rang him to check in. He said there'd been some issues. So, I thought I'd catch up with you. That's all.'

'Well, I'm fine. There was a disagreement, that's all. They happen.'

'Take me through it,' said Alicia.

'We have charged someone with murder and there's another avenue I wanted to check out. To be one hundred per cent sure that we've got it right. Rob and my partner disagree with me. That's it.'

'What makes you so sure that these three men are the same person?' asked Alicia.

Zoe shot Alicia a furious glare, incensed that Rob had told the psychologist the details of their conversation. These particulars should have been kept confidential, even within Homicide. She saw Alicia flush in response to her glare.

'Instinct,' said Zoe, 'honed by years of experience. But I'm not going to start discussing cases with people outside the squad. It's not ethical.' Zoe could feel her heart beating hard, and the air felt thicker. She could sense a panic attack coming on. *Not here, not now.*

Harry leaned in against her leg, his head against her thigh. Zoe looked down at him and placed a hand on his head.

'How've you been sleeping?' asked Alicia.

'Fine,' said Zoe. 'Sorry, Alicia, but I've got work to do. Come on, Harry.'

Harry jumped to his feet and followed Zoe to the door.

3 PM, FRIDAY 7 FEBRUARY

Zoe could feel the vibration through her desk. She sensed Charlie glancing across at her every minute or so from his adjoining desk.

'You right? Maybe give that jig you're doing under the desk a rest,' she said.

The vibration stopped. 'Yeah. Look, sorry about earlier with the boss,' said Charlie. 'I should have just backed you up.'

'No need to say sorry. Thrashing around theories—together—helps us get to the right results. Look, just forget about it and concentrate on getting the paperwork finalised on Dwayne Harley, okay?'

'Yep, you've got it.'

Zoe copied the case folders from the archives and saved them in a folder she named 'System Drivers' on a USB drive. She put on her headphones and listened to the recorded Crime Stoppers calls from the Ben Jennings murder case in Frankston. There were two calls.

On the first, the caller sounded young and nervous. *These two guys were having a blue outside the old Mechanics Institute building on the Nepean Highway*, the caller said. *I was walking towards the pub and they were coming towards me. I recognised the guy who got killed from when his photo was on the news. It was definitely him. At first they seemed to be getting along all right, but then they started to argue. The guy who got killed was saying 'Aaron, ten grand is ten grand, and I need it back'. I kept walking. Might not mean anything, but...anyway, my missus said I should let you know.* The caller didn't leave a name or number. Zoe opened up the original case file. Hannah and Angus had visited the Mechanics Institute after the call and looked for CCTV cameras, but there was nothing in the vicinity. They did find footage from outside a hotel a hundred metres away showing Aaron Smyth and Ben Jennings walking towards the Institute. They concluded that the call was genuine and that the information was relevant to the case.

Zoe opened the recording of the second call. This one was from a male who sounded significantly older than the first caller. *I was driving by and saw one of the people who lives in our street—Mica Street, Frankston—dropping something into another neighbour's bin a few doors down from where he lives. It was bin night last night so all the bins were lined up on the footpath. Anyway, this guy's bin didn't look to be overflowing or anything when I drove past his house, so I thought that was odd he was disposing of rubbish in someone else's bin. I don't know the gentleman myself, but he lives at number seven. The bin he put something in was outside number twelve. Anyway, with all the trouble a few streets over with that ghastly murder, I thought I'd best let the police know. You know, just in case. Okay, that's it.* Zoe knew from reading the report that the call had come in after the local patrol had noticed, by chance, what looked like a smear of blood on the side of the bin and had found the bloodied t-shirt that linked Aaron to the murder.

In the case file, Zoe read that Angus and Hannah had interviewed everyone living in Aaron's street to try to find the caller, without success. Every male denied having made the call.

When questioned, Aaron Smyth openly admitted owing the deceased man money, but denied they had argued about it. He also denied placing the bloody shirt in the neighbour's bin.

She listened to both calls again. She could not hear any similarities in the voices. She pulled her headphones off and stood up, stretching her arms.

Charlie looked up at her. 'Nearly there,' he said. 'It'll be beer o'clock soon.'

Zoe gave him a half grin, dropping back into her chair. She reopened the other case file, the murder of Eric Drum a year later. As with the murder of Ben Jennings, there were two calls. The first seemed to be an elderly man, his voice crackling. *I've never called about anything before, but I heard that Trevor Hill was…well, someone at the bowls club told me that this Trevor Hill fellow was, um, a hom-o-sex-ual and that the gentleman who died was apparently upset about it...That is all I know...All the best. My name is David Mc— Oh, I don't suppose it matters what my name is. Anyway, all the best, cheerio.*

Iain and Garry had been unable to locate the caller, despite contacting all the local bowling clubs and interviewing every member named David.

The second caller was male. He sounded middle-aged, and had a clipped English accent. *Hello, my name is Mark Wilson...Yesterday, I was walking through the King Creek Bushland Reserve in Hastings when I saw a man with a shovel and a bag. It was about two in the afternoon, maybe two-thirty. Anyway, I thought he looked suspicious, so I stood behind a tree to watch what he was up to. He dug a shallow hole and buried a bag, then walked off with the shovel towards a street called Mariners Way. I didn't go near where he'd dug the hole, but if you were to keep walking directly in from where the road ends and the reserve starts, it is about a hundred yards in, behind a spindly old eucalyptus...Not sure what it means, but I thought it proper to call...Okay, thanks. Goodbye.*

Garry had made a note that they'd been unable to find anyone with the caller's name, Mark Wilson, living locally.

Police searched the area the next morning and located the bag within two hours. It contained bloody clothes which had Eric Drum's blood on them. DNA linked the clothes to Trevor Hill.

When Trevor Hill was first interviewed he denied being gay, although he admitted it once the detectives showed him the taunting emails from Eric. Trevor also denied burying the rubbish bag with bloody clothes in the forest.

'Come on, Harry.' Zoe got up from her desk and headed for the elevator.

Zoe and Harry walked a block up La Trobe Street to Flagstaff Gardens, on the fringe of the central business district. His tail waving high, Harry ignored the coos of people walking around him. As soon as they had left the building, Zoe put on her large dark sunglasses and removed Harry's Service Dog vest, carrying it under her arm. She knew that it attracted too much attention when he wore it, with people soon starting to remember where they'd seen Zoe before. As soon as that happened, then the questions always started to flow.

Once they arrived at the gardens, Zoe said, 'Free.' Harry ran across the grass, sniffing the air, tail wagging. She pulled her phone from her pocket and dialled.

'Hey Zoe, long time no speak,' Rebecca Willis said, answering. Rebecca worked in the Forensics Department as an audio expert.

'Hi Bec. How's things at the audio lab?'

'Good. Busy. When did you start back?'

'Sunday, on a case right now. Hey, I've got a favour to ask. You got any free time?'

'For you, I'll find some. What are you looking at?'

'I'm doing a review of some old cases and I wanted to get some voices from Crime Stoppers tapes analysed. I want to confirm that the callers on the tapes aren't all the same person. The voices sound different, but I need to be sure.'

'When do you need it by?'

'Soon as you can.'

'Okay, email me the files. I'll try for Monday.'

'One more thing. Can we keep this one quiet? It's a hunch I'm chasing and I don't want blowback.'

'No drama. I'll keep it off the books until I hear differently from you.'

'Thanks, Bec. You're a champ. I owe you.'

6.30 AM, SATURDAY 8 FEBRUARY

Zoe woke from her dream, feeling the bed being thumped gently. She blinked twice, getting her bearings, before turning towards Harry, whose tail was doing the thumping. He laid his chin on her shoulder, looking straight at her from a few inches away.

'Hey there, gorgeous,' she whispered softly.

Harry lifted his head, his mouth falling open into an easy smile.

'Hey there, yourself,' said Tom sleepily from the other side of the bed. He yawned and rolled towards her.

Zoe smiled, still looking at Harry. 'How'd you sleep?' she asked, before turning to Tom and kissing him.

'Good. You?'

'Yeah, okay,' she said. It had been another warm night and she felt drained after her first week back at work. Zoe clambered out of bed and walked into the bathroom. She stepped into the shower, swung the mixer tap to cold and pulled it towards her. She shuddered as the water hit her body.

Afterwards, as she dried herself, Harry sat in the doorway to the bathroom. She couldn't stop thinking about the tapes, wishing it was already Monday and that she had an answer from Rebecca. She decided not to wait: she would go back down the peninsula and speak to Greg Enders. Zoe wanted to look him in the eye and convince herself he wasn't the same guy as the other two mourners. She knew that being wrong about her own theory was the best-case scenario. If she was right, there would be big ramifications for the squad, and for her.

She considered calling Charlie to let him know her plans, but decided to keep him out of it. At least until she knew one way or the other. Besides, he would be watching his son play cricket.

'How do you feel about a trip to the beach?' Harry jumped to his feet and spun in a circle.

'You talking to me or Harry?' Tom called from the bedroom.

'Um, both,' lied Zoe, her tone coy. 'I'm heading down the peninsula to check something out.'

'I'm guessing you were talking to Harry then,' Tom said, laughing. 'My place is overdue for a clean anyway.'

'No worries,' she said through the doorway, smiling down at Harry.

'Hey, isn't this a day off?' asked Tom.

'Yes, but there are some loose ends that need tying,' she said.

'Say hello to Charlie for me,' he called out.

'Will do,' she lied, staring at the bathroom mirror. She went into the walk-in robe and pushed a pair of shoes aside. She knelt down, lifted a small rug and placed her thumb against the fingerprint reader on her gun safe. Hearing the bolt click, she turned the handle.

Around eleven, her Ford Escape rolled into Rye. The weather was milder and more people were out, sitting outside cafes or walking their dogs. Zoe pulled up outside Greg Enders' house, leaving all the windows down. 'Wait here a second,' she said over her shoulder to Harry, who was ready to jump out.

Zoe felt different from the last time that she and Charlie were here. Lighter, freer. T-shirt and jeans suited her just fine. Maybe, she thought, working the Drug Squad or Organised Crime would be okay if she could dress this way every day. Zoe had her Victoria Police lanyard around her neck, so the locals wouldn't baulk at her Smith & Wesson M&P holstered in full view on her hip.

There was no car in the driveway. Zoe knocked on the door, tilting her head to listen for movement inside. She heard nothing. The curtains were slightly open, and she peered inside. The room was bare. She jogged to the window on the other side of the house and peeked in. Also empty. Zoe's gut tightened.

She looked behind her at her car. Harry was happily watching through the open window. Walking around to the side of the house, she called out, 'Police. Anyone home?'

There was no response. She went around to the back of the house. The room where she and Charlie had sat on Tuesday was empty. *Shit.*

Zoe retraced her steps. A woman, perhaps around seventy and wearing a flowery sun dress, was standing on the footpath and squinting down the driveway.

'Everything all right?' she asked.

'Yes,' said Zoe. 'Do you know the resident of this house?'

'I do, it's Greg something…Let me think, he did tell me…'

'Have you seen him recently?'

'He moved out yesterday. There was a white van here in the morning and he was loading stuff into it. When I stopped by around lunchtime, he was gone. He seemed like a nice man…Is something wrong?'

'No. I just needed to clear things up with him. Do you have any idea where he's moved to?'

'Not a clue, sorry.'

'You don't happen to know which real estate agent was renting the house out, do you?'

'Yes, it's Reagan Real Estate, up on the main road. They had their sign out before Greg moved in.'

'Thanks, that's very helpful.'

Zoe walked across the yard and tried the other neighbour, who didn't know Greg and hadn't realised that he had moved out.

Zoe got back in the car, and called the mobile number she had for Greg. A message told her that the number was disconnected. She drove into the main street of Rye, where she found the Reagan office. It was located in a shopping strip, between a pharmacy and a fish and chip shop. The smell of fried food was heavy in the air. Zoe and Harry walked into the office. It was a large open space, with three offices along the back wall. A young woman stood behind the counter, leaning over a computer, engrossed. She was about twenty, with long blonde hair that fell over the back of a blazer that was a size too big for her. After a moment, she looked up, first eyeing Harry, before she saw Zoe's gun at her waist.

'Detective Sergeant Zoe Mayer.' She held up her badge. 'I am looking for information on one of your renters.'

'Yes, I can help. I'm Helen, the property manager here. Who's the renter?'

'Greg Enders. Moved out yesterday apparently.'

'Yes, he dropped the key back in the afternoon. I was going to head down there this afternoon to make sure it's been properly cleaned. Is there a problem?'

'Do you have information on Greg from when he first rented the property? Former address? Driver's licence? That sort of thing.'

'Yes, sure.' Helen spun on her chair, got up and walked to a filing cabinet. She pulled out a thin file and came around to Zoe's side of the counter. She opened up the file. A photocopy of Greg Enders' licence showed his photo and former address in Mount Eliza.

'I remember him coming in to apply for the house. His hands were all bandaged up from some sort of accident. I had to fill in the form for him. He had trouble even signing his name at the bottom,' she said.

Zoe looked down at the scrawled signature that appeared to have been done by a four-year-old. *No fingerprints on the form. Very clever.*

'Can I get a copy of this? Any other ID?'

'I can give you a copy. No other ID. We did a reference check, though.' She flicked through some pages. 'Doug Jones, his former landlord. His number is here.'

Zoe dialled and got a message saying that the number was no longer in service.

'How did he pay for the lease? Card or bank transfer?'

'Cash. Six months up front. First time that's ever happened to me. The owner was really happy.'

'Did he drop the keys in himself yesterday when he left?'

'Yes, in an envelope.'

'Do you still have the envelope?'

'No, he did give it to me, but then asked for it back as he needed it to make a shopping list or something.'

'But you have the keys here?'

Helen pointed down at a set of keys sitting on her desk. 'Had them out to remind me to go check the place over.'

Zoe reached over the counter, picking up the key ring with her pen. As she brought them closer, Zoe was hit with the smell of bleach.

The young woman noticed Zoe wince. 'He said he'd dropped them in the sink when he was cleaning the place. Is he a criminal or something?'

'No, he may be a witness. Did he leave a forwarding address?'

'No, sorry.'

'Any chance I can have a look inside the house?'

The woman looked at the clock on the wall showing 11.50 am. 'I'm closing up at midday. I can meet you down there if you like.'

The smell of bleach overwhelmed them at once. The house had been meticulously cleaned. Zoe checked the bathroom for hairs, without success. The kitchen counters and cupboards all had streaks across them from being scrubbed. The wheelie bins outside were empty. Zoe could see streak marks on them too.

She contemplated calling Forensics to get them to sweep the place, but stopped herself. *Against what job would they put their time?* Every hour was accountable nowadays, logged a few different ways. Her instinct said that it was pointless. Greg had cleaned every surface. Plus, they hadn't pulled any DNA from Ray Carlson's crime scene to compare against anyway.

Zoe drove the short distance to Katie Harley's house and parked in the driveway. As she got out of the car, a teenage girl opened the front door and slouched against it, trying out a tougher version of herself. 'What do you want?'

'I would like to speak to your mother,' said Zoe.

She rolled her eyes. 'Mum. Cops are here again,' she called out, walking inside. Zoe opened up the back and Harry jumped down.

Katie Harley walked to the front door. 'No need to let the whole street know, Marie. What can I do for you, detective?'

'I wanted to have a chat. Do you have a moment? Maybe outside would be best,' said Zoe, looking over Katie's shoulder. Zoe wanted to talk outside so she could be closer to Harry, who was sitting in the shade near the car, but was happy to let Katie think it had to do with her privacy.

'Sure,' Katie said wearily, shutting the door behind her. They walked down onto the grass, under a large elm.

'What do you know about Greg Enders?'

'Greg? He's a mate of Dwayne and Ray's. He's a bit disabled. Not sure if that's the proper term for it nowadays, probably not. He got hurt at work and his neck and back are stuffed. Nice guy though.'

'How long have you known him?'

'Six, maybe seven months. Not too long.'

'How did you meet?'

'Dwayne met him, at the footy club at Sorrento, I'd say. That was Dwayne's regular. He played there for years. Why are you interested?'

'Do you know where Greg is now?'

'No idea. At home I presume. He doesn't work...His neck, you know.'

'He's not there. He's moved out. The house is empty.'

Katie frowned. 'He never said anything about moving. Then again, with everything that's been happening, it may have passed me by...Your people were here all afternoon yesterday. Didn't leave until after nine last night. Dug up most of the backyard, they did.'

Zoe didn't want to get sidetracked by Dwayne's drug charges. 'What's your impression of him?' she asked.

'Greg? You think he's got something to do with what happened to Ray?'

'No, we just have to finalise his statement and he didn't mention he was moving. All normal stuff. So, your impression of him?'

'Always friendly, upbeat. Generous, too. He got free tickets to the Grand Final and took Ray and Dwayne. Won a raffle for a boat charter and took a load of the guys out for the day. That sort of thing.'

'And the movies,' called Marie, who was apparently eavesdropping from behind the screen door. 'He gave us a USB with heaps of freebies.'

Zoe glanced towards the house before focusing again on Katie. 'I'm not really worried just now about him pirating movies. Do you know if he had family?'

'No, we never got into that sort of stuff. I never asked him.'

'Any other close friends?'

'Wouldn't know. He came around here a few times with Ray, but I didn't see him with other people. Dwayne would catch up with him at the footy club. I guess Greg would've known other people there.'

'Okay, thanks for your time, Katie.'

'No problem. Any news on Dwayne? He hasn't called us.'

'He's been charged with murder and remanded. Plus, you know he's been charged with meth production. What news were you expecting?'

Katie's face creased. 'I thought he might get bail, that's all.'

Zoe didn't know how to respond. *You've got a serious dose of privilege going on there.*

'He'll be remanded until the trials are finished. Sorry,' Zoe said, immediately regretting apologising.

'I guess it's all real, then. Keep thinking I'll wake up.'

'Someone will keep you informed.'

'Great. Thanks very much,' Marie called out from the background, her voice laden with sarcasm.

Three hours later, after visits to the footy club and the pub, Zoe and Harry were at Sorrento Beach, facing the bay. Despite the heat, Zoe wore a light rain jacket so that her holstered gun would not be visible to the public. She had Harry on a lead as the sand was packed with people. They walked a fair way along the sand before the crowds thinned, and she let him free. He ran into the water, jumping the waves with joy. Zoe took off her shoes and felt the warm, white sand squeak between her toes.

At the pub and the club, everyone had a similar story. An old Italian fellow named Serge told her how Greg Enders was a top bloke and would do anything for anyone. Others said similar things. Only been around for six months. No one knew anything about his background or family. No one knew he was moving house.

Her phone buzzed in her pocket. Tom.

'Hey,' Zoe said.

'Hi, where are you?'

'At the beach. Watching Harry learn to bodysurf.'

'There's something we need to discuss,' he said. Tom

sounded unsettled, unlike his usual unflappable self.

'Sounds scary. Everything okay?'

'Yeah, not really...Sally found out that we've been dating.'

Zoe laughed. 'What? It's eighteen years since you two broke up.'

'True, but the way she just went off at me on the phone, you'd think we broke up two weeks ago.'

'She called you? I would have thought her more an angry-email type of person.'

'I wish. She chewed my ear off about how she knew that I liked you back when we were dating. That I was just a typical man, yada, yada. She was relentless.'

'Sounds juvenile. Well, that's going to make life interesting for both of us,' said Zoe.

'More interesting for me than you, I'd reckon,' he said. 'I'm the one going up against her in court. She needs Homicide on her side when she's prosecuting cases. I'm just the enemy defence lawyer.'

'Sounds about right,' said Zoe. 'Anyway, there's not much we can do about it. Unless you want to break up?'

Tom laughed. 'Yeah right. It took me eighteen years to get together with you. I'm not walking away now.'

'So, you were keen back at uni after all?' asked Zoe, smiling.

'No comment. How good is Harry at bodysurfing?'

'Nice way to change the subject.' Harry was now trotting along the beach towards her. 'He's a quick learner. So, what are you going to do about Sally?'

'She's always been suspicious of people and doesn't give up easily...or ever, actually. She still thinks you spread the rumour at uni about her stripping up in Canberra.'

Zoe felt her neck tighten. 'Two things—she *was* stripping and it wasn't me who started the rumour.'

'Yeah, I know that's true, but we also both know what she's like. She never gives up on these things,' said Tom. 'Dinner?'

Zoe exhaled. 'Sure, I'll call you when I'm heading back into the city.'

Harry walked up beside Zoe and started shaking himself dry.

'Thanks very much,' said Zoe, wiping the salty water from her face.

6 AM, SUNDAY 9 FEBRUARY

They lay facing each other, Tom tracing a finger along the contours of Zoe's body. The ceiling fan whirred above them, cooling the heat of their skin. As they stared into each other's eyes, Zoe leaned towards Tom, kissing him softly at first, and then with passion. Tom started to slide his way down the bed, and Zoe felt a rush as she held Tom's head. She could smell sandalwood drifting in through the window. An old hippie couple had settled next door after years in India. Their golden days, they called them. The scent of the incense made her feel like she was somewhere exotic with a holiday lover eager to please her. She glanced towards Harry, curled up in his bed, as if sleeping. Zoe could see that he had one eye half open, watching her.

She pulled Tom back up towards her, and kissed him again. She pushed him onto his back and climbed on top. Using her hand, she guided him into her. Tom held her hips as she rode him, gently at first, then faster, shuddering with pleasure. She threw her head back, her eyes closed, rocking her hips slower and slower, letting the vibrations subside.

'You're a fine stallion,' she said with a teasing smile.

'I love you.'

Zoe's heart skipped. Tom had never said it. She looked into his eyes, knowing this was a special moment. 'I love you too.'

Zoe had spent the night waking every hour or so, thinking about either Greg Enders or Charlie and Rob talking behind her back. Zoe felt both frustrated and betrayed, but most of all worried. She needed to get to the right result, the truth, and fast. She'd tried everything to get some solid sleep, imagining the sound of waves crashing, counting imaginary sheep, even breathing in unison with Tom and Harry when they fell into sync. Nothing had worked. Now, she realised that the last half an hour may have been just what she needed all along.

She rolled off Tom, walking into the ensuite to take a shower. As soon as the cool water hit her body she felt herself jolted back into work mode. When she came back out, Tom was fast asleep again. She put on her jeans and a clean white t-shirt, and walked Harry at the park nearby. Back at the house, she gave Harry his breakfast and made two coffees and toast.

'Smells good,' said Tom, stretching in the doorway to the bedroom. 'Thought you would have taken the opportunity to lie in.'

'Thinking about the case. Lots of moving parts.'

Tom noticed Zoe's holster on the table.

'You going to work on a Sunday?' he asked. 'I was hoping we could get some lunch.'

'Sorry. I would have loved that too, but I just need to get out in front on this case.'

'I don't reckon Charlie's going to be so thrilled to have you back. Working him seven days a week and all.'

Zoe said nothing. She was planning on working solo today too. She ate her breakfast slowly, savouring her morning coffee.

Zoe turned off the freeway and drove east through farmland, across the top of the peninsula, and towards the town of Hastings. Stands of arthritic-looking trees lined the road, their limbs bulging and haphazard, stunted by droughts and beaten down by storms over the years. Zoe looked at them with respect. *Survivors.* Angling the rear-view mirror, she glanced at Harry, who had his chin resting on a paw, and was staring back at her.

Zoe drove into Hastings. Facing onto Western Port Bay, the town was a mixture of older houses and newer developments of larger houses, especially by the shoreline, where two-storey residences overlooked the water and the marina. It looked like a place where not much happened. *Probably just as they like it.*

Following her phone's directions, she slowed as she passed the house where Eric Drum had been killed. It was a white brick house with a charcoal-coloured roof. Pink climbing roses were growing up the pillars of the veranda, almost to the gutters. A hose was neatly coiled, hanging on a hook attached to the side of the house. The front garden was overgrown with long grass and there was no car in the driveway. The blinds were open, but it was dark inside and the scene radiated despair.

She drove on a few blocks and passed Trevor Hill's house. The lawn was mown and scattered with children's toys. The fence enclosing the front yard looked new. Zoe remembered Sarah Westbrook telling her that Trevor had sold his home to pay his legal fees.

Zoe accelerated, turning at the next corner. She stopped outside a weatherboard house painted white with grey trim. She got out and opened the back. Harry jumped down, and began to sniff around as Zoe walked up the pathway bordered by pink rose bushes.

Zoe opened the screen and knocked on the front door, holding her notepad and badge in the other hand.

The door opened slightly.

'Hello...' started Zoe.

'Not interested,' said the woman's voice, before the door slammed shut.

Zoe opened the screen door again and slapped her hand against the door. A bad night's sleep had left her too tired for this. 'Victoria Police, open up,' she growled, loud enough for the neighbours to hear.

The door opened fully this time, to reveal a wide-eyed woman in a white t-shirt and denim shorts. Her blonde hair was starting to grey. 'S-sorry, I thought you were a charity collector or a bible-basher. They sometimes walk around with dogs to get you on-side, especially on Sundays.'

'That's okay,' said Zoe, holding her badge up. 'I'm Detective Sergeant Zoe Mayer. Are you Andrea Milburn?'

'Yes, but what's happened?' the woman asked. 'I'm sure I paid that parking fine.'

'No, nothing like that. Detectives spoke to you following the death of Eric Drum last year, yes?'

'That's right.'

'We are working on a separate case and our software hit on a matching photograph in our system,' lied Zoe. 'We are trying to locate this man. Do you know him?' Zoe opened her folder and showed Andrea the solidly built, clean-shaven man with dark auburn hair who had been at Eric's funeral.

'Oh, yes, that's Eddie...Edward Nicholas. What's he done?'

'Nothing,' said Zoe. She couldn't remember seeing the name in the case notes. 'He may be a witness in another investigation.'

'Right.'

'Do you know Eddie's address?'

'Yeah, he lived in Tyabb, next town back up the peninsula.'

'Lived. You mean he's no longer living there?'

'That's right. He left ages ago. Made an Irish exit.'

'Sorry, what's that?'

'Took off without saying goodbye. A few people were pissed off, thought he was their mate, you know?'

'Do you have any idea where he went?'

'None at all. The guy vaporised.'

'He ever mention family? Where he'd come from?'

'Nah, he didn't talk about himself much. Was more of a quiet type.'

'When did he leave town?'

'Around the end of autumn, probably late April last year. I remember driving over there to see how he was and the house had been rented to a family. His neighbour said Eddie had left three weeks before that. Wasn't too impressed, myself. Thought we were friends.'

Zoe ran the date through her mind. It was after Trevor Hill had been charged and was in custody for Eric Drum's stabbing. 'How long was he around for?' asked Zoe.

Andrea shut her eyes momentarily. 'Probably about six months. Met him at the footy club one night. He'd won a grand on the ponies and was shouting drinks all round. Nothing like free drinks to make you popular. He was a good bloke, easy-going, mates with everyone. Funny, too.'

'Who was Eddie closest to in town?'

'Probably Eric Drum, the guy who died. He was mates with Trevor Hill as well. And with Jim Crowley.'

'Where could I find Jim?'

'Over there.' Andrea was pointing to a house three doors down, on the other side of the road. 'The one with the green letterbox.'

Zoe gave a grin. 'Small town.'

'You've got that right. Too small sometimes.'

'Where did Eddie live in Tyabb?'

Andrea gave her the address.

Zoe noted it down and then handed her a business card. 'Thanks for your help. Give me a call if you think of anything else.'

'Will do. Hope he's not in strife with the coppers.'

'No, just a witness. Nothing to worry about.' Zoe did not want to start a wildfire of rumours in a small town like this. She said goodbye and led Harry across the street.

A man around fifty was sitting on a chair on his front veranda as she approached. He wore khaki shorts and a blue tanktop. A dagger was tattooed high up on his left arm and Zoe could see that he was fit and strong. 'Jim Crowley?'

'Yep.'

'I'm—'

'I know who you are. I saw the news. You're a fricken hero for what you did last year.'

Zoe blushed.

'They got you a service dog, eh? What's its name?'

'Harry.'

Jim leaned down, letting Harry sniff his hand before giving him a pat on the head. 'Harry, nice to meet you.' He looked up at Zoe. 'Top dogs, golden retrievers. Smart and loyal. Mate of mine from the army has a service dog too. He got blown halfway to God in Iraq. We managed to keep him going. Medevac pulled him out.'

'How's he doing now?' asked Zoe.

'Some days are good, some not so much. That dog is keeping him alive, though, that I do know.'

'How about you? Army?'

'Yeah, infantry. Did tours in Iraq and then Afghanistan.

Did my twenty years and got out in one piece, more or less. Rest your legs.' Jim motioned towards the other seat on the veranda.

Zoe sat. Harry lay down by her feet. She used the same preamble about photo-matching software. She could see Jim was doubtful of the story, but didn't want to say so. She showed him the photograph from her folder.

'Yeah, that's Eddie,' he said. 'He just vanished one day. Strangest thing. Left a lot of people confused.'

'Andrea said he lived in Tyabb.'

'Yeah, I reckon she was keen on him. Saw him as a fixer-upper. A project, you know? She was a bit miffed.'

'You know who else he was close to around here?'

'Eric Drum, who got murdered. Shitty business that. And to Trevor Hill, who you guys locked up for it. Then there's Andrea. He was pretty popular down at the footy club, always buying drinks for people.'

'Do you know what Eddie did for work?'

'Said he worked in construction. Must have been a decent job as he was flush all the time.'

'Ever mention family?'

'Nah.'

'Or romantic relationships?'

'As far as I know he was single the whole time, but I've no idea about before that.'

'Okay, thanks for that.' She pulled out a card. 'If you think of anything else, give me a call.'

'No worries, will do. You sure this has nothing to do with Eric's murder? Trevor's trial starts soon.'

'No, nothing at all.' Zoe could see that Jim was still in two minds.

'You know,' he said, 'there was a reporter fishing around a few weeks ago. She was making one of those podcast thingies.'

'Well, the trial's coming up. There will be stories in the media,' said Zoe, wanting to dampen Jim's instinct. 'It must have been a rough time around here then.'

'Yeah, we were pretty shocked. Eric being killed and then finding out that Trevor did it. Sorry, allegedly. That's what you're supposed to say, isn't it? And all because Trevor was gay?' Jim looked off into the distance. 'No one would have even cared. Not nowadays. Just a waste.'

She was approaching Somerville, halfway across the peninsula towards Frankston, when Harry gave an urgent bark from the back of the car. Zoe checked her rear-view mirror, then flicked on the indicator and pulled over. She punched at the button for the hazard lights. She knew what that bark meant.

As she turned back towards Harry, her eyelids flickered and she felt the pressure build in her chest even before she heard the thumping sound. Then the car went black and her head slumped.

Zoe could see the vapour from her breath. She looked at the cold blue September sky. And then a gap in the crowd caught her eye, revealing a bulging blue backpack beside a wooden bench. She walked across to get a better view.

There was no one near it.

She touched the side of her earpiece to activate the microphone. 'Suspicious bag, sector eight. Blue backpack, unattended.' Zoe peered up at the roof of the stadium. The spotter was scanning the area, looking for her location. Zoe took off her baseball cap and waved it, as if signalling a friend.

Time seemed to stand still after that. They cleared the crowd quickly from the area and waited, listening to the humming sound of the Bomb Squad's robot as it made its way to the backpack. She waited for the explosion, but could only hear the sound of her own breathing.

'All clear, all clear,' came the voice through the earpiece.

And then Zoe heard another sound.

She came to in the car, pulled over to the side of the road, with Harry yelping and straining to reach her in his harness. She remembered where she was, and listened. The chopper was gone. 'Good boy, good boy,' she said.

Harry looked at her. His mouth opened into a smile and he sat down, now relaxed.

Zoe headed back into the traffic and went over what she had heard in the past few hours.

After Jim Crowley's place in Hastings, she went to the footy club and heard the same story from the regulars at the bar. Eddie Nicholas was a top bloke. Disappeared off the radar. Then she called by the local real estate office, which was closed. She rang the mobile number plastered all over the front window. The real estate agent came in reluctantly and dug up Eddie's rental file. First six months' rent paid up front, all cash. A phone number for a rental reference that was disconnected. Everything was the same as she had discovered about Greg Enders the day before in Rye, fifty kilometres down the peninsula. When Zoe looked at the photocopy of Eddie Nicholas's driver's licence she gasped. She might have been looking at Greg Enders. At least, a clean-shaven version with different-coloured hair.

Zoe drove through Frankston's back streets. The suburb, once almost exclusively working-class, was changing fast. Every third or fourth house had a luxury car parked in the driveway. Zoe pulled up outside the house she was looking for. It had recently been rendered and was freshly landscaped. She hoped that Ben Jennings' widow still lived here.

Harry hopped down from the back of the Escape and they walked to the front porch. Zoe rang the buzzer.

A pale woman opened the screen door. Zoe knew from the file that Charlotte Jennings was about forty, but this woman looked much older, with dark rings under her eyes. She wore an old t-shirt with a coffee stain on the front and yoga pants.

'Charlotte Jennings?'

'Yes.'

'Detective Sergeant Zoe Mayer, Victoria Police,' said Zoe, badge in hand. 'Have you got a moment?'

'Did he escape?'

'Who?'

'Aaron Smyth. Did he escape from prison?'

'No. Sorry, I didn't mean to startle you. It's not about that. Can we chat?'

'I don't like dogs,' Charlotte said, punching each word out in a staccato rhythm. 'One bit me when I was a kid.'

'Don't worry, it's okay, he can stay out here. It should only take a minute.'

'Okay. You'll have to excuse the mess. I wasn't expecting anyone.'

Zoe gestured for Harry to lie down on the porch as Charlotte stepped back inside. Zoe followed her in. The house was dark, the curtains pulled shut. Charlotte turned on an overhead light to reveal a dishevelled room, with a quilt draped over the couch and magazines lying on the floor. Stained coffee cups littered the table. Charlotte pulled some newspapers off a chair and indicated for Zoe to sit. The air was stale.

'I wasn't sure if you were still here. Looks like you've had some work done outside recently.'

Charlotte looked confused for a moment. 'Oh yeah, we were going to fix the house up before...before what happened to Ben.' She stopped. 'Anyway, I thought I'd get it done. Thought it might cheer me up.' Charlotte's expression told Zoe that it hadn't. 'Dad did the landscaping. Put in all the yuccas.' The trees stood guard behind the shut curtain, lined up like spiky soldiers. 'Do you want some water or something?' Charlotte asked, without making a move to get up.

'No. Thanks though. This shouldn't take long.' Zoe opened her folder and held up a photograph. 'Do you know this person?' she said. It was the dark-bearded man supporting himself with a cane.

Charlotte took a sharp breath. Zoe realised that she knew the photo was taken at her husband's funeral. *Shit*. She should have prepared her first.

'Yes, that's…Alex…um…Alex Verdi. He was friends with Ben. I haven't seen him in a long time.' She shot a look at Zoe. 'Was he involved in Ben's murder, too?

'No. We believe that this man, Alex, is potentially a witness in another matter. Nothing to do with your husband's case.' Zoe felt the small pang she always experienced when lying at work. So much of her job was about misdirecting people to get a result.

'That's good. I couldn't take another trial. The first one…it kind of broke me, you know?' Charlotte's eyes grew moist.

Zoe waited for a moment. 'Do you know where Alex is now?'

'No, he dropped out of the scene after Ben died. Most people did. I felt like a leper for a long time.'

'I'm sorry about that. It must have been horrible,' Zoe said. Again she waited. 'Any idea where Alex lived?'

'Yeah. Hold on.' She pulled herself out of the chair and walked over to the kitchen bench. She shuffled through a stack of papers, pulled out a sheet and walked back over. 'I made a list of the people who sent cards or flowers when Ben died. I was going to write to thank them once I came good, but—I guess I'm not there yet.'

Zoe wondered how she would act, and feel, if she was

in Charlotte's position. It was two years since Ben had been killed, yet it obviously still felt raw for his widow.

'There,' Charlotte said, her finger resting on Alex Verdi's name and address.

Zoe wrote down the details. 'Thanks, that's great.'

'He went to the first day of the trial. Also, the sentencing,' Charlotte said.

'So he was still living around here then?'

'No, he left soon after Ben died, but must have come back for those two days. I was happy to see him. I just sort of said hello, gave him a hug and that was it. When I saw him at the sentencing he looked so different. He'd shaved off his beard and bulked up, like he'd been at the gym a lot. Took years off him, I remember thinking.'

'The trial would've been tough to get through,' said Zoe.

'Yeah, it was. Everyone was so tight-knit that I wasn't sure who was at the trial for me and who was there to support his killer, you know?' A single tear fell down Charlotte's face. 'At least we got the right verdict in the end.'

'I'm sorry,' said Zoe. 'I didn't come here to upset you.'

Charlotte waved a hand. 'Don't worry about it. This is just a normal day round here.'

'What was Alex like?'

'Average bloke. The guys liked him. He won some competition once and took a big group of the boys off for a day on a fancy golf course. They all got golf carts as Alex's leg was stuffed, you know, he had the cane to get around. They loved it. Ben said he'd never seen grass so perfect.' Charlotte smiled at the memory.

'Do you know what Alex did for work?'

'I think he worked as a surveyor...something like that. I seem to remember Ben telling me he'd smashed up his leg falling into a pit at a construction site.'

As Zoe noted it down, the two sat in silence.

'You know, it's weird,' Charlotte said. 'No one has spoken to me about what happened for months, and now two people in the last week.'

'What do you mean?'

'This woman called Sarah Westbrook came by on Friday asking all sorts of questions for a podcast.'

'I know who you mean,' Zoe said. 'What did you say?'

'I told her to piss off. Told her that Ben's life and death weren't for sale as entertainment.'

6.25 AM, MONDAY 10 FEBRUARY

Zoe opened her eyes. Her head lay on her crossed arms on her dining-room table, which was strewn with papers. A notepad was open beside her elbow. She blinked, trying to get her bearings. Just above her left ear she heard someone breathing. Instinctively, she jumped to her feet, kicking her chair away, and spun into an attack stance. From across the room, Harry jumped up at the same moment, rushing to Zoe's side.

'Whoa. Steady on. It's just me,' said Tom, taking two quick steps back.

'Shit, you gave me a fright,' said Zoe, before pulling the chair upright and stretching the kinks from her neck. Harry sat down, staring at Tom.

'What are you doing?' asked Tom.

Zoe tried to sweep the papers together and get them out of view. 'I couldn't sleep, so I got up to do some work.'

Tom pointed at the notepad. 'And what's that all about?'

Shit. On the notepad, Zoe had listed out the three cases in separate columns. The first read:

Frankston Murder
Victim: Ben Jennings
Offender: Aaron Smyth
Missing: Alex Verdi?

The second:
Hastings Murder
Victim: Eric Drum
Offender: Trevor Hill
Missing: Eddie Nicholas?

And the third:
Portsea Murder
Victim: Ray Carlson
Offender: Dwayne Harley
Missing: Greg Enders?

At the bottom of the three columns Zoe had scrawled, *Same person killed all three? What's the link? Who is he? Where is he? What's the motive? Why February?*

Zoe turned the notebook over. 'How long were you standing there before I woke up?'

'Long enough to read that. I thought you had charged someone for that Portsea stabbing? You think you got the wrong guy? You think it's a serial killer?'

'Look, I can't discuss this with you. I shouldn't have

left this information out. It's all confidential. Plus, it's just a scenario. It's not evidence, just an idea, okay?'

Tom said nothing.

Zoe put up a reassuring hand. 'Don't take it personally, Tom. You're a defence lawyer. You know I can't discuss it with you, or anyone else outside of Homicide, for that matter?'

'Yeah, okay. Just let me say one thing and then I'll leave it alone. If this scenario,' he said, pointing at the notepad, 'looks like being real, just be careful. Okay?'

Zoe nodded. 'I'll be careful as long as you forget what you saw here. Deal?'

'Deal,' he said quietly. 'I'll make the coffee.'

It was just after eight when Zoe and Harry walked into the Homicide office to find a huddle of detectives around Charlie's desk. Charlie, red-faced, was shaking his head.

Zoe felt a chill run through her.

'I don't know anything about it. I wasn't there,' she heard Charlie say.

'Ah, the great one has arrived,' spat Iain Gillies. 'What the fuck have you done?'

'What are you talking about, Iain?' Zoe said, trying to maintain a calm tone. 'Can you be more specific?'

Harry moved forward and stood between them, as more detectives stopped what they were doing and looked over.

'I received a call this morning from a bloke named Jim Crowley in Hastings asking why we were looking for some guy called Eddie Nicholas. He says he got to thinking after your little visit yesterday about the odds of two different detectives visiting him about two separate cases in less than a year. He thought they were somewhere between slim and fucking zero. Then he asks me if Trevor Hill is innocent and Eddie did the murder. That specific enough for you? Then Charlie here tells me that you're looking at one of Angus and Hannah's cases as well, the murder in Frankston. The one where a guy's already been found guilty. You've been back a week and you're already undermining the squad.'

Zoe glanced across at Hannah and Angus, who were staring hard at her. In the background, she also saw Anjali was standing against a wall, clutching a folder against her chest. 'Well, there are some elements that seem identical in all three cases and I decided to look into it. Charlie had nothing to do with it.'

Garry Burns crossed his arms, mimicking Iain. 'I thought you charged someone for that murder down at Portsea. What are you saying—that you've got the wrong bloke?'

'No, I'm not. What I'm saying is that I am examining every piece of evidence to make sure I get the right person. What exactly are you all worried about, anyway? If you are so sure you're right, what's the problem with me having a look?'

'The problem,' said Iain, 'is that family and friends of the victim and the accused get the idea that there is another person involved. Then the media grab hold of this and we reach a whole new level of chaos. That's the problem.'

Zoe knew that he was right and her stomach tightened. 'I gave them no indication that I was looking at Eddie Nicholas for Eric Drum's killing. Same with Alex Verdi for Ben

Jennings' murder. Zero. I told them my questions were about another case altogether.'

A grin formed at the corner of Iain's mouth. Zoe heard high-heeled footsteps behind her. She turned and saw Sally Johnstone strutting across the office, her black silk court robes trailing behind her like a cape. The expression on her face signalled war. Her blonde hair, usually pinned up, had fallen free. As she came to a stop, she crossed her arms and glared, thin-lipped, at Zoe.

'Well, Jim Crowley didn't buy it,' resumed Iain. 'Thanks very much. We have motive, opportunity and physical evidence that Trevor Hill murdered Eric Drum. The trial starts next week, for fuck's sake.'

'There's no mention of any Eddie Nicholas in the file,' Zoe replied, 'which is strange as he was good friends with both your victim and suspect. How'd you miss him?'

Iain laughed sarcastically. 'Probably because he had nothing to do with the case. And what are you doing fishing around in our files? If this prosecution gets wrecked because of your bloody meddling, I'll be coming for you.'

'If your case is solid, you've got no worries, do you?'

'You'll be creating reasonable doubt, and you know what that means. Maybe you should have become a defence lawyer, like your boyfriend, instead of a cop. You seem to be doing a good job of defending killers. Especially now you're a fucking basket case. How the psych signed you off to come back to work, I've got no idea.'

'What about Sarah Westbrook?' Zoe could feel the heat rising.

'What about her?' snapped Iain.

'She's doing an investigation for her podcast. You saying she hasn't reached out to you?'

'Yeah, she did. And I told her there's nothing in it. She's just some lefty journo trying to do an anti-cop podcast. And she's conned you into fucking helping her do it.'

'So, that's it then,' said Zoe. 'Nothing to see here. Is that the line? Sarah Westbrook isn't some random conspiracy theorist. She's a respected journalist with a podcast that is listened to by over a million people every week. If there's something in what she's saying, then we need to get in front of it.'

'But there's nothing in it,' Iain said. 'She's looking at cases that look similar and deciding that they're linked, while ignoring a ton of contradictory evidence. Just because she knew some of the people involved a lifetime ago.'

'My job is to get to the truth. I am doing my job.'

Sally gave a short jab of laughter. 'Your job? Doing off-the-book work on closed cases. Is that your job now?'

Zoe turned to Sally. 'I was looking into strong coincidences between three crimes. One of these put someone in jail for life, another will put someone in the dock in a murder trial starting next week, and someone has just been charged in the third.'

'I'm obviously aware of that,' said Sally. 'That's why I'm here. What I want to know is why? These cases are built on overwhelming evidence.'

'And what if that evidence has been fabricated, created to tick all the boxes and convict the wrong people?'

'Zoe, what if you aren't ready to be back at work?' Sally said slowly, venom on her tongue. 'You went through something last year. Maybe it broke you.'

Zoe stood a moment, waiting for composure to catch up with her, before she responded. 'Sally, there's something more important than winning cases.'

'Really? And what's that?'

'Justice. If there's even the slightest possibility that this is the work of a serial killer setting up innocent people, you should be asking how you can help, not sneering at me. Same goes for everyone else,' Zoe said, looking around. 'We should all be interested in the truth, not just closing cases. We need to investigate every lead. Sally, you're starting a murder prosecution in a week's time. If there was a surprise on the way, wouldn't you want to know?'

Sally said nothing, continuing to stare disdainfully at Zoe.

Zoe went on in a low, deliberate voice. 'Sally, the thing is, I don't really give a flying fuck about what you think I should be investigating. This feud you have with me—the one that clouds your judgment—is your invention. It lives in your head. I have nothing to do with it...and I never have.'

'Well, we'll see what you have to say once I've spoken to your DI,' snapped Sally.

From the back of the room, Rob Loretti spoke, 'No need, Ms Johnstone.'

Sally turned, scanning the room.

'I'm backing Zoe,' Rob went on. 'All the way. And I am sure you wouldn't want to try to impede the activities of this department. That *would* be a very serious overstep.'

Zoe felt like the cavalry had arrived.

Sally started to protest, 'Yes, of course, but—'

'I gave Zoe the okay to look at these cases,' Rob said, addressing the room. 'We have a person who *may* have been at all three funerals. I want to know if it's true and, if so, who he is. That's it. Now get back to work everyone. Zoe, I want an update in five minutes. Thanks.' Rob turned on his heel and headed back to his office.

Sally, her neck now pink, turned quickly and walked towards the door, while the rest of the squad broke up, returning to their desks. Iain and Garry muttered something Zoe couldn't make out.

When Zoe sat at her desk, Harry lay down under it.

She looked across at Charlie. 'You okay?' she said.

'Yeah.' He didn't meet her gaze, continuing to stare at his screen.

Zoe saw the light flashing on her desk phone. She listened to the message.

'Come on,' she said to Charlie.

8.25 AM, MONDAY 10 FEBRUARY

Zoe walked into the DI's office and found Rob leaning back in his chair, hands behind his head. 'Bloody hell, Zoe,' he said in a deep whisper. 'I told you to leave it alone.'

'Sorry, boss. You didn't have to back me up out there.'

Harry sat beside Zoe, also staring at Rob.

'Well, you didn't give me much choice. It was either back you or suspend you, Zoe. I'm responsible for the squad. What you do reflects on me, too.'

Charlie walked in, looking despondent.

'How are you doing, Charlie?' asked Rob.

'I'll be okay if Zoe's theory turns out to be right, otherwise we're both rooted.'

'Being universally loved is overrated,' said Zoe, not looking at Charlie.

'Tell me about it,' said Rob. 'So, what did you learn on this weekend fishing trip of yours?'

'Okay, I went to Portsea on Saturday to look for the

guy from Ray Carlson's funeral, Greg Enders. Went to his house, but it was empty. His neighbour said he'd moved out on Friday. His mobile number was disconnected.'

'You spoke with him after the murder, yes?'

'We spoke to him last Tuesday. No mention that he was leaving. Said if we had more questions, we'd know where to find him. He was friendly, but didn't seem to know anything relevant. What'd you think, Charlie?'

'He seemed like a normal bloke. He did give us a background on Joshua Priest, though, the guy that Dwayne and Ray were supplying with meth.'

'True,' said Zoe. 'Anyway, on Saturday I chased up the real estate agent. Enders, or whatever his name is, paid six months ahead, in cash, and was a model tenant. The place was meticulously cleaned. Every surface smelled of bleach. Even the wheelie bin was scrubbed. He left nothing. I rang the rental reference he gave the agent and the number was dead. She had a copy of his driver's licence showing his previous address in Mount Eliza. I checked it out on my way back up the peninsula. It was a vacant block. I also went to see Katie Harley. She was surprised Enders was gone. Like everyone else she said he was a top bloke, and got tickets to the Grand Final for Ray and Dwayne.'

'Small world,' said Rob.

Zoe was confused for a moment, before remembering Grand Final Day. 'Yeah, I suppose so.'

'So, what happened yesterday?' asked Rob.

Zoe went over her trip to Hastings and Frankston, detailing the similar behaviours of the men known as Eddie

Nicholas and Alex Verdi. 'Cash up front for the lease. Generous. Easy-going. Then there's a killing and they leave. The house is scrubbed with bleach both times. No one pays much attention. It's got to be the same guy.'

'Okay,' said Rob. 'If there's something to all this, we need to play it smart. Charlie, you keep wrapping up the paperwork in the case against Dwayne Harley. You don't need your career stuffed as well if this goes south. Zoe, keep investigating. We need to find this guy if we're going to be able to prove any of this. Okay?'

Charlie and Zoe nodded. The relief in Charlie's eyes was obvious.

Rob continued, 'Charlie, you get back to work.'

Charlie left, closing the door behind him.

Rob picked up the phone. 'Anjali, can you come in please? Thanks.'

Zoe gave Rob a quizzical look.

'Trust me,' he said.

A moment later there was a knock at the door.

'Come in,' said Rob. The door opened slowly. 'Come in and grab a seat, Anj. And shut the door.'

Anjali entered, closing the door behind her. She sat.

'I am assigning Anj to assist you. While you were away, I personally recruited Anj from the Fraud Squad. She's very good at finding people and keeping secrets.'

Zoe looked at Anjali, who gave her a humble smile in return.

'How can I help?'

'Okay,' said Zoe, thinking. 'I need you to run three

names. There's nothing on our database, but I'll get you to look at the tax office, motor registrations, immigration, the electoral commission, land titles office, Centrelink, Medicare, the works. Plus, the banks. Perhaps we'll get lucky.'

'No problem,' said Anjali.

'Also,' said Zoe, looking back to Rob, 'I have a friend in Forensics. I asked her to run a test—off the books—on the recordings of the phone tip-offs in each case. She just left me a voice message.'

'And?' asked Rob.

'There is an eighty per cent chance all of the voices are from the same person. There's a common inflection in certain words.'

Rob shook his head. 'Eighty per cent isn't enough. A good lawyer could tear that to shreds. Ninety-nine-plus per cent is what we'd need in court.'

'Agreed, but from an investigative viewpoint, it's a good indicator that we're onto something.'

Zoe and Rob stared at each other. Anjali waited.

Rob broke the stalemate. 'You're a hell of an instinctive detective, Zoe. I hope you're right, because otherwise the roof is going to come down on both our heads.'

'What other choice do we have?'

'Okay, but what's the hypothesis?' asked Rob. 'If the cases are all connected, how?'

'I don't know. But we need to find out fast. Trevor Hill's trial for the murder of Eric Drum starts on Monday.'

'The clock's ticking, then,' said Rob.

—

The message light was again blinking on the phone on Zoe's desk. 'Hi Zoe. It's Sarah Westbrook here. I know you said you'd get in contact only if you found anything, but... anyway. Hope you're well. Bye.'

Zoe replaced the receiver. *I have nothing I can tell her.* She looked across at Charlie, who was furtively glancing about the office. 'Listen,' she said, her voice low, 'if you want to win a popularity contest, you've got the wrong partner. Seriously. You're a good detective, but you can't always just go with the flow. Not with me, at least.'

Charlie was silent. 'Yeah, you're right,' he said after a while. 'I just hope you can prove all this, that's all.'

'Me too,' said Zoe. She checked her email. There was something from the real estate agent in Frankston. She clicked on the attachment. Zoe leaned in. 'Check this out.'

Charlie walked around to look. An ID photo from Alex Verdi's driver's licence filled the screen. In it, the man looked at the camera with blank, half-closed eyes, as if he were sleepy. He held his head back, and chin out.

'Okay,' said Charlie, 'It could be Greg Enders, minus the bent neck.'

Zoe keyed the address on the licence into the computer. 'According to the address on his licence, he was living at the Australia Post office in South Melbourne.'

7.45 AM, TUESDAY 11 FEBRUARY

The two whiteboards in the conference room had been scrawled all over. On one board, Zoe had listed everything they knew about the Portsea killing of Ray Carlson. On the other were details of the murders in Frankston and Hastings over the two years prior. It was a jumble of names, dates, alleged motives and evidence.

Standing there, arms folded, Zoe was willing new information to appear. She closed her eyes, going over everything she knew—that all the murders happened at yearly intervals in the summer heat of February; all the victims were male, all late thirties; the accused in each murder had motive and opportunity; evidence linked them to the killings.

Maybe my instincts are off. She smiled wryly down at Harry. 'Your mum might be out of practice.'

Harry tilted his head, leaning it against her leg, and looked up at her.

Zoe picked up the eraser. Then her eyes widened. She

turned to her laptop and punched the keys, bringing up the cases on her screen. She noted the date of birth of each of the victims. *Fuck.*

She rushed to the door, swung it open and looked for Charlie. He was walking towards his desk, morning coffee in hand. She waved him over.

'Hey Zoe—what's up?'

'Can you grab Anjali and meet me in here? And quietly, okay?'

'Sure.'

A minute later, the three of them were in the conference room. 'What've you got?' asked Charlie.

Zoe pointed at the board. 'I didn't see it at first because we just had their ages listed, but when you look at them in order of death, it all lines up. All three victims were born in 1982. The guys we have locked up were all born in 1982 as well. That's the key to this.'

'How do you mean?' asked Charlie.

'I'm guessing they were all at school together,' said Zoe. 'Anjali, can you do a search of Education Department records?' asked Zoe. 'We're looking for someone who was at school at some point with all three victims. Just keep it quiet around here for now.'

'Absolutely,' Anjali said, already halfway to the door.

4.45 PM, TUESDAY 11 FEBRUARY

The musty air was making Zoe nauseated. She and Anjali had been searching in the state Education Department's archives all day for records from schools on the Mornington Peninsula from the 1990s. The cavernous room was a large rectangular shape. Rows of shelves reached towards the high ceiling, crammed with archive boxes. The dust they had thrown up moving boxes around filled the ribbons of afternoon sunlight streaming into the room. Zoe doubted anyone had even entered the place since records went digital years ago. They had gone through box after box of dusty files, starting with the high school records. If they couldn't find a connection there, they would move on to the primary schools.

Once they finally located the correct archive boxes, they found a mixture of bound paper files as well as old-style floppy disks. Anjali held the discs up to the light like some sort of ancient treasure. 'I saw a photo of one of these once,' she said.

Luckily, the archives still owned a floppy disk reader, just in case the old files ever needed to be read. Zoe was relieved—getting a warrant to take the records out of the archive would have raised all sorts of questions.

Harry lay asleep on the floor. Occasionally his eyes would open slightly to check that Zoe was still there before he dozed off again.

They worked on the Frankston case first, pulling the data of Ben Jennings' years at Frankston High School from one of the floppy disks. Finding all the classes that Ben and Aaron had attended took time, as the records weren't in order, but once they did Anjali copied the data quickly into a spreadsheet. They could see that the boys were in the same class together in years eight, nine and ten. By year eleven, only Aaron's name remained.

It took longer to find the school records for the Hastings case. The relevant floppy disk for Hastings Secondary College was corrupted and they had to ferret through boxes of files to get the information they needed. Anjali typed the names in as they went.

'There's Eric Drum,' said Anjali. 'And Trevor Hill.'

'That's year nine, yes?' asked Zoe.

'Yep. But there is no sign of Trevor Hill in Eric's year eight class.'

Anjali kept typing but then stopped. 'Hold on. I think—oh my god,' she trailed off.

Zoe saw the same name. 'Ivan Raddich,' said Zoe. 'He is on both lists, in year eight with Ben Jennings and Aaron Smyth at Frankston, and in year nine with Eric Drum and

Trevor Hill at Hastings.'

Anjali was gaping at the screen.

'You did it, Anjali,' yelled Zoe. She scooped up a box of records from Rosebud Secondary College, where Ray and Dwayne had gone to school. 'We're looking for Ray Carlson's class for year ten,' said Zoe.

Anjali loaded one of the floppy disks, while Zoe flicked through the folders in the archive box.

'Got it,' said Anjali. She pointed at the screen. 'And there he is.'

Ivan Raddich.

Zoe pulled out her phone and called Charlie. 'We've struck gold.'

8.45 PM, TUESDAY 11 FEBRUARY

The cleaner made his way through the office, the vacuum strapped to his back, the power cord snaking its way behind him.

Zoe watched his feet travel past the glass of the conference room. Rob stifled a yawn.

'Okay, I've got nothing recent on Ivan Raddich,' said Anjali. 'He isn't in the database and his licence expired five years ago. It was issued almost ten years before that and his address at the time was the Grover Private Hotel in St Kilda.'

Rob, Zoe and Charlie knew all about the Grover. It had been the scene of multiple murders over the years.

'That bad?' asked Anjali.

'Yeah, boarding house,' said Rob. 'Druggies mainly. Almost everyone who's ever stayed there has arrived fresh from prison.'

'Almost, but not all, it seems,' said Anjali. 'Ivan Raddich has no record with Corrections. I've checked with the Grover and they had no forwarding address for him. The lady there can't remember him. She says she keeps a log of all troublemakers and his name's not on it.'

'What about welfare payments, child support, taxes?' asked Zoe.

'I'm checking all that now. I'll know more in the morning,' said Anjali.

Zoe nodded. 'I had a look and he has zero social media presence, at least under his own name.'

'How does a bloke who is living in the worst boarding house in the country, full of druggies and crims, start paying six months' rent in cash on houses all over the place?' asked Charlie. 'Even all these years later, it's a long way to drag yourself up. Dealing drugs?'

'Maybe,' said Zoe. 'I rang our friends in the Drug Squad and asked whether they knew of Ivan Raddich or any of his aliases. They have no record of him, but it doesn't mean he wasn't dealing under another name.'

'Okay, we need to add some resources to this,' said Rob.

Zoe let out a groan. After the last couple of days, the thought of getting help from the rest of Homicide didn't sit well with her.

Rob ignored her. 'Hannah and Angus have capacity.'

'But they were in charge of the Ben Jennings murder,' protested Zoe.

'And you and Charlie worked the Carlson case, so by that logic you should be taken off the investigation as well,' countered Rob. 'Plus, I really want this squad back working together. This will help, trust me.'

Zoe gave her reluctant agreement. 'Okay, let's work out a plan of attack and then we'll brief Hannah and Angus in the morning. Anjali, can you look for other family members as well?'

'We need,' continued Zoe, 'to find some of these classmates and see what they remember about Ivan. Anyone who was spoken to as part of the murder investigations should be put to one side for the moment, but there should still be plenty of ex-classmates left to speak to.'

'And what reason are we giving for wanting to speak to them about Ivan?' asked Charlie.

'We'll say he's a missing person. That's nice and neutral. Plus, it's true—we don't know where he is.'

'Okay,' said Anjali. 'I'll find the people we haven't yet spoken to. I'll have a list ready for the briefing tomorrow,' said Anjali.

'Well done, everyone,' said Rob, standing up and making for the door. 'Get a good night's sleep.'

Charlie was on his feet too. 'I'll see you tomorrow.'

'No worries, see you then,' said Zoe.

Anjali rubbed her face.

'Have you eaten?' asked Zoe.

'Not yet.'

'Come on, let's grab a quick bite.'

Anjali, Zoe and Harry headed down Lonsdale Street towards the restaurants and cafes in Hardware Lane. The sun had set and a southerly breeze was cooling the city.

'Fresh air at last,' said Zoe. 'I don't want to see another

room of archive boxes for a long time.'

Anjali said nothing.

'You okay?'

'Sorry, I was miles away. Thinking about Ivan Raddich. Just hoping we can find him.'

'You and me both,' said Zoe.

They had just crossed King Street, on the edge of Melbourne's legal district, when Anjali said, 'Don't look now, but your one-woman fan club is sitting across the road.'

Through the traffic, Zoe saw Sally Johnstone, smiling broadly, as she sat outside a bluestone pub. She reached over and touched the arm of the person across the table from her. Zoe stopped dead in her tracks. It was Tom.

8.30 AM, WEDNESDAY 12 FEBRUARY

Zoe walked through the car park below the City West Police Complex. Harry trotted alongside, looking up at her with concern. She had spent a restless night, obsessing about seeing Tom and Sally out together. He had texted her late to check in, but she'd replied saying she was busy working. Her instinct had been to ring and confront him, but she knew she was too worked up. She needed to get her thoughts in order. Get perspective. *Breathe.*

Rows of dark-coloured, unmarked criminal investigation vehicles were lined up, mainly late-model BMW, VW, Hyundai, Ford and Toyota sedans and wagons. Her Ford Escape was the least obvious CI car there, she thought. Probably made her look like a soccer mum. She was about twenty metres away when the elevator doors opened.

Iain Gillies and Garry Burns strode out, with Garry in mid-sentence. 'And we've been going out a few months and I start noticing this dark regrowth, you know, on her pussy, and I'm like "what's going on?" and she's like "my waxer is away". I thought she was a natural blonde, but apparently not. Then yesterday her eyes were hazel, not blue. So apparently she's been wearing coloured contacts this whole time. I thought I had a blue-eyed blonde, but I have a hazel-eyed brunette. I'm feeling fucking ripped off.'

Imagine, Zoe thought, *how she'll feel if she ever meets the real you.*

'Hey,' said Iain, 'Here comes DD, the Detective for the Defence.'

Zoe walked past them into the elevator. 'Always a pleasure to see you too, Runner,' she shot back.

'You fucking b—' she heard, the closing doors cutting Iain off.

Charlie spun his pen on his notepad as Zoe finished her briefing. Across from him, Hannah Nguyen and Angus Batch had scribbled pages of notes. Over the last half hour she had watched their curiosity grow and their doubts fall away.

Angus was staring at the whiteboard, which displayed enlarged photographs from the driver's licences of Alex Verdi, Eddie Nicholas and Greg Enders.

'What is it?' asked Zoe.

'He's a clever one,' said Angus. 'He's styled his hair so it obscures his ears. There are things you can do to change the appearance of a face. Gain or lose weight. Puff out your cheeks or suck them in, drop your chin down, that sort of thing, but you can't change the shape of your ears without surgery. If he had a crew cut in all three photos, you'd easily be able to tell if it was the same person.'

Zoe looked up at the photographs. In only one of them did his ears fully show.

The door swung open and Anjali rushed in. 'Sorry. Took a while to get everything printed.' She dropped a pile of stapled papers on the table. Her hair, usually neat, was unkempt and her eyes were puffy. Although she was wearing a jacket, Zoe could see that Anjali had the same shirt on that she was wearing the night before.

Zoe gave her a reassuring smile. 'Any joy?'

'Yes and no. Unsurprisingly, Ivan Raddich was on unemployment benefits around the time he was staying at the Grover. After that, he disappears. Checked with the ATO. No tax returns submitted since that time. No record of him anywhere else either. I'm about to start calling the banks, but my gut says we won't find him there either.'

'What about overseas? He may have gone abroad.'

'Yeah, that's the good news. No record of him leaving the country. The Immigration Department have a record of Ivan Raddich arriving in Australia with his family in 1990. Came from what was then Yugoslavia, now Serbia. Born in Belgrade. Ivan was eight when he arrived. I also checked the other names—Alex Verdi, Eddie Nicholas and Greg Enders—and they don't come up on the immigration records at all. Or any government records, in fact, apart from the driver's licences.'

'And his family?' asked Zoe.

'His parents are dead, but he has a brother, Marko, who's two years younger. Marko is alive, living in Melbourne.

He works as an IT consultant...works a lot with the state government. He is in the middle of a major project with the Department of Justice right now.'

Zoe smiled. 'Fantastic. He's our next stop. Let me know about the banks.'

'Will do. Also, I've gone through the list of classmates from the three schools Ivan shared with the murder victims. There are quite a few still around Hastings and Rosebud. Less in Frankston, but still enough, I think. The women were harder to find because of married names, so the lists are skewed towards men. There are at least six people for each school.' She pushed the papers into the middle of the table as she stifled a yawn.

'Thanks, Anjali. Great work,' said Zoe.

Anjali half slumped back in her chair, and grinned with relief.

'Okay,' said Zoe. 'Charlie and I will go and see Marko at the Department of Justice. Then we'll go to Frankston. Hannah and Angus, can you do Portsea and Hastings?'

'Sure,' said Angus. 'What do you need us to find out?'

'One—does anyone know where Ivan Raddich is? Two—what were relations like between Ivan, the victims and the guys we have locked up.'

'So,' said Hannah. 'Friends. Enemies. Incidents. That sort of thing?'

'That's it,' said Zoe, flipping her folder shut. 'Let's go and find him.'

10.30 AM, WEDNESDAY 12 FEBRUARY

Zoe and Charlie stepped out of the elevator and into the foyer of the Department of Justice in Exhibition Street. Harry walked happily beside Zoe.

The receptionist bounced up out of her seat as they approached. 'What a beautiful dog.'

Harry wagged his tail in response.

'Hi. Detectives Mayer and Shaw. We're here to see Marko Raddich.'

'Oh yes, just a moment, sorry.' She picked up the phone, scanned a list and punched in some numbers.

'Hi Marko. I've got two detectives here to see you... Okay...no...Okay.' She put down the phone. 'He'll be right out.'

'Thank you,' said Zoe. A moment later a door at the back of the lobby swung open and a tanned man with a neat crew cut walked confidently towards them.

Marko Raddich was leaner, three inches taller, and had

blue eyes, compared to Ivan's brown, but the similarities were there. Zoe and Charlie glanced at each other.

'Hi, I'm Marko,' he said, thrusting out his hand.

Zoe took a step forward, and shook his hand. 'Zoe Mayer and Charlie Shaw. Is there somewhere we can chat?'

'Yes, sure, come through to the office,' said Marko, before looking down at Harry. 'Hey there, what's your name?'

'His name's Harry,' said Zoe.

'Bit unusual, isn't it? A police dog that's not a german shepherd.'

'He's a specialist,' Zoe said, smiling.

They followed Marko to his large corner office. It looked both south and east, the view taking in the Yarra River bending around past the Melbourne Cricket Ground. Zoe took an extra moment looking towards the northern end of the stadium and the surrounding parkland. Around the office were a number of computer boxes, some opened, others not, and his desk was piled high with papers and reports.

'Apologies for the mess. I just got back from a week's holiday hiking up at Mount Baw Baw and I'm trying to catch up. You should see the email backlog,' he said, smiling.

'Did you only get back today?' asked Zoe.

Marko laughed. 'You'd think so. No, I drove up a week ago on the Saturday and got back Sunday night. Eight days camping was more than enough. I was badly in need of a long shower and a comfy bed.'

'What do you do here?' asked Charlie.

'I've been consulting on a major project for the past six

or seven months. Updating cybersecurity protocols. Stopping hackers basically. I do a lot of government work. So, what case do you need help with?'

'Sorry?' asked Charlie.

'The case you're working on. I presume you need me to help with some cybersecurity aspect.'

'No, nothing like that. We are here about your brother, Ivan.'

Marko's body jerked. His shoulders slumped and he closed his eyes. Zoe noticed Marko's ears turn red.

'What's happened? Is he hurt? Is he—'

'No, nothing like that. We want to speak with him in relation to an investigation. He may be a witness, that's all. How can we find him?'

Marko took several deep breaths as he recovered himself. 'I wish I knew. I've hardly seen my brother at all in many years. Not properly since just after my mother died. The last time I saw him,' Marko paused, looking away, 'yes, that's it, I ran into him by chance here in the city, in the Bourke Street Mall, about ten years ago. He said he'd been working up north, picking fruit. I gave him my number and asked him to call me to catch up, but he never did. I tried to locate him a few years ago through the government databases, but I couldn't find anything. Zilch. I'd be happy to help you find him. He's all the family I have left now.'

'Thanks, we appreciate that. We'll let you know,' said Zoe. 'What was the last address you had for him?'

'It was our family home in Noble Park. Ivan was still living there when Mum died. We decided to sell it a few months later. I thought it was a good idea at the time—Ivan was depressed as hell living there without Mum. He was kind of floating about, not doing anything.'

'What was the address in Noble Park?'

Marko gave it to her before adding, 'The house is gone now. Was bulldozed for townhouses.'

'What did Ivan do for work?' asked Charlie.

'He worked with Dad at my family's fruit shop once he left school. Ran it with Mum after Dad died. When Mum got sick, she decided to sell it. She didn't want Ivan to be shackled to it. Got a good price in the end. After Mum died, Ivan had half the money from selling the fruit shop, but that wasn't going to last forever. I don't think he worked for a while. As I said, he'd been picking fruit up near the Murray River somewhere. Other than that, I'm not sure.'

'Your parents have any other kids?'

'No, just Ivan and me.'

'Tell us about your childhood.'

'It was good. We arrived in Australia when I was six, Ivan was about eight. Dad worked construction jobs all over the place while he saved money to buy his fruit shop. We were a close family.'

'Did you move around a lot with your Dad's work?' asked Charlie.

Marko raised an eyebrow. 'Yeah, we did. How'd you know that?'

'Where did you live?' asked Zoe.

'Dad looked for long-term construction jobs so we could all stay together. Building schools, roads, that sort of thing.

We lived up at Bright in the high country, in Hastings, Frankston, Rosebud, and finally in Noble Park. That's where my parents ended up buying a fruit shop. Big Serbian community there then. Helped them feel more at home.'

'When you were moving around, what was life like?'

'It was okay. Bit unsettling having to make new friends and change schools all the time, but we saw a lot of places.'

'What about for Ivan? How'd he find it?' asked Zoe.

'I guess he found it tougher. He was older and the other kids were less open to newcomers. Especially back then. We were different and our English wasn't good for the first few years. Plus, he was smaller than the other kids—our mum said it was because food was a bit tight back before we came to Australia. I ended up taller than him by the time I was sixteen, even though he had two years on me. Anyway, we just got on with things, and our English improved. Once we moved to Noble Park, Ivan left school to work with Dad in the shop.'

'Did Ivan have any problems with specific kids at school?'

'What? No, I don't think so. What's this all about?' Marko shifted in his seat.

'Ivan's name has come up in an investigation. That's all I can say right now. Where do you think your brother is?'

Marko's eyes hardened. He crossed his arms. 'I don't know. I would have told you first up if I knew.'

Zoe held up a hand. 'Okay, okay, I understand.'

'Sorry,' he said, calming slightly, 'this has been a bit of a shock. It's been a long time since I've heard from Ivan. It's thrown me a bit, that's all.'

'I understand. One more question. Did Ivan ever have any issues with drugs?'

Marko grimaced. 'To be honest, I'm not sure. I often wondered about that. Even asked him once, but he denied it. He's got a lot of pride, my brother, and he can be hard to read, but deep down he's sensitive. Gets easily upset by things, you know.'

Zoe pulled out her card. 'If you remember anything or think of anywhere we could find him, please give me a call.'

'Will do,' Marko said. 'He's a good person. Just never found his place in the world, I suppose. When you find him, can you get him to call me? Please.' He gave his card to Zoe. She tucked it into her folder.

3.30 PM, WEDNESDAY 12 FEBRUARY

'Ivan Raddich?' Carol Simmons was leaning against her front door, nose screwed up. 'Nah, can't remember him, sorry.'

Behind her, two children were chasing each other in the hallway, yelling.

'He'd just immigrated from Yugoslavia,' said Zoe, her voice raised above the noise. 'He was only at Frankston High for a year.'

One of the children, a boy of about five, came up beside his mother, and stared at Harry. He looked up at Zoe. 'Are you blind? Is that why you've got a blind dog?'

Carol pointed at Harry's vest. 'Gareth, that's a service dog. He's not a guide dog. Now, don't be rude to the lady. Go and watch your brother.' The boy ran back into the house.

Carol looked at Zoe. 'Sorry, what were you saying?'

'Ivan. Spent a year at Frankston High.'

'Oh wow,' she said. 'Now I remember. *Ivan the Yugo*,

we called him. Strange kid. Crap at English. What's he done?'

'Nothing. It's a missing persons case.'

'Shit. Sorry.'

'Was he ever picked on at school?' asked Charlie.

'You kidding?'

'What do you mean?'

'Immigrant kid back in those days—in our school. It was dog eat dog back then. Sorry, no offence,' she added, looking down at Harry.

'Any examples?' asked Zoe.

'There were a few in our year who gave him a hard time. Guy called Ben Jennings used to bash him a couple of times a week, just for the fun of it. Ben got stabbed a year or two back. Read about it in the paper. He was a prick back then, so that was no big surprise.'

'Anyone else,' asked Zoe.

'Hold on,' Carol said. 'Let me get my yearbook.' She walked back into the house. 'Shut it, you two,' she barked.

She came back out, book in hand. The fading type on the front said Frankston High School. She flicked through it before reaching a page of photographs. She studied the faces, row by row. 'Okay, yeah, that's right. There were two other guys who hassled him. Greg Spanno and Aaron Smyth. Greg is dead. Took on a power pole with his car when he was about nineteen and lost. Aaron is locked up for killing Ben. So, I don't reckon they're involved in this bloke going missing.'

'Was Ivan in that class too?' asked Charlie.

'Nah, don't reckon he was,' said Carol, her eyes skimming over the rows of students. 'Hold on,' she said, flicking through a few pages. 'There he is. Same year as us, but in a different class.' Carol put her finger against the chest of a small boy at the end of the second row. 'Ivan Raddich.'

The face peered forlornly out at them, a look of almost pleading despair in his dark eyes. The boy seemed smaller than the others, his face more a child's than a teenager's.

'Did Ivan have issues with anyone else in the school?' asked Charlie.

'Don't think so. Ben, Aaron and Greg were the thugs in our year. Ivan was their personal punching bag for a while.'

'You mind if I take a photo of Ivan's face?' asked Zoe, getting her phone out.

'Be my guest,' said Carol. 'You reckon that Ivan going missing has something to do with high school?'

Zoe focused and clicked. 'No, we don't, but in missing persons cases we look from every angle. We're all the sum of many parts,' she said, almost wistfully.

'I guess. There a reward or anything?' asked Carol.

'No,' said Zoe, smiling, trying to dampen her expectations. 'We are still in the process of working out if he's actually missing or has just gone on holiday without telling anyone.'

'Right, fair enough.'

Zoe and Charlie were in the conference room with Hannah and Angus. Anjali sat at the head of the table, her laptop open.

Angus flipped through his folder. 'Immigrant kid, victimised by schoolmates for being different. I interviewed four old school friends from Hastings who all told the same story. Eric Drum and Trevor Hill were troublemakers and they bullied the hell out of Ivan Raddich so much that Ivan wouldn't leave the classroom at recess or lunch. Teachers didn't do much to stop it.' He walked to the whiteboard and stuck a blown-up photo of the young Ivan on it.

'Same story at Frankston,' said Zoe, adding her photo of Ivan to the board. 'Saw five of the old schoolmates. Everyone gave a similar account, depending on how much they liked or disliked the bullies.'

'Almost identical story from the old students of Rosebud Secondary College,' said Hannah, pulling her photo of the high school-aged Ivan from her folder and sticking it on the board. His face was marred with acne and he was looking down. They stared at the photos of the maturing boy. 'Ivan was apparently up for fighting back by that stage, but it didn't seem to help. His life sounds like it was torture, with Ray Carlson and Dwayne Harley in charge of the bullying. They'd pick fights with him, give him royal flushes, that sort of thing.'

'I hate to even ask,' said Zoe.

'A royal flush is when someone picks you up, turns you upside down and sticks your head in the toilet while someone else flushes it,' said Hannah. 'Charming, eh?'

'Like water-boarding for high schoolers.' Zoe looked at the sad photos of the teenage Ivan on the board.

'I think we have answered the motive question,' said Angus.

'Yeah, but why wait twenty years to get revenge?' said Charlie. 'You'd think he'd have acted earlier or got over it. One or the other.'

'Something is driving him,' said Zoe. 'We'll find out what once we catch him.'

'He must have had a growth spurt,' mused Charlie. 'He was in the second to front row in all these pics, one of the shorter boys. The guy we met as Greg Enders was taller.'

'And we met with Ivan's brother, Marko,' said Zoe. 'He told us he doesn't know where Ivan is, and hasn't seen him in years.'

'You believe him?' asked Hannah.

'Yeah, I reckon,' said Zoe. 'What do you think, Charlie?'

'He came across as truthful to me,' Charlie said. 'We told him Ivan could be a witness in a case and Marko offered to help in any way he could. He said he was keen to reconnect with him.'

'Let's get his alibi checked,' said Zoe, 'to make sure he isn't involved in helping his brother. Just in case. Anjali, can you get a data dump for the phone tower closest to Mount Baw Baw? Marko told us he went hiking there. He said he left here on Saturday morning, the second of February, and returned last Sunday. Map it out, it's probably about three hours by car.'

Zoe pulled Marko's card out of her folder and slid it over to Anjali. 'The mobile number on there should be in the metadata from the tower.'

'Will do,' said Anjali.

8.45 AM, THURSDAY 13 FEBRUARY

Harry walked underneath Zoe's desk and sat on his dog bed. The office was busy. A new case had come in overnight.

Zoe saw Rob enter the office. He looked across at her and she cocked her head towards the conference room.

'Update time,' she said to Charlie.

A few minutes later, Zoe stood at the whiteboard. Rob, Charlie, Angus and Hannah were on the other side of the table. Anjali sat at the end, eyes sparkling.

'Okay, Zoe,' said the DI, 'what's our theory?'

Zoe pointed at the blown-up driver's licence in Eddie Nicholas's name, stuck to the whiteboard. 'What we know: Ivan Raddich, born April Fool's Day, 1982, in the former Yugoslavia, arrives in Australia in 1990. Father works on big construction projects and the family moves around a lot. Ivan gets badly bullied in three high schools: Frankston High, Western Port Secondary College in Hastings and Rosebud Secondary College. Years eight, nine and ten.

Ivan leaves school after that and works in his parents' fruit shop until his dad dies and his mum sells the shop. He goes through a period of heavy depression, living with his mum until she passes away. His brother, Marko, decides to sell the family house as Ivan seems to be going downhill living there on his own. From there, we don't know much else. He has a fair bit of cash from the sale of his parents' assets, enough for a few years. Marko isn't sure, but it's possible Ivan was on drugs, which may explain why he ended up living at the Grover in St Kilda.'

'Does he have any form for drug crimes?' asked Rob.

'No,' said Anjali. 'No charges at all, in fact. Not even a speeding ticket. At least under the names we think he's been using.'

'Right, and then?' asked Rob.

'Something triggers him. Maybe he met someone from his high school days, maybe he saw a shrink, who knows? He decides that he is going to get revenge. Take them all out.'

'Wouldn't someone recognise him from high school?' asked Rob.

'His face has changed a lot,' said Zoe. 'He was short and baby-faced early on, and by the time he hit year ten he had severe acne. He shot up after leaving school. Plus, the kid they all knew back then couldn't speak English very well and had a heavy accent. The Ivan they met later on would've sounded and looked different.'

'Okay, then what?'

'He decides he'll kill them in order—first, his tormentors

from year eight. He creates a fake identity and rents a nearby house, stakes out his victims, learns their habits and ways, finds out everything he can about them, becomes their friend. He works out who he will kill and who he'll set up for the murder. He manages to get some clothing from the fall guy's house, a pullover or a hoodie, full of DNA. Probably taken from a laundry basket when he was visiting. Then he waits for a perfect day, when he has access to the victim, and when he knows the fall guy will not have a solid alibi. He wants to be looking into their eyes when he takes revenge, probably telling them while they're dying who he is and why he's doing it. Once they are dead, he gloves up and pulls out the hoodie, soaking the front of it in the victim's blood. Then he scrunches it up and puts it back inside the bag it came in. Now he has the victim's blood all over the outside of the clothing and the fall guy's DNA on the inside. Once it's done, Ivan cleans up, probably changes clothes and exits.'

Zoe waited for a rebuttal or question.

'Bloody hell,' said Angus, his mouth falling open.

'But he could've easily left DNA at the scene, despite all that preparation,' said Rob.

'Yes, but it would only be a small amount. He could've explained that away as he was friends with the people he was targeting. He was in regular contact with them and he'd been in their houses plenty of times.'

'Keep going,' said Rob.

'Then he waits. Someone discovers the body. Maybe the police speak to him, maybe they don't. He doesn't really care. That's not his main game. He waits a day or two and then calls Crime Stoppers with a tip-off about the fall guy. A little while after that, he plants the pullover somewhere and then makes another call to Crime Stoppers, telling us about the evidence. We arrest the fall guy and he waits for charges to be laid. After the funeral, he disappears. With everything that has gone on, no one pays much attention. Then he starts to plan his next victim.'

'So, if he's done this three times, is he finished? Are there more victims to come?'

'According to his brother, Ivan left school after they lived in Rosebud and started working in the family fruit shop in Noble Park. So unless he was bullied later, he might be done.'

'Okay, that all makes sense as a theory, but how do we catch him?' asked Rob.

'I was lying awake this morning and I remembered Ben Jennings' widow telling me that Alex Verdi, Ivan's alias in that case, turned up on the first day of the trial and then at the sentencing. I suppose he wanted to gloat at his success. I hope Ivan will be at Trevor Hill's trial when it starts on Monday.'

'Unless he hears we're searching for him,' Charlie said.

'True,' said Zoe, 'but the only person we're aware of who knows the real Ivan is his brother, Marko. He seemed to be in the dark when we spoke with him. Anjali, did you check the phone tower data from near Mount Baw Baw on the days Marko said he was travelling?'

Anjali sat up. 'Yes, his phone was pinging off the tower there from 10.30 am on Saturday the first of February until

Sunday the ninth at 4.35 pm. It's around a three-hour drive from Melbourne, so that all lines up. He was at Mount Baw Baw when Ray Carlson was murdered and the entire week following that, nowhere near the crime scene.'

'Okay, Marko's in the clear,' said Zoe. 'So, unless Marko happens to run into his brother by chance, Ivan won't know we're after him.'

'I really would have preferred to get Ivan into custody this week,' said Rob. 'Waiting until the start of the trial will complicate everything.'

'If we can arrest Ivan on the courthouse steps,' said Zoe, 'we should be able to get the trial postponed by twenty-four hours to give us time to interview him.'

'You know who's prosecuting the case, don't you?' said Rob. 'Sally Johnstone isn't our biggest fan right now.'

Zoe bristled. 'Yeah, I know.' She felt her phone vibrate. It was a text from a number she didn't recognise: *Have you got five minutes? There's something you should know— Sarah Westbrook.*

Zoe and Harry walked out the front of the City West Police Complex on Spencer Street. She spotted Sarah near the side of the road, waving to catch her attention, and made her way through the pedestrian traffic to where she was standing.

'Thanks for coming down,' said Sarah. 'I know you're busy.'

'No worries. Harry is overdue for a walk,' said Zoe. Zoe felt her phone buzzing. It was Anjali.

'Sorry, I need to get this. Should be quick.'

Zoe shuffled to the kerb as people rushed by. Sarah followed her. Zoe shortened Harry's leash by winding it around her hand.

'Hi Anjali, what's up?'

The roar stunned her. She saw a flash of the driver as the car surged onto the footpath. Harry barked and jerked on his lead, pulling Zoe away from the road. Spun by the force of her dog, she tripped, dropping her phone. The side of the car glanced off her left leg. All around her, people were screaming and running. Zoe lay dazed on her back, staring up at the seagulls circling high above the city in the blue sky.

Harry was close by, whimpering. She could hear different voices calling for an ambulance or police. Her hair felt damp and warm.

A minute later, the pedestrians had been cleared away by a swarm of uniformed officers. She shut her eyes. When she opened them again, half of Homicide stood around her. *Anjali was on the phone when it happened. They must have looked down and seen me.*

Zoe jerked, trying to get up quickly. 'Where's Harry? Is he okay?' She was beginning to hyperventilate and the world was spinning. Tiny flashes of light flickered.

'He's okay. He's right here,' said Anjali. Zoe turned and saw that Anjali held his lead. She let it go loose and Harry rushed to her, licking her face.

'It's okay, Harry. It's okay. Good boy.' She stroked his head, calming him. 'Where's Sarah?'

About three metres away, Sarah lay still, with people kneeling around her. *Fuck.*

Sirens filled the air. Two ambulances and a Mobile Intensive Care Ambulance Paramedic unit pulled up. The road was blocked to traffic. Zoe knew that Sarah was in a bad way if the MICA had been called.

While four of the paramedics rushed to Sarah, one knelt down next to Zoe.

'I'm okay,' said Zoe, before he could speak.

'Hi. I'm John,' his voice calm, 'but your head says otherwise. You've got a nasty gash there. Where else hurts?'

'My left leg. The front fender hit my calf.'

John pulled up her trouser leg. There was an area that was red and darkening. 'Can you move your foot?'

Zoe kicked her foot forward and back, before rolling it clockwise and then anticlockwise.

'Okay, that's great,' said John. He gently moved her leg as she winced. 'It's not broken, but you'll need an x-ray to make sure there's no fracture.'

'No need, I'm fine,' said Zoe, looking across at Sarah, now wearing an oxygen mask. One of the paramedics was drawing liquid into a needle. Zoe saw Sarah's arm move. 'Is she going to be okay?'

'Not sure,' said John, 'but she's conscious, which is a good sign.'

'Did you see the car?' asked Rob, standing above her.

'Not really. Red SUV, maybe a Ford Everest. Driver was Caucasian. Wearing a black hoodie. Face was covered, it looked like a bandana, but his hands were white. It was over in a second. Didn't get a look at the plates.'

'Okay, Anjali, can you get onto the CCTV footage? Pull

every tactical intelligence officer you can find and get them on the job. Find that car.'

Anjali was on the move before he had finished speaking. 'I'm on it,' she called back.

'Let's get your head cleaned up,' said John, and helped her onto her feet. Zoe walked gingerly with him to the back of the ambulance as Sarah was on a gurney being fed into the back of the other ambulance. 'How is she?' John asked another paramedic.

'She'll be okay. She's smashed up, but she'll live.'

Zoe felt a flush of relief. *Thank god for that.*

John worked quickly on Zoe's head, while simultaneously asking a series of questions to see if she was concussed. After five minutes he was done. 'No concussion, but just to be safe, don't drive home tonight, and if you start feeling strange at all call an ambulance. Okay?'

'Understood. And thanks.' Her head again felt clear and alert.

'You will not be walking too well tomorrow. The bruising will set in and it'll ache like hell for a few days. Get it elevated and iced for the next few hours. You'll need anti-inflammatories and pain relief, so go to your GP.'

'I will. Thanks again.' She hopped down from the back of the ambulance, taking her weight mainly on her right foot.

She hobbled off. Charlie stepped beside her and formed a triangle with his left arm.

Zoe laughed softly at his impromptu show of chivalry. 'I'm good, Charlie. Thanks though.'

'No worries,' Charlie said, letting his arm fall loose.

'Could you do me a favour and take Harry up to Flagstaff Gardens? I was on my way there when all this happened. He needs a wee.'

'Sure, no problem at all.'

'Thanks, you'll probably need these too,' said Zoe, pulling some black plastic bags from her pocket and handing them to him. He wrinkled his nose.

'All part of the job. Thanks, Charlie. Keep him on the lead, though,' said Zoe, bending at the waist and stroking Harry's head. 'You be a good boy for Charlie.'

Harry wagged his tail.

The two detectives, one older and one a young man, from Melbourne CIU rolled the CCTV footage back and forth. Zoe watched their screens with them. Harry lay beside her.

The footage showed a red Ford Everest swerving onto the footpath, hitting Zoe and Sarah as it swerved back onto the road. The car hit Sarah front on, while Zoe was hit by the car's fender, Harry having pulled her away. They opened another view, from the front of the police complex, and saw it side-on. Zoe felt her body tighten, watching how close she had been to death. Sarah had been thrown like a rag-doll along the footpath. The same thing would have happened to her if Harry hadn't pulled her away. She smiled down at him in gratitude.

'We've found the car down by the West Gate Bridge. It's a smouldering wreck now. Completely burnt out. We ran the number plate and it's stolen,' said the older detective. 'In the

CCTV we can see the driver's hands on the steering wheel, which confirms he's Caucasian. Was this someone driving around drunk or on drugs or was this a deliberate attempt on your life? Or on Sarah Westbrook's life?'

'No one knew I would be out there then,' said Zoe. 'I got a text from Sarah to ask if I wanted a coffee and decided I'd take Harry for a walk. It's not like I do it at the same time every day. I'm not even in the office at the same time every day.'

'Yeah, maybe it was random, but we need to run at this one assuming it was deliberate. What are you working on at the moment? It could be related to one of your cases.'

Zoe didn't want to let the world know that she was conducting what was basically an undercover investigation of closed cases. 'We are closing out a job down at Portsea. Fatal stabbing. Guy has been charged and remanded. Drug Squad have also charged him for meth production.'

The two detectives shared a look that Zoe recognised.

'I really don't think it was me they were after,' she said. 'This is my first case back from leave. I was off for a few months…'

'We know all about that. What about before then? Any old cases?'

Zoe didn't want to tell the detectives how to do their jobs. She would have been asking similar questions. Zoe took them through the main highlights from the last few years.

'Okay, we'll check them out. We want to release the footage to the media. With luck someone knows who this is and dobs him in.'

Zoe groaned. 'Can we blur my face and not ID me? I don't want any more publicity after last year. And Sarah, for that matter.'

The two detectives shared another look.

'Understood. We'll keep your name out of it. Once we've spoken to Sarah Westbrook, we'll see if she wants us to do the same for her. You never know, she may want the publicity. Why were you meeting her anyhow?'

'She texted me five minutes before the crash to ask if I wanted to grab coffee with her. I don't think it was anything important.'

'You friends with her?'

Zoe hesitated. 'Yeah, kind of...more like acquaintances.'

'Right. Thanks. We may need to chat with you again.'

'No worries. Let me know if you find anything,' said Zoe.

'Don't worry, we'll find him,' said the younger detective, eager to impress.

Zoe wasn't so confident. She stood, and pain shot through her leg. She hobbled towards the elevator, Harry trailing behind her.

The light turned yellow and Tom pushed hard on the brakes, bringing the BMW to a sudden stop.

Zoe winced. 'Shit, that hurts.'

'Sorry. You okay?'

'Yes. I'll need a bath when I get home.' Zoe had been surprised when Tom rushed into the squad room. She had been about to summon an Uber to take her home. Charlie must have called him. Zoe still wasn't ready for the argument that had been brewing inside her since she saw Tom out with Sally.

Harry yawned in the back of Tom's car, his vest attached to the seatbelt buckle. Zoe half turned and smiled at him. 'Good boy.'

'Good boy, sure. You nearly got killed today because you were out there with him.'

Zoe dug her fingers into the armrest. 'No, I was saved because he was there. He pulled me out of the way. Look, I'm in too much fucking agony to deal with you having a go at me. Just leave it, okay?'

They drove on for another half a block in silence. 'Yeah, okay,' he said. 'Any update on the car that hit you?'

'Stolen plates on a red Ford SUV. Now sitting burnt out down near the river. White male—he had a hoodie on and a bandana across his face.'

'So it wasn't an accident. He was going for you.'

'It's not like Harry and I keep a regular schedule when we go to the park,' said Zoe. 'If anything, it's more likely they were targeting Sarah Westbrook. Someone with a grudge against her. She was an investigative journalist for a long time. She will have enemies.'

Tom was about to say something, but stopped. Zoe was relieved. She knew he was going to suggest that she leave her job.

They pulled up outside Zoe's house. 'Let me help you,' he said.

Zoe was half out as he reached her side. 'Can you get Harry?'

'Sure.' Tom opened the back door and unhooked Harry. He jumped onto the footpath and stood beside Zoe.

'Let's get you into that bath,' said Tom.

Zoe turned to him. 'What the hell were you doing with Sally on Tuesday night?'

Tom took a step backwards. 'What...what are you talking about?'

'Don't play dumb with me. I saw you with her, sitting outside that pub. What's your game?'

'Nothing. I caught up with her for a beer, that's it. Just work talk.'

'She's a prosecutor and you're a defence attorney. You're on opposite sides.'

'We passed each other walking on Lonsdale Street, near the courts, and she suggested we have a quick beer.'

'You know what she's been like. I told you she'd been screaming the squad room down a few days ago. Seems a bit coincidental to me.'

'Come on, Zoe. Don't be like that,' he said, trying to put an arm around her.

Zoe shrugged him off. 'Don't you get it? She'll do anything to undermine me.'

'I think you're overreacting,' he said. 'We hardly even mentioned you.'

Zoe gave a wry grin. 'I'll call you, okay?'

She hobbled towards the front door, Harry by her side. Tom stood by the car, palms open at his sides.

8.30 AM, FRIDAY 14 FEBRUARY

Zoe stared at her diary. Trevor Hill's trial was three days away. The wound on her head throbbed under the bandage and her calf felt as though she'd been hit with a baseball bat. Harry came out from under her desk and laid his head on her knee. She gazed at him and stroked his fur. *Such a good boy.*

'Morning,' Charlie said.

'Morning. You look like death.'

'Thanks,' he said, managing a smile. 'I could say the same about you. How's the head?'

'Feel like someone's using a jack-hammer on it.'

A plain envelope was jammed under her in-tray. 'Zoe' was scrawled on it in an elegant script, with a small hand-drawn heart in the corner. In her peripheral vision she could see Iain and Garry furtively looking in her direction.

'What's that?' asked Charlie.

'Valentine's Day admirers,' said Zoe. She picked up the envelope and tossed it in the bin.

Charlie's phone buzzed. 'Hi Mum...yeah, what's up? I'm at work...what? It's those bloody movies you're watching on the computer. You've got a virus or something. Don't touch it and I'll come around tonight and fix it.'

'Everything okay?' asked Zoe.

'Yeah. Mum's been watching pirated movies she borrows from her neighbour's son. Sounds like she's got herself a virus from one of them.'

Zoe stared at her desk.

'What is it?'

Zoe said nothing, raising her hand to buy a few more seconds, running her thoughts through her head.

'What?' asked Charlie again.

'When I was talking to Katie Harley on Saturday about Greg Enders, her daughter said that he'd given them movies on USB sticks.' Zoe tapped her pen on the desk. 'Is that how Ivan's finding out secrets to use to set people up when he calls Crime Stoppers?'

'Sorry, what do you mean?'

'I reckon he is using some sort of spyware program. I saw something on TV about it. Once they plug the USB into the computer, the spyware installs itself in the background. Ivan might have used it to read emails, eavesdrop on video chats, look at their social media, that sort of thing.'

Zoe picked up the phone to call Anjali. At that moment, the squad room door swung open and Anjali ran through the office towards them, half out of breath. She held an iPad in one hand and a file of papers in the other.

'I found a...cabin,' she exclaimed, breathless.

'What?' asked Zoe.

Anjali leaned against the desk, composing herself. 'I was doing a property title search and came across a cabin in Ivan's dad's name. He bought it a couple of years after they set up the fruit shop. It's near a place called Three Bridges.'

'Where's that?' asked Charlie.

'South of Warburton. An hour and a half east of here. Just past Yarra Junction. Middle of nowhere. It's down a track off Mount Bride Road.' said Anjali. 'Here, have a look.'

Anjali held the iPad so that they could all see the screen. She used two fingers to zoom in. For a moment, all Zoe and Charlie could see was an aerial image of forest. Then they saw it. A small clearing with a cabin. A water tank sat beside the building.

Zoe took the iPad. 'Well, someone's been using it in the last few years.'

'How can you tell?' asked Charlie.

Zoe pointed at the image. 'Solar panels.'

'Off grid, maybe?'

'Definitely,' said Anjali. 'I checked. The building's not connected to mains power or gas. Not connected to town water either. There'll be little in the way of landmarks out there, so I printed this.' She put a map on the desk with latitude and longitude coordinates. 'It's the only cabin for miles.'

Zoe felt the weight ease off her shoulders a little. 'And the property never transferred ownership since then?'

'No, still registered in the dad's name.'

'Can you find out from the local council who pays the rates every year?'

'Will do. I'll call you when I know,' said Anjali, already heading towards the door.

'Hold on, there's something else.'

'What is it?'

'Ray Carlson's computer. Can you pull it out of evidence and have another look at it. I want to know if there's spyware installed in it.'

'Will do. It's with the Drug Squad at the moment, but I'll head over there and get it checked out.'

'Thanks,' said Zoe, turning to Charlie. 'Let's have a look at this cabin.'

Zoe was regretting not getting Charlie to drive. Her left leg was aching. They were passing through Yarra Junction when the phone rang. Zoe hit the answer button on the steering wheel.

'Mayer.'

'Zoe, its Anjali. Couple of things. Firstly, I found a program called *Operation BugDrop* installed on Ray's PC. It's a type of malware program that allows you to access the information on an infected computer. You can also eavesdrop on people using their computer's microphone or webcam if the computer is on in the background.'

'And could you plant it by giving someone a USB stick full of movies?' asked Zoe.

'Yes, you'd need to disguise it a bit, but it can be set up to install itself. It can be easily hidden if there are a lot of folders with multiple files in each.'

'Can we see who has been accessing the information?'

'Not yet. These systems use cloud-based storage services to save the information. We may be able to trace that, but the account used is probably a free account in a fake name. Plus, with a VPN, a virtual private network, it would be hard to work out who was accessing the site.'

'Okay, thanks. What was the other thing?'

'Oh, yeah, I rang the Shire of Yarra Valley, which is Three Bridges' council. Rates for the property are paid in cash every year. Woman there remembers the guy paying a few months ago because only a couple of people pay by cash nowadays. He's in his late thirties or early forties and always wears a plain black cap, is always unshaven—a bit scruffy was what she said—and he doesn't like chit chat. Just comes in staring at the floor, pays and leaves. She remembers him because she thinks he's a rude prick. Her words. I asked about CCTV and they only keep recordings for a month before they re-record over the top.'

'Okay, thanks, Anjali. Good work,' said Zoe. She hung up.

'Sounds like Ivan to me. Up-front payments in cash,' said Charlie.

'I'm feeling more positive that we could finally get some physical evidence linking Ivan to all this. If we find his computer we should be able to link him to that malware.'

They drove on in silence, before Zoe noticed Charlie shaking his head.

Zoe glanced across. 'You okay?'

'Yeah,' he said sheepishly. 'It's just...I shouldn't have doubted your instincts. I feel like shit about it.'

'Don't worry about it. What's past is past.'

Twenty-five minutes later, they pulled off Mount Bride Road onto a dirt track. Zoe let the car coast to a stop. All around them were rainforest and scrub. A small mob of kangaroos bounded off the track, disappearing into the bush. Charlie looked at the map Anjali had printed for them. 'It's not far. Less than a hundred metres around that bend,' he said.

Zoe opened the car door and listened. All she could hear were the song birds.

'Let's walk,' she said.

Charlie gave a small involuntary moan.

'We'll have a quick look. No point calling in the cavalry if it's empty. Be careful shutting the door, though. The sound will travel out here.'

Charlie got out, and quietly closed his door. Zoe opened the back and Harry jumped down beside her. They started walking towards the bend on the track. She pulled her pistol, and held it low. Charlie noticed and pulled his gun too. The air was silent, except for the cicadas.

Slowly the cabin materialised through the trees. Painted dark brown, it stood in a clearing about the size of four tennis courts. At the front were two small windows on either side of a door. The side of the cabin that they could see had no windows, and the roof was corrugated iron. The solar panels were out of sight on the far side of the roof.

Zoe winced as she dropped into a crouch. Charlie moved down next to her. She leaned in close, whispering into his ear. 'The breeze is behind us, so we need to be really quiet.'

Charlie nodded.

'I'm going around the back,' said Zoe. 'You stay here and cover me. Wait for my signal. If there's no car there, we'll look through the front and back windows, okay?'

'Got it.'

Zoe limped around the edge of the clearing, her gun trained on the house. Harry kept pace just behind her. There were no vehicles parked at the back.

Zoe peered back at Charlie. She pointed two fingers towards her eyes and then in the direction of the cabin. Charlie nodded and walked into the clearing, gun at the ready.

Zoe could see no movement through the old sheer curtains that covered the two back windows. She looked in. The room was empty. She walked across to the other window. It was a kitchen. Also empty.

She opened the screen door and knocked. 'Victoria Police, anyone home?'

There was no movement inside. She knocked again. Zoe turned the doorknob slowly and pushed. It opened. She took one step inside before stepping out again. She indicated for Harry to drop down and stay.

'Charlie,' she called out. 'You'd better get around here.'

11.15 AM, FRIDAY 14 FEBRUARY

She had recognised the smell as soon as she opened the door. Charlie came running around the back and was now standing, wide-eyed, one hand across his nose and mouth, gun in the other hand.

'Victoria Police. We're coming in,' called Zoe, as she re-entered through the open back door. She pointed her gun as she walked through the dull light. Charlie was behind her, his pistol also drawn. Behind them, Harry gave a whine from where he'd been told to lie. The cabin was small, with a combined living and kitchen area. A large freezer stood next to the kitchen, its cord pulled from the socket. There was a bedroom at the front. They checked it, but it was empty. They walked over to the bathroom.

He was lying in the bath, fully clothed, a tourniquet tied around his arm, a needle beside him. Although the skin had turned grey and his body was bloated, she recognised him immediately. His neck was still angled down towards his shoulder. She didn't need to check him for vital signs. A swarm of flies hovered above the body.

Charlie walked in behind her before turning away. 'Oh, fuck.'

Zoe looked at Charlie. All the colour had drained from his face and she knew he was about to be ill.

'Come on, follow me, quick,' she said. Charlie chased her out the back door. He walked over to a nearby tree and bent over, throwing up violently. He then started sucking in deep breaths of air.

'Sorry, that smell,' Charlie said, still hunched over. 'I haven't got used to it yet.'

'You won't, either. We'd best get on the phone and tell the DI, Forensics and the pathologist. I'll call Rob. Can you call Forensics?' She pulled out her phone and looked down at the screen. She had no coverage.

'I haven't got a signal. You?'

'I've got nothing either.'

'Can you get Forensics and the pathologist on the radio? Also, get some local uniforms up here to guard the scene until they all get here.' Charlie set off towards the car.

Zoe kept her mouth closed, glancing at the sky, trying to compose herself. Her frustration was boiling over and she wanted to scream. With Ivan dead, everything just became much harder.

They drove for ten minutes before they got phone coverage again.

Zoe immediately phoned the DI.

'Hi, Zoe, How'd you go?' asked Rob.

'Not great. Ivan's dead. Overdose. Needle was next to him in the bath. Looks like he's been dead a few days. I'd say he bolted from Portsea and went to the old family cabin. He could have been there for years if Anjali hadn't found the cabin.'

'Fuck.'

'Yeah. Now we have nothing physically linking Ivan to any of the murders. It's all just circumstantial. We couldn't find his computer anywhere in the cabin.'

'Where are you now? Still in Three Bridges?'

'No, we're on our way back, coming up towards Yarra Junction. The local police are guarding the scene until the pathologist and Forensics arrive. I want to get to Ivan's brother and let him know face to face. He'll need to ID him.'

It was almost two when they arrived back in the city. They drove straight to the Department of Justice offices in Exhibition Street.

'Harry's back,' the receptionist said, grinning over the top of the counter. Her smile faded when she saw Zoe's and Charlie's expressions. 'Are you looking for Marko?'

Zoe nodded.

The receptionist picked up the phone. 'Marko, the detectives—' she said before looking at the phone. 'I think he's coming straight out.'

Marko appeared through a door. 'Did you find him?'

Zoe could hear the hope in his voice. 'Can we chat privately?' she asked.

'Yes, yes. Please.' He rushed back to the door, opening it for them. 'Same office as last time.'

They walked into Marko's office. He shut the door. 'Have you found him? Ivan. Have you spoken to him?'

'Take a seat, Mr Raddich,' said Charlie.

Marko eyed them suspiciously and sat. 'What's happened?'

'I'm sorry to say we have some bad news for you.' Zoe paused. 'We have found what we believe to be Ivan's body in a cabin. It looks like it has been there several days.'

Marko put his face in his hands. He started to rock, forwards and backwards. 'No, no, no,' he whispered.

'We're sorry for your loss,' said Charlie.

Marko sucked in three quick breaths. 'You said he was in a cabin. Where?'

Zoe gave him an incredulous look. 'At your family's cabin, outside Three Bridges.'

'Bloody hell, the cabin. How'd you find that? I haven't thought about that place in years. Dad bought it after we moved to Noble Park.'

'When were you last there, Marko?'

'At the cabin? It would be over twenty years ago. At least. Ivan and I used to go with Dad sometimes. We'd leave after he shut the shop up at lunchtime on a Saturday and spend the weekend up there in the forest. I went once after Dad died, but it was weird without him there.' Marko looked down at the floor, shaking his head, as if lost in his thoughts. 'Who owns it now?'

'What? You do,' said Zoe. 'You and Ivan.'

'No, Mum sold it. I remember her telling me. Was at the same time she decided to sell the fruit shop. Ivan was all cut up about it. It was one of the reasons we grew apart. It became kind of a wedge between us. Everything was changing too fast for him, with Dad dying and the shop getting sold.'

'There's no record of the property changing hands,' said Charlie.

'Fuck...and, what, Ivan was living there?'

'We're not sure. We will find out, but we believe that he's been paying the rates notices every year, even though they are still in your dad's name. There is a fairly new solar system and battery. The place is completely off the grid. Tank water, the lot.'

'I feel like...I don't know what,' said Marko. 'This is all very confusing.'

'We will need you to come in soon to identify Ivan's body,' said Zoe. 'It may be later this afternoon or tonight.'

Marko sucked in a deep breath before responding. 'Of course. When I heard you were here, I thought that you'd found him and we'd be able to catch up and...I don't know, reconnect. I've been thinking a lot about him since you were here. It would've been good to get close to him again. I can't believe he's dead.' Marko leaned forward and started sobbing into his hands.

'Is there anyone we can call for you? Your wife or a friend?' said Charlie.

'No, I'm not married. I'll be okay. So, what happens now? I'll have to arrange a funeral...Shit, how do you do that?'

'Just take things one step at a time,' said Zoe. 'We'll call you about the identification. Once that is done, call a funeral director and they'll be able to help you make arrangements. Okay?' She looked down at Harry, who wagged his tail slightly, looking up at her.

'We'll be in touch,' said Zoe, standing. She nodded at Charlie, who followed her and Harry out of the room.

In the elevator, Zoe turned to Charlie. 'We've got another problem.'

2.45 PM, FRIDAY 14 FEBRUARY

'What problem?' asked Charlie, as the elevator descended.

'Harry didn't react.'

'What do you mean?'

'When Marko started crying, Harry just sat there. He reacts to emotions. Mine especially, but if someone is upset, his instinct is to comfort them. Marko was bawling and Harry didn't flinch. So it makes me wonder if Marko was faking it.'

'I understand that, but Harry's reaction isn't evidence,' said Charlie. 'You know, if he hasn't been close to his brother for years, maybe he was laying it on thick because he thought that not reacting would look weird to us.'

'Maybe, but it still feels wrong to me. The other thing he said—how he didn't have the first clue about organising a funeral. He would have helped to arrange his parents' funerals. Ivan doesn't sound like the most organised person, so Marko would surely have been involved. Why would he say that he had no clue about what to do?'

'That was a long time ago and he's in shock. Are you sure we aren't just grasping here, now that we missed catching Ivan?' asked Charlie. 'I mean, we know Marko was up in the mountains when Ray Carlson was killed so he had nothing to do with Ivan's crime.'

'I dunno. All I know is that it didn't feel right to me.'

They reached the ground floor and Zoe pulled out her phone, dialling Anjali as she walked.

'Anjali, can you do me a favour?'

'Sure, shoot.'

'Can you rerun the data analysis of Marko's trip to Mount Baw Baw? See if he went past Yarra Junction on the way. There'll be a phone tower in town that he would have pinged if he passed through. It's probably the closest to the cabin.'

'On it,' said Anjali.

Marko was still dressed in his clothes from work. Zoe had called him at 8 pm to say that they could do the formal identification of Ivan's body the next morning. He had asked to do it at once. He'd wanted to get it over with, he said.

Zoe and Harry were in front of the morgue in South Melbourne when Marko approached. He was shaking slightly and looked pale.

'Are you going to be okay to do this?' she asked.

'Yeah, it's not something I ever thought...' His voice trailed off.

'I understand.'

An attendant met them and led them to the viewing area. Marko and Zoe stood in front of a window, with a curtain on the other side of the glass. The curtain was pulled back and they saw the body lying under a white sheet. Marko jerked. Zoe nodded and the attendant pulled back the sheet, uncovering Ivan's face.

Zoe watched Marko. At first he looked confused, then his face contorted. He shut his eyes, and then rested his forehead against the glass.

'Is that your brother, Ivan Raddich?'

Marko swallowed. 'Yes.'

Zoe nodded again to the attendant, who pulled the sheet back over Ivan and then closed the curtain.

'Why...why does he look like that?' stammered Marko.

'What do you mean?'

'The colour. His skin's all grey.'

'He'd been there a few days before we found him and it has been hot. I'm sorry you had to see him like that.' She looked down at Harry, who was sitting calmly beside her.

7.30 AM, SATURDAY 15 FEBRUARY

Marie Harley stood defiantly at the front door in her pyjamas, reluctant to pass over the USB stick. Once Zoe told her that she could be arrested for receiving stolen goods, her mother stepped in and told Zoe she could take it.

Zoe stopped off at the beach at McCrae to let Harry have a swim, texting Anjali to let her know she'd need to analyse the USB first thing Monday morning. Out in front of her, Zoe watched as Harry swam in the crystal blue water of Port Phillip Bay. Two minutes later, her phone buzzed.

'Morning Anjali,' she said. 'Sorry to bother you on a Saturday.'

'No worries. Is this the USB that Ivan Raddich used to deliver the malware?'

'I believe so. I just retrieved it from Dwayne Harley's daughter. I'm certain we'll find the same malware that you found on Ray Carlson's computer. And we need to find Ivan's computer. Anyway, I don't want to wreck your weekend. I'll see you Monday and you can look at it then.'

'Are you going into the office today?' asked Anjali.

'Yes, I'm driving in now.'

'I'll be there when you arrive.'

Zoe smiled. 'Thanks. I should be back in just over an hour.'

There were about ten detectives working when Zoe and Harry walked into the Homicide office. She suddenly felt a bit underdressed in her jeans and t-shirt.

Anjali came into the squad room. 'You got it?'

'Yes, it's here,' said Zoe, holding the evidence bag out.

'Fingerprints?'

'I wouldn't waste your time,' said Zoe. 'That USB has been passed around the Harley girl's high school for months now. The original prints, even if he left any, are well and truly gone.'

'Okay, I'll start analysing the files using a PC that's not online or connected to our server. I'd hate to open a door into this place for hackers.'

'Good thinking,' said Zoe, who knew that she might well have gone searching through the USB on her own networked laptop before considering the ramifications.

'Give me thirty minutes, okay?'

'No worries,' said Zoe, walking to her desk. She sat as Harry wandered under the desk and lay down. Zoe knew that time was against her. She cupped her face in her hands. Harry lifted his head and laid it on her foot.

Her phone buzzed. Sarah Westbrook. *Hey, weren't we going to have coffee? Lol.*

Zoe grinned and dialled.

'Hey there,' said Sarah.

'How are you feeling?'

'Sometimes I feel like I've been hit by a car. Other times I feel like I am floating. Depends on when they give me drugs.' Sarah giggled.

Zoe guessed she was currently floating. 'What's the damage?'

'Two broken ribs, fractured right leg—plus plenty of scrapes and cuts. I laughed when they told me I was lucky.'

'I'll bet. When are you getting out?'

'Tomorrow, I hope. Told them I need to be in court Monday morning. They said, we'll see. And I said, yes, we will.' Sarah was almost singing the last part.

'Well, I'll find you there,' said Zoe. 'Hey, what was the information you wanted to tell me?'

'I can't remember. I'd have written it down…I'll have a look and let you know if I find it.'

'All right, take care,' said Zoe, 'and make sure they give you the good stuff, eh?'

'No doubt, no doubt at all. Bye-de-bye,' said Sarah.

The line went dead. Zoe smiled, glad that Sarah was recovering well.

A moment later she heard the door swing open and bang hard against the doorstop. Iain and Garry walked in, an air of triumph about them. They grinned in unison when they saw her.

'Perfect,' said Iain. 'Good news. Trevor Hill confessed in full last night to his cellmate. Said he'd stabbed Eric Drum and was happy he was dead. We took his cellmate's statement this morning. Sally Johnstone is thrilled. Positively buzzing. Looks like we'll be able to repair our relationship with the DPP after all.'

'What'd you offer the cellmate?' Zoe asked.

'Come on, Zoe, don't be like that,' said Iain, his voice dripping with sarcasm. 'The confession is good news for everyone. You included. It means that three killers won't be set loose based on your crazy conspiracy theory. You might even save your career. Maybe.'

'If you two are running around offering inducements to prison snitches and you push through a wrongful conviction, how are you going to live with yourselves?'

Zoe knew she'd hit a nerve. There was a look of cold determination Iain's eyes.

'If you want to accuse us of something,' he said, 'feel free to call Professional Standards. It'll give them a nice insight into a detective who has lost the plot.'

Zoe narrowed her eyes, setting her jaw tight. 'Gillies, you're a fucking coward,' she said.

Iain wheeled back, instantly flaring up. 'What did you say to me?'

Zoe noticed Garry step to one side, out of the line of fire.

'You heard me,' said Zoe. 'It's not my fault you chose to run away that day.'

'What are you talking about?'

'Don't give me that crap. You shoulder-charged me, *running away*.'

Iain opened his mouth to respond. Zoe could see the veins on his neck pumping. She knew he had no comeback.

'But I don't actually blame you for running,' she continued. 'That's a survival mechanism. What I blame you for is hating me for *not* running. That's why you're a coward. You're trying to destroy me because you're ashamed.'

'Screw you, Mayer. I'm going to make an official complaint and get you chucked out of here. You and your bloody therapy dog. For good, this time.' He spun around and made for the door.

Garry hesitated, not sure what to do.

'Go on, you run off too. Help Iain with the creative parts of his complaint.'

Garry glanced up at her, before he looked away again, turning to follow Iain.

Harry, still lying down, was watching her intently. Zoe realised the exchange had not made her anxious. She gave Harry a grin, then spotted Anjali standing frozen in the corner.

'You okay?' asked Anjali.

'Yeah, no problem.'

'I don't think I've ever seen someone that angry. I thought he was going to keel over.'

'Sorry about that. I promised myself I wasn't ever going to mention what went on with him that day. Best forget you heard it. Anyhow, what did you find on the USB?'

'The malware is there, buried in one of the folders. Ivan hid an old Yugoslavian movie from the 1960s among about twenty new movies. Doesn't even have subtitles. I guess he thought no one would bother looking too closely at it.'

'Ivan liked to amuse himself, didn't he?'

'I doubt he thought we'd get this close,' Anjali said, 'but this is good news. We've got proof that...' She stopped short.

'Exactly. We have proof that Ivan was spying on Ray's and Dwayne's computers, but that's not proof of him killing Ray. It's not enough.'

Anjali opened her folder. 'I've got other news. I've been over the metadata from the phone tower near Yarra Junction. Marko didn't pass through the town, according to his phone data. I checked the other most likely route he might have taken, going through Drouin, and the tower data shows him passing through on the way there and on the way home.'

'Well, okay, but doesn't that just back up Marko's story?'

'Sorry, there's more,' said Anjali. 'I also found two other phone numbers that passed through at the exact same time as Marko, on the way there *and* the way back. The only reason...'

'...would be if they were all in the same car,' said Zoe. 'Marko didn't mention going with anyone else. Can we trace the numbers?'

'Already done,' said Anjali. 'The numbers belong to William and Mary Rogers, a couple from Bentleigh. I've got their details here.' She held out a piece of paper. 'One other thing—they live next door to Marko.'

'Anj, you're a legend,' said Zoe, grabbing her arm. She looked down at Harry. 'Let's go.' She called Charlie on her way to the elevator.

Zoe parked a few doors away from the house, down a slight incline. Charlie was already getting out of his car. They walked up to a neat 1940s art deco house with a row of white roses along the front fence. The scent reminded Zoe of her grandmother. Charlie rang the bell before taking a step back.

A fit-looking woman in her sixties answered, her neat grey hair cut just above her shoulders. 'Hello,' she said cheerfully. She smiled at Harry. His tail wagged in response.

'Mrs Rogers?'

'Yes, call me Mary, please.'

'Detectives Mayer and Shaw,' said Zoe, holding up her badge. 'And Harry. Can we have a word?'

'Oh, come in,' she said, looking flustered. 'Is everything okay?'

'Just some general enquiries. Is it okay to bring Harry in?'

'Of course, we love dogs here. What a beautiful boy.'

Zoe, Harry and Charlie walked into the living room. A man was standing next to a sofa, looking perplexed. Around six foot tall, with hair cut short, he had the bearing of a military officer. He wore fawn-coloured slacks and a blue polo shirt with a golf club insignia.

'This is my husband, William.' They shook hands and everyone sat down. Harry sat next to the sofa at Zoe's feet.

'We believe you took a trip between Saturday the first of February and Sunday the ninth—is that right?'

'Yes,' said William. 'Were we speeding or something?'

'No, nothing like that. Tell me, who did you travel with?'

'No one, it was just the two of us,' said Mary. 'We do

the same trip every year. We have some friends from Gippsland and we meet them each year for a week or so. Camping and bushwalking up at Mount Baw Baw.'

'Sorry, I heard that your neighbour, Marko Raddich, went with you,' said Zoe.

'Marko? No, he didn't come with us. Who said that?'

'Ah, we must have our wires crossed. Someone up the road thought he'd gone with you,' said Zoe, feigning confusion.

'I mean, Marko is a good friend of ours. He helps us if we need a hand with something around the garden. He even helped us pack the car for the trip.' Mary started to laugh. 'That's it—someone must have seen the three of us loading stuff into the car and assumed he was going with us. But no, Marko didn't come.'

Zoe was trying to appear calm, but her heart was pumping. Harry turned his head towards her. 'Does Marko live alone? I believe he's got a brother?'

'I didn't know that,' said Mary, looking across at her husband, who was shaking his head. 'He's never mentioned having a brother. He lives alone. Doesn't really socialise much, what with his big job with the government and all. No time for a girlfriend. He's away a fair bit for his job, interstate for months on end sometimes. We keep an eye on his place when he's away. William mows his lawns, that sort of thing.'

'Sorry to have troubled you,' said Zoe. 'We'll push on. Thanks for clearing that up.' She stood up, causing everyone else to do the same.

'But what's all this about? Is Marko in trouble or something?' asked William.

'No, there was a burglary in the next street and we are just trying to work out who was around at the time. We've been talking to other people in the street. That's where I got my bad information. Nothing to worry about. The suspect's in custody,' lied Zoe.

'Oh, okay, that's good. Thanks for everything you do,' said Mary.

They said their goodbyes and walked out onto the footpath. Zoe glanced up towards Marko's house. Her phone buzzed.

'Mayer.'

'Zoe, it's Oliver Nunan from the morgue. We started working on Ivan Raddich's body and there's something strange going on. He did die from a heroin overdose, but not recently. His body has been frozen. When you found him in the bath, he had been defrosting for at least four days. He's probably been dead for years.'

Zoe stopped. Charlie turned and stared at her.

'Zoe, you there?' said Oliver.

'Yeah, sorry. Do you know where he died?'

'I'd say he died in the bath, where you found him. The *livor mortis*, you know, where the blood pools after death, is consistent with him dying exactly the way you found him, but I think he was moved later when rigor had set in and his body was stiff. He was frozen and then he was moved back to the same place, probably four or five days ago.'

'Oh, god. How sure are you about this?'

'The frozen part? A hundred per cent. Freezing changes the cell structure through expansion and crystallisation.'

'Thanks, Oliver.'

Zoe looked at Charlie. 'It's Marko,' she said. Then she took off.

'Wait, what?' asked Charlie, but Zoe was already metres away, running with a heavy limp towards Marko's house, Harry at her heels. Charlie took off after her.

The driveway was empty. Once they had climbed over the low fence, Zoe signalled for Harry to drop flat on the grass and to stay. She and Charlie then approached the house slowly. Zoe kept a hand on her holstered gun, watchful. She was conscious that Charlie had come straight from home, and was unarmed.

Zoe went to the front door, knocking twice, instinctively standing to the side, listening for any movement. Charlie peered into the window to the right of the door. Catching Zoe's eye, he shook his head. Zoe peered in through a gap in the curtains on the window to the left. The room was basic, with a television and two sofas. There were no pictures and no coffee table. She walked over to Charlie and saw an unmade double bed, and a wardrobe with one door open. It was stuffed with clothes. There were a number of small boxes below the clothes. Zoe strained to read the labels on the boxes.

Together they walked around the house. Zoe looked into the kitchen through the back window. A couple of dirty dishes were in the sink, but there was no sign of Marko.

They returned to the front of the house. Zoe called

Harry over to her, before peering up and down the street, hoping somehow Marko would appear.

'Okay,' said Charlie. 'You want to tell me what's happening?'

4 PM, SATURDAY 15 FEBRUARY

Zoe was in the conference room, her head in her hands. Harry lay on the floor beside her, glumly mirroring her mood.

Rob entered, followed by Anjali. 'You okay?' he asked.

'Yeah,' she said. 'Not sleeping, that's all.'

Charlie came in. 'I've checked Marko's work history. He's an independent IT contractor and has been the main guy the state government has used for cybersecurity for at least the last eight years. He's gone from one department to another on projects, each usually lasting between six and eight months. The current project is for the Department of Justice. Apparently it has got three months left to run.'

'So he can change his appearance,' said Zoe, 'and people don't really notice because he's moving between departments, working with different groups.'

'That's right,' replied Charlie.

'Speaking of changing appearances,' said Rob, 'you met Marko at the Department of Justice soon after you met Greg

Enders on the peninsula. Didn't you suspect they could have been the same person then?'

'Marko resembled him,' said Zoe, 'but Enders looked a good three inches shorter, and had brown eyes. Marko's were blue.'

'How'd he manage all that?'

'Enders was slouched, neck bent, apparently because of a work accident. Then, today, through Marko's bedroom window, I saw boxes containing lifts—inserts to put in your shoes to give you more height. Plus, Marko had cut his hair and cleaned himself up when we saw him at the DoJ offices.'

'Okay,' said Rob. 'And the eye colour?'

'Coloured contact lenses. I overheard Garry Burns whining to Iain Gillies about his girlfriend wearing them.'

Charlie opened his folder. 'I also found out that he managed a big IT overhaul at VicRoads about four years ago. That's how he was able to create his false identities so easily. He knew the back end of their system, so he was able to produce as many driver's licences as he wanted, whenever he wanted. He still has access. He'd log in and enter his new details, upload a photo, and the system would automatically create and send him out a new licence.'

'Any idea what he's earning for this work?' asked Zoe.

'Based on what he's charging the DoJ, I'd guess it's well over half a million a year,' said Charlie.

'Now we know how he can afford six months' rent in advance on these properties.'

'Okay,' said Rob. 'Catch me up on your current thinking.'

'Right,' said Zoe, 'here's the chronology. After the

parents die, Ivan, who's already dysfunctional from being bullied at school, goes off the rails and gets involved in drugs. He dies from a heroin overdose at the family cabin at Three Bridges, probably around four years ago. Despite what Marko told us, I believe that the two brothers had remained close. Marko worries when he can't contact Ivan, goes to the cabin and finds his body. He decides to avenge Ivan's death, blaming the kids who bullied him and stuffed up his life.'

Zoe looked up at the photographs of the three victims lined up on the whiteboard. 'The way he sees it, there are three pairs of bullies to deal with and he decides he'll take out one pair per year. Marko puts his brother's body in the large freezer in the cabin. It's an insurance policy to use if we ever got too close to the truth. Marko finds the old school bullies using the VicRoads licence database and decides the order in which to deal with them. No one recognises him—he was a couple of years below them at school. He commutes to his job as normal, having gradually changed his look, growing his beard or his hair. He inches his way into each community, making friends, buying beers and handing out pirated movies. He uses malware to spy on them, and also finds a way to steal clothing from the person he's going to frame, so he can plant it as evidence. Then one day he kills one of them and sets about framing the other, whom we arrest and charge. Easy—two birds, one stone. One bully dies; the other does twenty years. And he gives himself an alibi.'

'How's that?' asked Rob.

'The neighbours take holidays every year in February,' said Zoe. 'He plants his silenced phone in their car, probably stuffed up underneath their car seat, and they head off on their trip unaware. He knew we could check the pings from the phone towers, just in case we somehow linked him to all this, and that gives him the perfect alibi. He takes time off work and tells everyone that he's going hiking in the mountains and will be out of contact. Then he does the killing and is around all week while we're investigating, in disguise and under his assumed name, acting as the concerned friend, all the while calling in tips, planting evidence and waiting.'

'And then he retrieves his phone when they return,' said Charlie.

'He thinks the chances of us linking him to this are maybe one in a thousand, but he creates the alibi, just in case. Then when his neighbours return, he helps them again, gets his phone back and then listens to the story of their trip. If he ever needs to, Marko can give a detailed account of a hiking holiday, even describing the weather.'

'The guy's a fricken genius,' mumbled Charlie.

'Yeah,' agreed Zoe, 'he thought of almost everything. The only thing he didn't count on was Anjali searching for other phones pinging in sync with his phone.'

Rob turned to Anjali, sitting off to the side. 'That's great work, Anjali. Well done.'

Anjali half nodded, blushing and looking down. 'Thank you,' she said.

'The other failsafe Marko had was Ivan's frozen body. After Ray Carlson was killed, Marko would have headed out to the cabin, pulled his brother out of the freezer and put him back in the bath where he first found him. Ivan would thaw out over a couple of days. We'd eventually find out about the cabin—perhaps Marko would suddenly *remember* the cabin in a month or so and tell us himself—and go and find a decomposed brother who only looked recently deceased. Not the four years he's actually been dead. The only thing he misjudged is that we found Ivan's body too soon. After another few weeks of this heat, his body would have been too decomposed for us to determine that it had been frozen.'

'Seems disrespectful to his brother. Leaving him out there rotting in a bathtub,' said Rob.

'It was the cost of Marko's war against Ivan's bullies,' said Zoe. 'Don't forget, Marko found his body in the first place, so he knew that otherwise it would've been out there rotting anyway. Probably saw it as Ivan's contribution to getting even with the past.'

'It all works as a theory,' said Rob, 'but we need to find him and his computer. The DPP won't want to know about any of this unless we've got a living, breathing criminal to put away.'

'I've got surveillance watching Marko's house. If he turns up there, they'll call me.'

'What about the neighbours? Might they tip him off?'

'I spoke to them again before I left,' said Zoe. 'Told them that we were looking for Marko with regard to a homicide and to not tip him off, but to call me if they heard anything. The husband used to work as a prosecutor in Canberra. They'll be fine.'

'Should we put out an alert for him? Start speaking to his colleagues at work?' asked Charlie.

'No,' said Zoe. 'If he gets wind that we're looking

for him, he'll be gone. He'll have a stack of licences with different versions of himself. This guy's too organised. He'll have contingencies in place.'

'Have you thought about the possibility that he's started working on another target?' said Rob. 'Maybe he's already in some other town, preparing.'

'Maybe, but after school Ivan went to work with his dad at their fruit shop,' said Zoe. 'If Marko has a vendetta against someone else, it won't be to do with a high school Ivan attended.'

Charlie spoke up. 'Plus, I'd say him putting Ivan's body back in the bath tells us that he's taken care of everyone on his list.'

Rob nodded. 'Okay, let's hope he either goes to work on Monday or shows up at Trevor Hill's trial. We can pick him up at either place.'

'I hope it's that easy,' said Zoe. 'I need a warrant to search his house and his office. He may have kept his personal computer at work. I also want to get a warrant to triangulate his phone to at least tell us the area he is in. That'll be better than nothing.'

'Leave the warrants with me,' said Rob. 'I'll try and yank some strings.'

'Thanks, the sooner the better,' said Zoe.

Rob stood up.

'I think we have another problem,' said Anjali softly from the end of the table.

They all turned to her. Anjali was staring at the screen of her laptop.

'What is it?' asked Zoe.

'I...I think someone's been in the case file archives, deleting stuff.'

Zoe moved around behind Anjali. Over her shoulder, she could see the open folders for all three cases.

'The sub-folders containing the images and video from the funerals,' said Anjali. 'They're all gone.'

Rob sat down again. 'Charlie, give me your laptop for a second?'

Charlie passed it across. Rob quickly logged himself in. Everyone sat in silence as he worked. After thirty seconds, he looked up. 'The sub-folders are in the back-up. Those files can't be deleted without a higher clearance. I can view them, but I can't trash them. Good news is that we'll be able to get them back.'

'And I took a copy of all the folders on a USB,' said Zoe. 'I can restore them later. But who deleted them?' She felt the heat rise in her face. *Tom was with Sally. Did he tell her about the notes he'd seen the morning he found me asleep at the dining-room table? Did Sally find someone—someone with a vested interest—to delete the evidence? Iain? Garry?*

'Zoe, you okay?' asked Rob.

Zoe shook her head. 'Sorry, I was miles away. Anjali, can you work some magic and trace who deleted the files?'

'I can try,' said Anjali.

Zoe exhaled. 'It's an inside job,' she said finally.

10 AM, SUNDAY 16 FEBRUARY

Zoe lay on her couch, staring at the white ceiling. How could they find Marko and his computer? His house was under surveillance. She'd spoken to the morgue in case Marko contacted them about collecting Ivan's body for burial. She'd had the data log for the Department of Justice offices checked—neither Marko nor anyone else had entered or left the office since late Friday.

Harry was fast asleep on his back beside the couch, his legs in the air. They had been on two walks to the park already. She grabbed the remote and turned on the television. She flicked through the channels, past sitcom repeats, sports wrap-ups and shopping channels, until she stopped on a nature documentary. The screen was filled with kangaroos on the edge of a rainforest.

Zoe sat upright, staring at the screen, energised. 'Harry, wake up, we've got to go.'

She grabbed her phone and called Charlie.

It was just before noon when she parked outside the supermarket in Yarra Junction. She looked at her watch, checking her side mirror for any sign of Charlie. A minute later her phone buzzed.

'Charlie, where are you?'

'I was almost there when I got a tip that the witness in one of my other cases, that DV homicide in Toorak, has popped up having brunch at a cafe in Malvern. I'm on the way there now. Can you get a couple of the local uniformed officers to assist? I'll be tied up with this witness for a few hours. Sorry, Zoe.'

'Don't sweat it. Do what you need to do,' she said, trying to hide her disappointment. 'Good luck with it.'

'You be okay getting some local uniforms to help?' he asked.

'Yeah, all good,' she said.

Zoe drove slowly up Mount Bride Road into the rainforest. She'd decided to take a look and then radio for back-up if she needed it. She thought that Marko was too smart to be hiding out in the cabin, but she knew it would be a good hiding place for his computer. In the roof cavity. Or under the floor.

With the overhanging rainforest darkening the winding road, Zoe felt her stomach tighten. She hadn't seen another car since Yarra Junction. She could feel her quickened pulse throbbing through her injured leg. She slowed her breathing down to get her heart rate under control. Harry sat in the back, studying her reflection in the rear-view mirror.

Zoe saw the small opening to the left, half obscured by gigantic ferns fanning the entrance, and she coasted onto the rough dirt track. She turned off the engine and the car rolled silently to a stop. She opened her window. Apart from the birds singing in the trees, there was no other sound.

The cabin was a hundred metres down the track. Zoe got out of the car, leaning against her door to shut it quietly. By force of habit she felt for her gun in its holster, and then opened the back door. Harry stared at her hesitantly, sensing her anxiety. 'It's okay,' she whispered. 'We're just going to have a look, that's all. Let's go.'

Harry jumped down and stood at her side, his tail down. Zoe pushed the door shut.

With a hand on her still-holstered gun, she walked cautiously along the side of the track, Harry in tow. Her leg was causing her pain. Every ten metres she would stop, listening for unusual sounds. Harry kept pace, stopping whenever she stopped. There was nothing. The cabin wasn't yet visible through the forest.

They'd walked a few more metres when a branch cracked to her right. She spun and drew her gun, levelling it in the direction of the sound. A small grey kangaroo stood blinking at her before bouncing away through the undergrowth. Zoe shook her head, looking back towards the cabin. 'Come on,' she whispered to Harry.

As they got closer, Zoe started to bend at the waist, her weapon still in her hand. The track began to widen into the clearing in front of the cabin. Once again, she stopped and listened. Nothing.

Zoe walked off the track towards the giant ferns growing near the clearing. Harry followed as she found cover beneath an ancient tree, its base the width of a car. Edging around the trunk, Zoe peered at the cabin. There were no signs of life. Everything seemed to be the same as when they'd found Ivan's body. She made her way through the bush until she was directly across from the windowless side of the cabin.

'Wait,' she said to Harry, before gesturing to him to lie down. 'Stay.'

Zoe walked alone into the clearing, gun raised. Facing the cabin, she walked around to the back. The area was clear. She waited, considering her next move. A kookaburra startled her by breaking into its long cackling song. *It's probably laughing at how recklessly stupid I am.* She walked backwards a few metres, out of the clearing and into the large ferns. Switching her gun into her left hand, she reached down and picked up a fist-sized rock. She stood up, wincing as pain shot through her injured leg.

Harry was lying still where she'd left him. He was watching her intently, head tilted. Zoe tossed the rock high towards the cabin. She swapped her gun back into her right hand just as the rock crashed onto the corrugated iron roof. Zoe waited, listening intently for any sound. Nothing. She breathed out, unsure whether she was relieved or disappointed.

Training her gun on the back door, she walked into the clearing. She reached the cabin and found the back door unlocked, just as it was when she and Charlie discovered Ivan's body. She called Harry over and told him to sit outside the door. She opened it quietly and ducked under the blue-and-white police tape that was stuck across the doorway. Her finger remained on the trigger, ready. The odour of death lingered. Going from room to room, she found the cabin empty. She checked the fridge, which was on. There was nothing in it.

Her eyes moved to the large freezer. It remained unplugged. She walked over, raising her gun in readiness. In one motion she lifted the lid and thrust the gun into the freezer space. It was empty.

Zoe went from room to room, looking up at the ceiling, searching for an access panel. She found it in the bedroom. She grabbed a rickety chair from the living area, dragged it into the bedroom and stood on it. As she pushed the cover out of the way, Zoe felt a surge of anticipation. Reaching up with both hands, she pulled herself up into the darkened roof space.

Zoe sat on the edge, her legs hanging down from the ceiling, and used her phone to light up the area. Cobwebs hung between beams. She spun around, searching. Nothing. She pointed the phone's light down around the entrance. All she could see were her own handprints in the thick dust. *Shit.*

Zoe spent another fruitless hour checking beneath the floorboards in the cabin, before she decided to head back. She was driving along a hedge-lined road through Gladysdale when her phone picked up a signal and buzzed that she had a voice message. She pulled over to play it.

'Hello...Detective...My name's Serge. You spoke to me at the pub after Ray was killed. Anyway, you told me to call you if I thought of anything else. Look, I don't know...maybe it's nothing, but I am in Warburton visiting family and I saw Greg Enders. I went up to say hi, but he told me I was mistaken. He had sunnies on, but it was him. His car's got a deep scratch near the fuel cap and I remember seeing it at the footy club. Anyway, it was definitely him. I thought that was bloody odd, especially seeing how nice he'd always been. My missus said to call you about it. Anyway, all the best.'

The line went dead.

Zoe went over her memories from interviewing people at the hotel until she could picture Serge. Older man. Short and stocky. Faded Italian accent. Firm handshake. Yes, that was him. She called him back. He answered after two rings.

'Serge, it's Detective Mayer. I got your message. Thanks for calling.'

'No problem. I don't know if it's even relevant, but it was just that Greg was always friendly. Anyhow, today he stared at me like I'm a lunatic. Told me he's not Greg. I just thought it was odd.'

'What sort of car was he in?'

'Blue Camry. Fairly new. Probably only a year old. I got the rego.'

Blue Camry.

'Great,' said Zoe, reaching for a pen. 'Go for it.'

'ELP 886.'

'Thanks. Where was the car?'

'In the main street. There's a tourism info building there—got a big waterwheel on the side of it—he's parked outside of it right now.'

'What? Are you still there?' asked Zoe.

'Yeah, I'm parked down the road a bit. Thought I'd keep an eye on him until you called back.'

Zoe felt a rush of appreciation for the man. 'That's fantastic, Serge. You've done a great job. Don't approach him again. I'll be there in ten minutes.' She said goodbye and turned on her siren. 'Harry, lie down.'

Slowing as she rolled into Warburton's main street, Zoe turned off her siren and the flashing lights hidden behind the car's grille. The town was surrounded by forested mountains that towered above it. In the distance she could see a large plume of smoke, no doubt from a bushfire. At the far end of the street a fire truck was driving off towards the fire, its red-and-blue lights flashing. The street was busy and she scanned it for Marko and his car. On her right, she saw the waterwheel turning at the side of the tourism office. The blue Camry was there, parked on her side of the road. Further on, a late-model Ford pulled out and did a quick u-turn, travelling away from them. *Thanks, Serge.*

She decided to drive past and confirm it was Marko before she called in the cavalry. As she approached, the blue Camry darted out and sped off. She instinctively turned on her lights and siren as she started her pursuit. She concentrated on the road for half a kilometre until she reached the outskirts of town, then grabbed her radio to call in for assistance. It was dead. She tried again. Nothing.

She sped up. 'Harry, lie down,' she said, keeping her eyes on the road. Harry lay flat in the back. 'Stay.'

They were headed up a winding road. Marko drove wildly, cutting corners. Victoria Police policy was to abandon dangerous pursuits, but without a radio she couldn't organise local officers to block the road ahead. Something told her this was her last chance to catch Marko.

Watching him take another bend, she reached into her pocket and pulled out her phone. She glanced at the screen before a truck flashed past her. She fumbled the phone and it fell down between the seats. *Shit.*

They came to a stretch of relatively straight road and Zoe tried the radio again. Nothing. *What the fuck is happening?*

Marko pulled off sharply onto a dirt road. Zoe was thirty metres behind. The fine dust thrown up by the Camry made it hard to see and she bounced in and out of potholes, causing the car to lurch across the road as she went. To her left, a large family of grey kangaroos bounced away into the bush, fleeing the noise of the siren. A secondary track loomed up on the left. Marko swung the Camry onto it at the last moment, the back end of his car sliding out. There was a No Through Road sign. She slowed to a stop, and parked her SUV diagonally across the track, blocking it. She turned off the siren, leaving the red-and-blue lights flashing on her front grille and back window. She tried the police radio again. Nothing. She checked the lights on the radio. Everything looked normal. She reached around under the seat and found her phone.

She got out of the car and listened. In the distance she could hear sirens competing with each other as they raced towards the bushfire. She glanced down at her phone. No coverage. She looked at the dense forest surrounding her and the mountains towering above. Only then did she notice the haze of the smoke in the air, being blown down the track as if following in Marko's wake.

Zoe thought about leaving Harry in the car, but decided it was too risky. Marko could try and make a run for it and smash into her car. 'Harry, let's go,' she said, opening the back. She knew that Marko pulling off here was no mistake. *He wants a confrontation.* She drew her gun and walked slowly along the track for a few metres, feeling completely exposed. She could feel her anxiety levels surging. All around her was lush rainforest, with large ferns the size of cars. She listened hard but, apart from the birds, she could only hear her own breathing.

Zoe walked a few metres into the rainforest to give herself some cover as she followed the track off to her right, Harry alongside her. She could see around the trees and ferns for about fifty metres ahead, but there were thousands of places Marko could be hiding, waiting to ambush her. Her leg began to throb again. She could now smell smoke. She walked as quickly as she could without making noise, stopping every twenty metres to listen. Then she would do the same thing again, edging her way alongside the track she could now barely see.

Zoe had travelled about a hundred metres when she felt another great wave of anxiety surge through her. Her vision flickered and she felt a huge weight on her chest. A massive firefighting helicopter roared low overhead, its tanks filled with water, blades thumping the air. Zoe fell to her knees, and her world turned black.

The sound was bouncing off the curved concrete wall of the stadium. Zoe looked up at the hovering black police drone. But this was a different sound, higher pitched. Then she saw it. Another drone was flying in from the northwest, over the parkland, headed directly towards the packed Melbourne Cricket Ground. It was silver and smaller.

Zoe felt her stomach tighten. Oh, fuck.

She grabbed at the microphone in her sleeve. 'Silver drone flying in from the north. Approximately a hundred and fifty metres elevation.' Her voice was desperate and loud.

A second later, Zoe heard a single gunshot. Distant. High-calibre. Sniper.

'Suspect down. Suspect down,' she heard through the earpiece.

Above them, the drone gave off a sudden screeching sound. Its propellers stopped. People were looking up and pointing. Zoe saw the drone wobble as it lost momentum.

The now silent device began to fall.

People began to scatter in all directions. In the chaos, Zoe judged that the drone would hit the ground about ten metres from her. Iain was directly beneath it, staring up at the device.

Before Iain had even begun to run away, Zoe knew what was going to happen. She burst forward, sprinting. Her eyes were fixed on the drone, as it fell like a stone. In her peripheral vision, at the last moment, she saw the solid mass of Iain, who was about to collide with her as he ran for his life. She stepped to the side just as his shoulder hit hers, jolting her sideways.

Time seemed to slow and everything went quiet inside Zoe's head. There was just one goal. Keeping her eye on the drone, she dived forward and caught it at waist level. It was small, about half the width of her shoulders. Iain had vanished.

She tightened her grip on it as her body was about to hit the concrete. Don't. Drop. It.

Zoe smacked into the concourse hard, her knees and elbows taking most of the impact. Crying out from the pain, she managed to keep her elbows bent and her wrists cocked through the impact. The drone stayed just off the ground. Then she felt a secondary wave of agony rush through her and she let out an involuntary scream.

A young constable in uniform ran over to her, her voice cracking in panic. 'Fuck, you okay?' she asked, crouching down beside her.

The drone had two thin glass cylinders attached to its base. Both were filled with clear liquid, which was now sloshing around.

'Yeah,' moaned Zoe, her voice wavering. 'Hey, what's your name?'

'Rachel.'

'Okay, Rachel,' said Zoe, keeping her attention fixed on the cylinders of liquid. 'I need you to clear the area. Fast.'

Zoe's body throbbed. She lay flat against the concrete, her elbows bent, arms jutting up. The drone sat dead in her hands, its four propellers still and silent.

She half expected it to come to life and take off again at any moment. It was so heavy. Under her jacket, Zoe could feel warmth and wetness around her elbows: blood.

The tremor in her hands was getting worse. She saw small waves roll back and forth in the clear liquid.

The concourse was now deserted, though she could hear the crowd, unaware, in the stadium. To her right she heard the humming sound of the bomb disposal robot speeding towards her. A male voice came from the speaker attached to it.

'Hi Zoe. I'm Joel. This will all be over soon.'

'Hi Joel. Good. I'm feeling sore.'

One of the robot's arms swivelled low. It had a camera attached to it, recording the action. The arm made a broad sweep, taking in the scene from multiple angles.

'What are we looking at here, Joel?' asked Zoe, trying to sound upbeat.

There was no answer.

The robot's arm swung away from her and up into the air. 'Just give us a sec,' said Joel, his voice solemn over the robot's radio.

'Sure, take your time,' said Zoe, deadpan. Her stomach was in knots and she could feel her heart pumping. Blood from her injured elbows had seeped through her jacket onto the concrete. The drone seemed to be increasing in weight every second. Zoe shut her eyes and tried to meditate, concentrating on controlling her breathing. The robot reversed a couple of metres. The arm with the video camera swung up and pointed straight at her, now a silent witness.

Zoe looked at the camera. 'Hey Joel. Any chance you could tell me what the fuck I'm holding?'

'We're trying to work it out. Give us a moment.'

'Great,' said Zoe, under her breath. Inside the stadium the crowd gave off a cheer.

Zoe stretched her head from side to side, trying to release the tension in her neck.

'Zoe, two members of our team are approaching from your right.'

Zoe looked under her armpit to see a man and a woman walking quickly in dull grey bomb disposal suits. Their helmets had large visors.

The man carried a small toolbox and the woman held a piece of thick foam, the size of a briefcase.

They came up close to Zoe.

'Hi Zoe. I'm Sophia. This is Richard. We're here to help.' Her voice was calm.

'Hi Sophia. What's the plan?'

Sophia got down onto her knees, hunching over so that she was at eye level with Zoe. 'I'm going to slide this foam underneath the drone and then you can put it down. Very, very gently, okay?'

'Okay.' Zoe could feel her hands trembling. She held firm. 'Don't suppose you want to tell me what this is?'

'Let's just concentrate on putting it on the foam.' Sophia slid the foam underneath the drone, so it touched Zoe's forearm.

'Okay, Zoe, lower it. Nice and slow.'

Zoe's arms felt locked in place at the elbow. She took a breath and pushed through the pain, settling the drone onto the foam. She pulled her shaking hands clear, and rolled away onto her back, gasping.

'Okay, bring in the chamber,' Sophia said into her radio.

The two bomb techs were peering at the cylinders under the drone. A couple of their colleagues approached, pulling a small trailer. On it was a domed chamber, like a portable cement mixer.

'So, what is it?' asked Zoe.

'We think it's sarin,' said Sophia.

'Fuck,' said Zoe, remembering grainy news footage of a sarin gas attack many years ago on the Tokyo subway.

'They wanted to fly it above the MCG and drop it into the crowd, but the guy piloting it by remote control was taken out by the sniper. That's why it fell early. Once those two cylinders smashed, the liquids would've combined, reacted and created a sarin gas cloud. The cloud could have killed thousands. Plus, with the stampede to get away, who knows how many more.'

Zoe felt numb. She went to push herself up but felt light-headed and slumped back down. Richard and Sophia placed the drone, still on the foam mat, into the dome chamber, before closing its door. 'We're all clear,' said Sophia into a microphone. 'We need an ambulance up here though, asap.'

Zoe felt her body start to shake. She was trying to moderate her breathing when a police helicopter swooped in above her, hovering, its blades thumping the air. The downdraft pushed her onto her back and she lay there staring up at the chopper for a second before she passed out.

—

Zoe blinked, the air was still again. She felt something pushing at her side and she jerked herself up and spun away, bringing the gun back around. Harry stood there, staring at her, whimpering softly. She had no idea how long she'd been out for.

Hugging him with her left arm, she kept her gun up, sweeping it in arcs around her.

It was too dangerous to take Harry with her. 'Lie down,' she whispered in his ear. 'Now stay. Stay.' Zoe held her hand flat. 'Good boy, I'll be back,' she said, before kissing him on the head.

She got up and went forward, stopping just before she lost sight of Harry to check he was lying in the same place. The smoke haze muted her view, giving it an eerie quality. Again she thrust her hand out flat in his direction. He reluctantly laid his head down on his paws, keeping his gaze on her.

She walked out of Harry's sight, turning from side to side. Marko could be anywhere and she had no cover. He had all the advantages.

Then she saw it through the trees. The Camry was parked downhill from her on the track. The car looked empty. She crouched down. It seemed like the perfect ambush. He wanted her to walk up to the car to check it and then he would attack. Zoe shook her head. *This guy thinks I'm an idiot.*

Zoe saw a large boulder, probably three times her height, ten metres ahead. Part of the face of it had fallen away, creating an overhang. She moved to it, low to the ground. With the rock behind her she had some protection. Marko could only attack her from the front.

She knew that he was hiding in the forest, within attacking distance of the car. If he had a knife, he'd be within five metres. She remembered Ray Carlson, and the knife with its etched silver handle. If Marko had a gun, he'd probably be within thirty metres.

Trying to slow her breathing down once more, Zoe started scanning the area, back and forth. On the third sweep she saw it. One of the ferns on the far side of the track moved almost imperceptibly up and down, when all the others were swaying sideways in the breeze. *Gotcha.* Zoe brought her gun up. She left the safety of the rock and moved her way down towards the track, using her peripheral vision to tell her where to put her feet. Her focus remained on the group of ferns on the far side. She reached a large old log lying beside the track, covered in moss. Zoe crouched down behind it, and stretched her injured leg out.

'Marko, it's time to give yourself up. I know what happened with Ivan, about the bullying, about his overdose, about your brilliant plan. You played the long game almost perfectly. I know what you did for your brother...'

There was silence.

'I'm not coming.' Marko's voice was deep, defiant.

Zoe shifted, her leg throbbing. 'Come on, Marko. You need to come with me and get your brother's story out there. Those kids bullied the life out of him and his story needs to be told. Your story, too. Or else they'll just pigeonhole you as a lunatic serial killer and that'll be your place in history. You don't want that, do you?'

Silence. The smoke was now thickening. Zoe could feel it in her throat.

'I've got back-up on the way, Marko.'

Marko's sudden burst of laughter reverberated back off the mountains. 'Sure you have. Did you call for back-up with your radio that doesn't work? I killed the system. All it took was for me to delete some code as I saw you driving up the street. I've got access to the system, you know. They won't have it fixed for at least an hour. Or did you call for back-up on your phone with no coverage? It's not by chance that you've ended up on a dead-end track. There's no one coming to help you, Zoe.'

Now it was Zoe who was silent.

'Didn't you think that getting that message today from Serge was a bit odd? I know he was there that day you were fishing around for info on me—I was following you—so I used his name when I called your phone this afternoon. You fell nicely for that. I saw the news. That CCTV footage of you diving for that drone in the Grand Final attack. You're famous, Zoe. And brave. You're not like most cops. They'd have special operations group police searching for me with machine guns and snipers. Not you though. I knew that you wouldn't think twice if you saw an opportunity to catch me, that you'd take the bait if I put out a lure for you, that I could trap you here. You don't think twice. Your courage makes you reckless.'

Zoe cursed at the thought of having been manipulated so easily, but was determined not to show fear. 'What's the endgame, Marko? My leg's still aching from where you tried to run me over the other day and I'm not crouching down here forever.'

Marko started to laugh. 'I was actually gunning for that journo who's been chasing down the story. Westbrook. Seemed like serendipity when I realised she was heading to meet you. You know, two birds, one stone. A bit like what I did to the bullies, eh? Two-for-one specials all around.'

'We never bullied your brother,' Zoe called out. 'How do you justify trying to kill Sarah or me?'

'Collateral damage. Happens in every war. Big or small,' Marko said, his voice momentarily softer.

Zoe could feel her heart beating. 'So, what's your plan for today? Are you going for *suicide by cop* or is it more a *kill a cop*-type scenario?' She was trying her best to sound in control.

'I may be going to hell, but those guys are staying in jail, Zoe,' Marko yelled, his tone bitter again. There was a blast as Marko fired his gun, the bullet cannoning into the log Zoe was crouched behind. She felt the vibration of it through the wood against her shoulder. Two more shots followed, each thudding into the log near her head.

Zoe knew she had to think fast, to find better cover.

It was then that Zoe heard a soft thumping. She glanced across as Harry flashed by through the scrub, a couple of metres away, teeth bared. Zoe pushed herself up, but Harry was already past her, halfway across the track, cutting a path through the smoke.

Zoe saw Marko stand up and aim his gun at Harry.

In one movement, Zoe levelled her weapon and fired.

Marko was hit in the shoulder, shunting his body sideways, before he fell heavily to the ground. Zoe hobbled quickly over to where Marko lay face down on the ground. Harry was snarling in his face.

Marko reached out, towards where his gun lay. Zoe moved across, her weapon on Marko, kicking his away. Harry was still snarling in Marko's face when Zoe put her right foot into the middle of his back and pushed him face-first into the ground. She moaned in pain as she dropped her knee hard into his back and pulled his arm around to handcuff him.

6 AM, MONDAY 17 FEBRUARY

Marko Raddich was handcuffed to his bed in the secure ward used for prisoners at St Vincent's Hospital. It looked like any other hospital ward, except for the bulletproof glass and bars on the frosted windows that should have overlooked the city. His eyes were open, but it was hard to say what he was looking at. Zoe sat in the corner of the room watching him. Harry was snoring quietly on the floor beside her. A uniformed officer stood guard outside the room.

Zoe's phone buzzed. A text from Anjali: *Not his main computer. No relevant data.* Zoe sighed. She had given Anjali the laptop she had discovered in Marko's car, hoping that it would contain information linking Marko to all the cases. She looked up to see Marko staring at her.

'You ready to talk?' asked Zoe.

'You should have killed me while you had the chance.'

Zoe said nothing, giving Marko an exhausted half-grin. She shot a glance at the clock on the wall.

'You got somewhere to be? That's right. Trevor Hill's trial starts this morning. You going?'

Zoe ignored the bait. 'No, I'd rather chat to you. What's that mean?' she asked, pointing at the script tattooed on his arm, with the year 1984 beneath it.

Marko maintained Zoe's gaze. 'It's the Serbian spelling for Belgrade, where I was born.'

'Your plan was amazing, Marko. Deploying the malware to find out their secrets. Killing one bully and setting the other one up. Using your neighbours for your alibi. Having Ivan on ice, just in case you needed someone to take the blame,' said Zoe.

When he heard Ivan's name, Marko's gaze darkened.

'But I'm guessing you didn't expect us to find the cabin so quickly. Probably thought you had much more time to let him rot away out there. So we wouldn't know he'd been frozen solid for years. What was it? Three or four years? That would make it at least six months before you killed Ben Jennings.'

Marko said nothing.

'You almost got away with it,' said Zoe. She waited. 'You know, you can still control the narrative if you want. All you need to do is tell me your story.'

Marko let his head sink into the pillow. He looked at Zoe. He opened his mouth as if to speak. Zoe leaned forward. Marko smiled. 'What I'd like, detective,' he said, 'is a lawyer.'

When they arrived at Homicide, Harry made a beeline for his dog bed. He lay down with a contented moan. Charlie was in front of his computer, typing fast.

'Hey,' said Zoe.

'Hi, has Marko talked yet?'

'No, and he's lawyered up. We won't be getting much out of him now.'

'Shit,' sighed Charlie. 'Rob got the warrant sorted and we went through Marko's house first thing this morning. Nothing. Checked inside the roof, in the cellar, and everywhere in between. We're waiting for someone to unlock the door at the Department of Justice so we can get into his office.'

'I don't like our chances finding anything there. He's too careful,' said Zoe.

'Probably, but I don't think he expected us to come this close to catching him. Let's hope he's made an error.'

'I like your optimism. What are you up to?' asked Zoe.

'Trying to find somewhere else he could be keeping his computer. His neighbours said he didn't socialise much. No girlfriend either. I started thinking that he could have a storage locker somewhere where he has it stashed away. I'm compiling a list of storage places around his house, as well as between there and the city.'

'That's good thinking,' said Zoe.

'The complicating factor is that the storage could be under any name.'

Zoe sat down. 'The guy's a planner. Look for a storage locker that's been rented for at least three years. He's been at this for at least that long.'

She looked at her watch. Seven-thirty. Two-and-a-half

hours until the trial was due to start. Something caught her eye and Zoe looked up.

Anjali was standing just inside the office. She took half a step before stepping back. Harry jumped up out of his bed and ran over to her. He circled around Anjali and sat in front of her. She looked down, a sad smile on her face, before patting him.

Zoe went to her. 'Anj, are you okay?' She could see tears welling.

'Come with me,' Zoe said, taking her quickly by the arm. Two tears fell down Anjali's face as they walked. With Harry alongside, they went into the conference room and Zoe closed the door. Anjali slumped down into a chair.

'What is it?' asked Zoe.

Anjali sucked in two deep breaths to try to get herself under control. 'I thought he'd confess, that's why I didn't say anything. I thought he'd—' She put her face in her hands and sobbed.

7.35 AM, MONDAY 17 FEBRUARY

'Anjali, what are you saying?' said Zoe.

'Marko Raddich...he was an old boyfriend of mine. A bad one.'

Zoe shook her head. She was fuming, but was trying to stay composed. 'Why didn't say you anything?'

'When we found Ivan's name in the Education Department files I was stunned. I knew he was Marko's brother. Marko had mentioned him once or twice.'

'But why didn't you say something?'

'I was caught off guard. I'm sorry. Marko had implied that his brother had gone off the rails, and that he didn't see him anymore. If I'd known...'

'Fuck, Anjali. You know Marko tried to kill me, don't you?' growled Zoe. 'Yesterday, up at Warburton and the other day when he tried to run me and Sarah Westbrook down.'

Anjali's tears began to flow again. 'Yes, I...I know that now, but until Saturday I thought that it was Ivan we were chasing,' she stammered. 'I know what Marko's like. It took me six months to get away from him. He was stalking me everywhere. I was terrified. I told him I would get the police involved and then he sent me a video, a video he had recorded of us...an explicit video. He was threatening to post it online and send it to my family. Then he sent me another. Said he had hours of tape. I didn't know it but he had high-definition video cameras set up all around his place, recording everything. Bedroom, bathroom, everywhere.'

'And did he ever follow through and send them to your family?'

'No. I think he just wanted to hold them over me. The guy's evil.'

'Didn't you think when you saw the driver's licences that it was Marko?'

'There was some similarity, but no, those guys looked different. Marko was leaner, clean cut, six foot one, with blue eyes. He had a different bearing to him. He was confident and just looked different.'

'When was this relationship?'

'We split up in the middle of last year. In June. We'd been dating less than a couple of months. It took until the end of December to get him out of my life. It was before I transferred to Homicide. He'd appear once every couple of weeks, knocking on my windows at three in the morning, or following me around on the weekend. That sort of thing. He was always either threatening me or trying to get me back.'

'Why are you telling me now? We've got him in custody.'

'I was digging around yesterday trying to work out who

deleted the case files from our server and I found out it was at 2.45 am on Saturday, the ninth of February. It was before the rest of Homicide found out so it wasn't any of them.'

'Who was it then?'

'The person deleting the files was logged in remotely under my name. It was Marko.'

'Fuck. How'd he get your log-in details?'

'Before I came over to Homicide, when I worked with the Fraud Squad, I'd sometimes do extra work from home on the weekends. I'm guessing that one day I logged in from his place while he had his video cameras on. He must have been spying on my password.' Anjali wiped away a tear. 'I was so stupid.'

Zoe leaned back in her chair. 'The bit about being taped is on him. But that you didn't tell me straight away when we found out Ivan's name, that's another story.'

'I know. I'm sorry. I just didn't want Marko back anywhere near me. I thought that when we got Ivan, everything would work out. He would be in custody and Marko would never find out I was involved and he'd stay out of my life. I didn't know about Marko being directly involved until late Saturday, after you got the call from the pathologist saying that Ivan had been dead for years.'

Zoe shut her eyes. Anjali was right—they didn't know it was Marko until then. Harry sat by Anjali, resting his head on her thigh, looking up at her. She patted him gently.

The conference room door swung open and Charlie walked in. 'The Department of Justice office doors have been unlocked for us. We should get our skates on and get over there.'

'You head over. I'll be there in a bit,' said Zoe.

From behind Anjali, Charlie gave Zoe a puzzled look. She met his eyes with a solemn glance, tilting her head towards the door. Confused, Charlie nodded and left the room.

'We'll need to come back to this later,' Zoe said to Anjali. 'We've got two hours to find Marko's computer. It's the missing piece of the puzzle. Charlie is searching for a storage facility. Do you know if he used one?'

'No, not that I know of.'

'All right, you know Marko better than anyone in our reach. Tell me everything you know about him.'

'Okay,' she said. 'He isn't all that social. We didn't go out much. We met at an IT conference. He likes opera, art galleries, that sort of thing. He fancies himself as some sort of intellectual. We'd eat out every now and then, but mainly it was just takeaway at home. What else? He has a thing about libraries. He loves them. After he arrived in Australia, he said, he used to spend a lot of time in libraries. Reading to teach himself English. Even when we were together, he'd often go to the State Library here in the city, mostly on his lunch break. There's a section on Serbian history and he liked browsing there. I remember he called it his sanctuary. He also said one day that it was where he did his best work.'

Zoe looked up. 'Did you ever go there with him?'

'Yes, once. He wanted to show me, so I met him there.'

'Let's go,' said Zoe, standing.

Even with full lights and sirens, it took them fifteen minutes to get across the city during the morning peak hour. Zoe pulled up at the La Trobe Street entrance to the library, opening the back for Harry as Anjali got out of the car. Together, they ran to the automatic door, which stayed shut.

'What the heck?'

'We're too early,' said Anjali, looking at the opening hours by the door.

Zoe smacked her hand flat against the door several times, drawing the attention of a female attendant inside. She shook her head and pointed at her wrist.

Zoe pulled out her badge and slammed it against the glass. 'We need to get in. Now,' she yelled.

The librarian walked over, kneeling to unlock and open the door. As she did, she smiled at Harry, wagging his tail on the other side of the glass.

'Thanks,' said Zoe. 'I'm Detective Sergeant Zoe Mayer and I need to look at one of your...'

The woman cut her off lethargically, 'Knock yourself out. Just let someone know when you need to leave.'

'Thanks,' said Zoe and turned to Anjali. 'You lead the way,' she said.

Anjali broke into a jog. As they ran through the building, Zoe pointed her badge at every confused-looking staff member they passed. Harry trotted alongside Zoe.

Two minutes later, Anjali slowed. 'Yes, this is the spot.' In front of them were two metal bookshelves devoted to Serbian history.

'Okay,' said Zoe. 'Start searching. It's got to be here somewhere.' She scanned the walls. 'No CCTV in this section.'

Anjali was pulling books out one by one.

'Do it like this,' said Zoe, putting her hands around eight books at a time, squeezing them together and stacking them on the floor. She used her phone to light up the area at the back of the shelves, looking for a hiding spot. Anjali did the same thing.

Zoe's phone buzzed. She glanced at the screen. Tom: *I'm sorry. Can we talk?*

They made their way down the shelves. Zoe pulled out the books on her side and shone her phone in. Nothing. Anjali knelt down to pull out the books on her side, knocking her knee against the base. 'Shit,' she muttered. She pulled out more books. 'There's nothing there.'

They were both on their knees, surrounded by books, when Zoe looked at the steel base of the shelf and started to push and pull at it. Anjali saw what she was doing and did the same on her side. The base fell away in Anjali's hands. Then the one on Zoe's side did the same.

Zoe dropped down and looked under the base. She could see a black nylon strip leading back into the darkness deep under the shelf.

Punching a code into her phone, Zoe opened the video function, hitting record. She gave it to Anjali. 'Video everything.'

'Okay,' said Anjali, pointing the camera down at the opening at the base of the shelf. Zoe pulled a pair of latex gloves from a pouch attached to her belt and slipped them on.

'This is Detective Sergeant Zoe Mayer from the Homicide

Squad, along with Tactical Intelligence Officer Anjali Arya. It is 8.10 am on Monday, the seventeenth of February. We are in the State Library of Victoria and have located evidence we believe is connected to a series of murders here in Victoria.'

Zoe then reached down, pulling the nylon strip until a flat black bag appeared. Zoe tore the velcro strip open and grabbed the laptop out of the bag, along with a power cord.

9 AM, MONDAY 17 FEBRUARY

The Forensics officer was running through the library, a case in her hand. 'Zoe Mayer, are you here somewhere?'

Zoe stood up. 'Over here,' she called out, and waved.

'Came as fast as I could. I'm Bianca,' she said, hand outstretched towards Zoe, while also smiling down towards Harry.

'Good to meet you,' Zoe responded, shaking her hand. 'This is Anjali.'

Bianca looked up from Harry, nodding to Anjali.

'Let me show you what we've got,' said Zoe. Books were strewn everywhere. Harry stood up, wagging his tail. 'We are on a tight clock, so we need this laptop fingerprinted first, and then the area around the base of that shelf.'

Bianca looked down at the shelf with the steel plate at the front removed. 'Got it,' she said, kneeling down and opening her case.

Zoe's phone vibrated. It was Rob. 'Hi boss.'

'Hey. Where are we at?'

'Forensics is here now taking prints. We should have the laptop in our hands in a couple of minutes.'

'I don't suppose he left the password written on a sticky note,' Rob said.

'That's our next problem,' she said, looking down at the computer being fingerprinted. Bianca had it open. 'It looks newish and I can see it has a fingerprint reader. What are our chances of getting a warrant to make Marko unlock it for us?'

'We'd need to prove it was his. A good barrister will argue that finding his fingerprints on it doesn't mean it's his computer. But how did you know where to look for it?'

'Anjali,' said Zoe. Anjali shot her a resigned look. This was the sort of thing that could end her career. 'She discovered some intel that told us Marko was into Serbian history and spent his lunch breaks at the State Library. Seemed as good a bet as any.'

'Tell her well done,' said Rob. 'Where's Charlie?'

'He's still at Marko's office. I've told him we found the laptop but he's checking if there's anything else there.'

'Okay, I'll meet you at the court.'

Zoe ended the call and looked up at Anjali, whose eyes were full of tears. 'Thank you,' she mouthed.

'Okay, all done with the laptop. The thing's covered in prints,' said Bianca, from behind Anjali. 'You want an evidence bag?'

'That'd be great,' said Zoe.

Bianca slipped the laptop and its case into a large paper bag and handed it to Zoe.

'Thanks Bianca. We've got to go.'

'I don't know what to say,' said Anjali, as they sprinted towards the library's exit. 'Why didn't you tell Rob?'

Zoe remained silent as they approached the doors the attendant was already unlocking. She waited until they were outside before she answered. 'Marko put you in a hard position, where you had to choose between your job or having your sex life exposed to your family and friends. You made a big mistake in not telling me earlier, but we couldn't have caught Marko without you...Let's just say we're even, okay?'

'Thank you, Zoe.'

'Just don't fucking mess up again. I don't give second chances.'

'I won't. I promise.'

'Do be prepared, though. It may come out some other way,' said Zoe. She unlocked the car and opened the back for Harry to jump up. Anjali slid into the passenger side with the evidence bag. When Zoe opened the driver's side door she looked across at her. 'What is it?' asked Zoe.

'I think I may know the password for the laptop.'

'What?'

'Marko's got a tattoo in Serbian Cyrillic on his arm. It says "Belgrade"—that's where he was born—and "1984" below that. "Belgrade1984" was his wi-fi password at his house.'

'Shit. I saw the tattoo this morning in the hospital. Try it. Put some gloves on, though—there's a box under the seat.'

Anjali pulled out a pair of latex gloves and put them on. She then took the laptop from the evidence bag and opened it. She turned it on and punched in 'Belgrade1984'. The computer gave her access. 'We're in,' exclaimed Anjali.

'I think we should buy a lottery ticket.' Zoe started the car. 'Buckle up. We're off to the Supreme Court. See what you can find before we get there.' She pulled out into La Trobe Street, siren blaring.

Anjali clicked through the folders as Zoe negotiated the traffic. As Zoe turned left into William Street, Anjali called out, 'Bingo. It's all here. Marko's got everything organised. There's a folder marked "Ray and Dwayne" and it has a heap of emails between Ray Carlson and Katie Harley. And there's a map with their houses marked—even the bin at the beach is marked.' Anjali clicked a few more times. 'There are other folders here: "Aaron and Ben", "Trevor and Eric". Same kind of information in both.'

'Fantastic,' said Zoe, turning left into Lonsdale Street. 'We've got him.' She parked the Escape and glanced across at Anjali, who was staring at the screen. Anjali had a folder open with dozens of files in it.

'Are they the videos of you?'

'I think so. The folder is called "Anjali". There's so many of them.'

Zoe looked across at her. 'Listen carefully…I need to ring Rob back and let him know we got into the computer. I'll do that while I'm getting Harry out of the back, okay? I don't think those videos are relevant to our cases. Do you understand me? I think they'll, um, be distracting. I'm going to the back of the car now.'

As Zoe opened the door, she saw Anjali shut her eyes in relief.

9.45 AM, MONDAY 17 FEBRUARY

Charlie waved as Zoe, Harry and Anjali approached.

'We got it open,' said Zoe.

'What, no password? I thought this guy was a cyber-security genius,' said Charlie.

'Anjali guessed it. I told her about the tattoo on Marko's arm and she had a hunch. Everything we need to charge him is in there.'

Thirty metres away, down a corridor, Zoe saw Sally Johnstone leaving the bathroom and walking away in her black silk court robes.

'Let's go,' said Zoe. Harry walked alongside her, with Charlie and Anjali following. Zoe circled around Sally, and stopped directly in front of her. Zoe could see that Sally had a distant look in her eyes and knew she had been going over her opening statement in her mind.

After a moment, Sally reacted. 'You? What do you want?'

In her peripheral vision, Zoe saw Iain Gillies and Garry Burns, who were sitting in the waiting area, turn towards her. 'The charges against Trevor Hill are going to be dropped,' said Zoe in a hushed tone.

'What are you talking about?' shot back Sally. 'It's not even your case. Why are you telling me this now? The trial's starting in ten minutes.'

Iain and Garry walked over. 'What's this latest drama, Mayer?' Iain asked.

Zoe ignored him. 'We have evidence that Trevor Hill was set up for the murder of Eric Drum as revenge for a bullying attack by both Trevor and Eric from their school days. We've got a suspect in custody, Marko Raddich, and he will be charged with three counts of murder today. The murder charge against Dwayne Harley will need to be withdrawn for the same reason, and Aaron Smyth's conviction for killing Ben Jennings will be overturned. One person committed all three killings. We know who it was, how and why he did it.'

'But we've got so much evidence against Trevor Hill,' sniped Iain. 'How do you know your evidence is even real?'

Zoe stared down her nose at him. 'Because your evidence was fabricated and fed to you by Marko Raddich, and the proof is all here,' said Zoe, pointing to the evidence bag being carried by Anjali.

Sally was about to say something when her phone rang. 'Yes,' she snapped, answering it. She said nothing while she listened. 'Yes, okay, will do.' She ended the call.

Her face ashen, Sally turned to Iain and Garry. 'That

was the Director of Public Prosecutions. We're going to request an adjournment to consider new evidence.' Without looking again at Zoe, Sally turned and walked towards the courtroom.

'What just happened?' asked Garry.

'Your case collapsed,' said Zoe.

Iain turned and followed Sally. In turn, Garry followed him.

Down the corridor, Zoe could see Sarah Westbrook in a wheelchair. She was staring at Zoe, intrigued by the commotion.

Zoe turned to Charlie and Anjali. 'Wait here for a sec.' She and Harry walked across the waiting area towards Sarah.

'Hi. What's happening?' Sarah asked.

Zoe smiled at her. 'It'll be better when you hear it from the prosecutor in the courtroom. I just wanted to say that you've got good instincts, that's all. Let's catch up for a wine or two when you've recovered.'

11.30 AM, MONDAY 17 FEBRUARY

'I was wondering when you'd be back,' Marko said from his hospital bed, eyes narrowed at Zoe. 'This is my lawyer, Stefan Thomas.'

The lawyer nodded. From the quality of his suit, Zoe quickly guessed that Stefan would be charging close to a thousand an hour. Harry sat down on the floor, staring up at Marko.

'This is the cop who shot me,' Marko said. 'We are going to sue her arse.'

Zoe felt slightly giddy with tiredness. She pushed her lips tightly together for a second. It was all she could do not to burst into laughter.

'What are you so fucking happy about? You chased me into the mountains in your car. You didn't identify yourself as a police officer. I was scared for my life and then you shot me without reason. Get prepared to lose everything.'

Charlie walked into the ward wearing blue latex gloves

and carrying the large evidence bag.

Marko stared at the thick paper bag, confused.

Zoe looked at Charlie. 'What have you got there, Charlie?'

'Let's see,' said Charlie theatrically. He opened the bag and lifted out the laptop.

Marko's eyes bulged. 'That's not mine. I've never seen it before,' he stammered, looking at his lawyer, who had his hand up, gesturing for Marko not to say anything else.

'Your fingerprints are all over it,' said Zoe. 'You must have unlocked it thousands of times.'

'It's not mine, so I don't have a clue about how to unlock it. Sorry.'

'Marko,' Zoe said, 'the password is tattooed on your arm. We've already opened it up. We've got it all.'

Marko stared at her. 'I should've run you over properly last week,' he snarled.

Stefan's face showed alarm.

'Probably,' said Zoe. 'Charlie, you can do the honours?'

'Marko Raddich, you are being charged with three counts of murder, the attempted murder of Sarah Westbrook, as well as two counts of attempting to kill a police officer. You do not have to say anything, but anything you do or say...'

Zoe felt free. She couldn't remember the last time she'd felt this good. Harry came over and leaned against her thigh and looked up at her. She pulled out her phone and looked at Tom's text again. *I'll call you tomorrow*, she typed. *Taking Harry to the beach.*

ACKNOWLEDGMENTS

I would like to thank Michael Heyward and all of the talented team at Text Publishing for their passion and support in bringing *The Long Game* to readers. It is an absolute pleasure to work with them all.

Much gratitude also to Rebecca Ettridge, Sophia Grewal and Gwyn Beaumont, who read various drafts along the way and gave valuable feedback.

In addition, the team at the Victoria Police Film and Television Office were very helpful in providing guidance to some of the technical aspects of policing.

Finally, special thanks to my wife, Karen, who read countless drafts of this book and provided thoughtful and patient advice throughout the process. Without her, *The Long Game* would not exist.